UNDERCOVER

Also by Laurinda D. Brown

Fire & Brimstone

The Highest Price for Passion

UnderCover

Laurinda D. Brown

SBI

Strebor Books
New York London Toronto Sydney

Published by
SBI
Strebor Books
P.O. Box 6505
Largo, MD 20792
http://www.streborbooks.com

This book is a work of fiction. Names, characters, places and incidents are products of the author's imagination or are used fictitiously. Any resemblance to actual events or locales or persons, living or dead, is entirely coincidental.

Originally published in trade paperback in 2004.

ISBN-13 978-1-59309-220-7
ISBN-10 1-59309-220-2
LCCN 2006923553

First Strebor Books mass market paperback edition May 2008

1 0 9 8 7 6 5 4 3 2 1

Manufactured in the United States of America

For information regarding special discounts for bulk purchases, please contact Simon & Schuster Special Sales at 1-800-456-6798 or business@simonandschuster.com

DEDICATION

For Rose Rita

ACKNOWLEDGMENTS

The other day I wanted to reach out to my mother and shower her with all the love I felt flowing through me when I saw her for the last time. I wanted to tell her that her granddaughters were growing into beautiful young ladies, each with an eternal memory of what "Ganny" meant to them. I wanted her to know how much I looked like her whenever I tied my hair up at night and put on one of her old robes. I wanted her to know that I've never worn any of her old suits; they're still hanging on the same hangers she put them on four years ago, and just the other day, I found a strand of her Indian-like gray hair around the collar of one of them. I wanted to explain to her that I'd chosen to be happy with my life and not just content with it. I wanted to tell her that I've learned to think before I speak, for carefully chosen words have the power to heal someone in their time of need. I wanted her to feel me thinking of someone else first before thinking about myself. I wanted to let her know that my relationship with God is the best that it has ever been, for I look to Him for the wisdom, knowledge and patience that have become constants in my life. When it was all over, said and done, I couldn't do any of that. Instead, I thumbed through the pages of my life and found those angels my mother had sent here for me. So, for my acknowledgments, since I couldn't get to my mother, I chose the next best thing…

To Daphne, thank you for being my champion. Your strength and courage have influenced every thought I've had since the day we met. Every word you've ever spoken to me has made me stop and think about where I am in my life and what I'm supposed to be doing with it. At each juncture, it was always something you said that made me choose the right path. Since the day we met, you've made many senseless days worth something.

To Olivia, thank you for being my friend.You've never judged me despite my "oops, I did it again!" screw-ups and cries for attention. When I think about what my life would be like if I'd never met you, I feel empty inside because your presence has always filled a void that no one else ever could. I've thought the world of you since the day we met, and that will never change.

To Bunny, thank you for giving me vision and for guiding me with words of compassion and wisdom. You were the one who taught me to never put anyone on a pedestal "because if that pedestal ever falls and breaks, then you will never be able to put it back together just like it used to be."

To Michelle, thank you for your cheery personality and overwhelming support of my endeavors and me. I'm so proud of you and what you've accomplished. Just remember good things come to those who wait.

To my wonderful girlfriends from Howard University—Vangee, Danielle, Martrice, Kelley, Karen, Kathy, Michele, Joya, and Lisa—the classes of 1991 and 1992. Thank you for being so supportive and accepting of who I am.

To Mrs. Patterson, thank you for teaching me the power of words. It was you who told me that no matter how many times you apologize for your chosen words, you can never take them back.

To Charlotte H., thank you for being such an amazing mentor over the years. Your philosophical way of telling me right from wrong has always been greatly appreciated.

To Joyce and Kathleen, thank you for helping my adjustment to new surroundings worthwhile and carefree. It only takes one kind word or gesture to know when a person is for real. I've found that in the two of you, and it means more to me than you'll ever know.

To the Ladies of Delta Sigma Theta Sorority, Incorporated—particularly, the Newport News Alumnae Chapter, thank you for the worldwide bond of love and sisterhood that no one can ever break.

To the 36 G.E.M.S., I love all of you—Yvette Ayala-Richards, Marion Barnett, Doris Battle, Alicia Coles, Chastity Corbett, Brooke Daniels, Deborah Griffin,

Quanda Griffin, Rosalyn Hardaway, Erica Hill, Lalanda Johnson, Suzette Johnson, Jeneen Joyner, Yolandis Lumpkins, Natasha Muldrow, Nadiyah Murray, Cassandra Murphy, Shirley Norwood, Renee Ragland, Oriel Robinson-Taylor, Giselle Russell, Sherry A Scott, Jerri Smith, Kim Smith, Titinesha Smith, Rory Stapleton, Roshonda Tabb, Ann Taylor, Lisa Taylor, Annie Thomas, Tamika Vincent, Natalie Ward, Michelle Webb, Bernie White-Morton, Chioma Wilkins—thank you for having my back. To Nyema, thank you for being a wonderful soror and a fabulous friend.

To Whitman-Walker Clinic, thank you for your overwhelming support and endorsement of this project.

To Dora, thank you for the plates of collard greens that you've given to me over the years. You looked beyond all that "other stuff " and opened your heart and kitchen to the girls and me.

To Zane, Charmaine and the Strebor family, thank you for the opportunity to let me do my thang!

To Brandy, simply thank you.

To L'Ornya, thank you for being brutally honest with me about the way I USED to be when it came to our friendship. Hindsight is 20/20.

To Kevin and Latonya, thank you for reminding me that family IS real.

To Dr. Rita Dorsey-Flowers…(hee-hee!)

To my grandmother, I love you!

To Daddy, I love you, too!

To my sister, Nyree, Momma left us here to deal with each other, so I guess we have to make the best of it. I love you.

To Cantaloupe, thank you for walking beside me and for helping me keep my quick temper in check. Thank you for coming into my life and making me realize that beneath all the anger and frustration within me, there was a human being with feelings. Most importantly, you've taught me to love, and that there's nothing wrong with expecting it in return.

To Jhoilan and Cydney, my beautiful babies, life meant nothing until I had you.

And, saving the best for last, thank you, God, for blessing me with talents beyond my wildest dreams and for directing me on a path that I know is not my own.

The Menagerie
Presents
Miss Nay's
Revue
Saturdays at Midnight

MISS NAY'S REVUE

Patrick sat at the bar waiting for the love of his life. The house was packed as usual with folks in from Atlanta and St. Louis for the holiday weekend. Cars were lined up on both sides of Front Street that night—which wasn't a big deal to many. But, to Patrick, it meant the world.

It meant that everyone had come out to see his baby perform at the club. Men from all walks of life handed Patrick's lady dollar bills, five-dollar bills, ten-dollar bills, and, on the first of the month, maybe even some twenties. But none could surpass Patrick. Every Saturday night, dressed to the nines, he would watch those other men walk to the front of the stage, fanning bills and pieces of paper with phone numbers scribbled on them. Often tripping over themselves to do it, some even borrowed from their dates just to be able to touch the silken hands of The Menagerie's biggest star. But it was Patrick who made a hush fall over the crowded room. Leaving his double B-52 and Lite Beer, he rose from his VIP booth and pulled out his Coach breast wallet that Nay had gotten for him while on a trip to California. He was seductively smooth, suave, and anything else that a gay Black man with the most amazing smile and the whitest teeth could ever be. Fragranced with imported cologne and always clad in custom suits, Patty was the center of attention. With every stride—waving that bill in his hand, eyes followed him, wondering what dead president he'd pulled from his wallet. By the time he reached the stage, the bill was creased across Ben Franklin's face, gently resting on his index finger. And Miss Nay? She would lean over and smile as her man first kissed the paper and then placed the crisp one hundred-dollar bill between her breasts.

Tonight, though, Patrick was not all right. He didn't get his usual table in the center of the dance floor and, knowing he wouldn't be staying long, he didn't bother to remove his jacket. Instead, he sat slumped over the bar and nursed a flat ginger ale that had succumbed to the three ice cubes that the bartender had so graciously offered. He hadn't been to the club in over two months.

About that fact folks had begun to talk. "Patty, you wan-anotha drink?" someone offered. But Patrick remained silent and kept swirling his straw around the bottom of his glass. "Guess not," snorted the waitress as she sashayed her way to the other end of the bar. Patrick sat practically stock-still with his back turned to the stage. The frigid air around him warned the usual passersby to stay away, to stay far away.

Three years seemed barely like three days to Patty, for he and Miss Nay were lovers at first sight. They'd traveled the world together: Cancun, Montego Bay, Paris, and London. Patty insisted that Nay allow him to occasionally get his dick sucked by nameless strangers, and she was assured things would go no further. In exchange for that luxury, Nay was given the world, and she flaunted it. But privilege came with a price that Nay didn't mind paying. She wasn't allowed to take anyone home with her, nor was she allowed to accept phone numbers or business cards. Those weren't the club's rules. They were Patty's. As she performed, Miss Nay electrified the crowd with her sultry moves and finesse, but outside of work Nay was strictly off limits. Everybody knew that. That was the way Patrick wanted it.

Patrick, with long and lovely supermodel eyelashes, sat with sullen eyes, agonizing over what he'd finally gotten the nerve to do. Closing his eyes, he whispered to himself, "Now, let's practice this one more time." With the music blaring at deafening levels from one corner of the club to the other, no one heard him thinking out loud. *Take a breath.* "Nay, Baby, you know that I love you more than life itself. Nothing else in this world mattered to me when we were together. I allowed everyone and everything to come second to you and me, and at times, that even included my family. Since Mama died, the whole world has been looking a lot different to me. Those things that didn't matter before mean a whole lot now, and I've got to do the right thing. My family is expecting it, and so is God. I promised Mama on her deathbed that if she would just surrender to Him so that she could finally be free of her pain, then I would dedicate my life to serving Him and would leave *this* life alone. The things that I chose to turn the other cheek to have come around and smacked me in the face. I can't continue to act like the world around me is grand when my insides are about to fall out. Every time I think about you, touch you or kiss you I feel like I'm dissing Mama. So, every time I get that way—the devil's way—I go to church. I've been scrubbing the floors, cutting the grass, cooking in the kitchen—anything to keep me from thinking about you. The next thing I knew I'd found my way into the pulpit and realized that I had something to say. I mean it's like my soul just opens up when I'm there. All these people around me…hundreds of them, and, with all that, I still feel like it's just me and God. When I'm there, I like what I see. I like what I feel." Even with his voice rising at times to octaves just above a whisper, it seemed as if no one had heard a word Patty uttered. He continued, "Nay, I realize now that love is more than just what we have. It's more than what I ever thought we had. The last thing that I've ever wanted to do was to hurt you, but, after all these weeks of Sunday School,

Bible study, and worship services, I now know that life is about the choices you make, and right now...today, I have to choose God."

Patty's heart transformed his emotions into tears that flooded his eyes and overflowed down his cheeks. And just when he'd reached the point of locking out all else in the club around him, just when he'd felt there was no one else in the room but him and God, Patty opened his eyes amazed and bewildered to see that there was also Miss Nay.

This epitome of refined elegance and style was exemplary of regal stature; yet this woman of grandeur, this mega diva worthy of applause until her last breath, simply sat there, and, with her now former lover, shed the same tears. She shared the same pain. The once flawless make-up was carelessly smeared, revealing the mustache fuzz and facial hair. Nay, displaying divine class and stature to the end, slowly removed the silk scarf that had been a gift from Patty. Speechless, Nay gently reached for Patty's cheek and tenderly kissed it. She draped the scarf around Patty's neck, rose from the bar stool, and dejectedly strolled towards the dressing room to gather her things. There would be no more encores. This was her final curtain call.

Once out the club door, it would be the first time in years that she would have to face the world as Nathaniel Chamberlain Alexander.

FIVE YEARS LATER

MAINTAINING THE CONNECTION

MOCHAMD: Hi

CreolSista: Hey you. Long time no see ;)

MOCHAMD: Not true. You saw me exactly 19 hours and 47 minutes ago. Sorry for being late. Had to work an extra shift last night.

CreolSista: Never thought anyone could work more than me.

MOCHAMD: I know. It's always good, though, to come home, sign on and see you here. Makes it all worthwhile. I have a surprise for you.

CreolSista: ;) What is it?!

MOCHAMD: How's everything? How are you?

CreolSista: What's my surprise? And stop changing the subject!

MOCHAMD: LOL ;)

CreolSista: Okay! Okay! I'm doing well. Work is good, and everyone here is doing okay. Getting ready to go out of town.

MOCHAMD: Out of town? Again?

CreolSista: Yes, again. A combination of work and vacation. Mostly vacation, though. I was waiting until everything was confirmed before saying anything to you.

MOCHAMD: Well, darn!

CreolSista: ???

MOCHAMD: My surprise was that he and I were actually coming there for a month. He wants to take a look at some real estate to redevelop, and I was hoping to get a chance to finally meet you. When do you leave?

CreolSista: Ummm, next Thursday. I'm planning to be gone for almost two months.

MOCHAMD: Now that's what I call a vacation! I don't think that we even leave for another three or four weeks. Any chance you'll be back a little early?

CreolSista: It depends on how things are going. I've been working nonstop for the past two years, and some down time would be wonderful. The university is on break, too, so I just decided to take some vacation time as well. The kids are out of school for a few weeks, and even though it's beautiful here, a change of scenery would be nice.

MOCHAMD: Well, maybe the trip back will get delayed, and I'll still be there when you return. It would be great to meet you.

CreolSista: Same here. You have my phone number and address. Use it for a change!

MOCHAMD: I will. I promise.

CreolSista: So. How are things at home?

MOCHAMD: Better, I guess. He's probably never going to change. Business comes first, then him, and then me.

CreolSista: Lemme ask you something.

MOCHAMD: What?

CreolSista: Are you happy?

MOCHAMD: Yes.

CreolSista: Liar.

MOCHAMD: What?

CreolSista: If you were happy, you wouldn't get so much joy from chatting with me. You might be content, but you're definitely not happy.

MOCHAMD: I resent you saying that.

CreolSista: So, it's the truth. You have no idea what you're getting yourself into.

MOCHAMD: How about we change the subject?

CreolSista: You know, I'm not surprised. You always want to do that when you're about to be outted.

MOCHAMD: Anyway, do you realize we've been chatting for almost three years now?

CreolSista: ;)

MOCHAMD: You actually mean a little something to me.

CreolSista: A little?

MOCHAMD: Okay, a lot then. I get butterflies when- ever I see you here.

CreolSista: Trust me, the feeling is mutual. I'm about to start my day while you're ending yours.

MOCHAMD: I like that feeling, too.

CreolSista: And what feeling is that ;)?

MOCHAMD: Having you on my mind before I go to bed at night.

CreolSista: ;)

MOCHAMD: Do you feel the same way?

CreolSista: I do but with reservation.

MOCHAMD: Why the hesitance?

CreolSista: I have my reasons, but I don't want to get into them.

MOCHAMD: ;(

CreolSista: No need to pout about it.

MOCHAMD: Please tell me.

CreolSista: I'll admit that you bring something really special to my life. I think that we established that some time ago. "Seeing" you just as I'm about to face the day is really a nice feeling to have first thing in the morning.

MOCHAMD: That's all you have to say?

CreolSista: I don't know what else you're looking for me to say. I mean you're in a relationship...one that you've been in for quite some time. The flip side is that I'm not. I'll be almost whatever you want me to be for you, but for personal reasons, I have to protect me.

MOCHAMD: oic

CreolSista: As much as I like chatting with you, I'm still careful. You're practically married, so I know this will never go anywhere. We're both professional women with very busy schedules. C'mon now, let's be real. Where do you honestly believe this can go?

MOCHAMD: I don't know. I think that we have a connection that is worth maintaining. I do miss you when we're not talking, and, on those nights when "home" isn't all that it should be, I miss you even more.

CreolSista: Having said that, don't you think that you've got some things you need to work through?

MOCHAMD: I don't know.

CreolSista: Well, you'll have two months to work it out. It's getting late, and I have to run some errands before I go to work.

MOCHAMD: Now you're pissed.

CreolSista: A little bothered but not pissed. Got too much to do to be upset about this today. Let's face it. We've never met, and it doesn't seem like we ever will. We've only talked twice in a three-year period, and that's because I called YOU. I even wrote you a letter!

MOCHAMD: It's too hard to try to call you with him always scanning the phone bill with fifty thousand questions, and putting things on paper around here might not be such a good idea either.

CreolSista: Awfully damn funny you manage to find time to hop on here to chat with me when God-knows-who could walk in on you! So what's the difference?

MOCHAMD: That's not the point.

CreolSista: The point is that you're trippin' and that you've NEVER called or written. I'm tired of this being a one-sided whatever. We need a break. Gotta go.

MOCHAMD: I'll talk with you later?

MOCHAMD: Creol?

CreolSista is not currently signed on.

Amil sat and watched the computer screen waiting to see if CreolSista was going to sign back on. Amil knew she'd pissed her off. Their conversations had started off quite innocently. Amil had just been looking for some harmless company while Manney worked long hours at the firm. So one evening she perused the member profiles of BlackVoices.com and sent out about ten e-mails. She thought that it would be easy to keep up with e-mails from ten strangers, and it was likely that she'd only get two or three responses, if any at all. Five e-mails were sent to straight men—the harm in that was the possibility of them wanting more than just casual conversation. Four of the messages were sent to straight women—maybe one of them would be in search of the same thing: a little attention while the man in her life was away. But then there was the last one, sent to a woman whose sexual preference was listed as, "That's my business." She, CreolSista, was the only person that had responded. For three years, Amil had nurtured this Internet relationship because it had provided a consistent outlet from Manney's selfishness. CreolSista knew when to ask if anything were wrong at home. She knew when to stop asking questions once MOCHAMD's answers had become short and snappy. She knew when to give a virtual hug when a real one wasn't possible. A kind word, an eCard, or maybe even just a simple smiley face was enough for Amil to know that somebody else loved her, and, those simple tokens of thoughtfulness had won Amil's heart, mind, and soul. Getting up the nerve to exchange addresses and phone numbers with a complete stranger took a little while, though. For all she knew, the screen name could have been a man disguised as a woman or could've more easily been a serial killer. Never hiding who she was, CreolSista had made being loved by a stranger so easy for Amil. The two times that CreolSista had called she'd greeted Amil with "This is CreolSista." Their conversations lasted only a minute or two and had never gotten any deeper than the usual pleasantries. CreolSista, always on the speakerphone, had made it a point to be too busy to really talk but not too busy to stop and say hello. The intrigue kept Amil wanting more.

Two weeks after they both graduated from New York University, Manney and Amil were engaged. Amil went right into medical school at Howard University that fall and graduated at the top of her class four years later. While she did her residency at Georgetown Hospital, Manney put in long hours at both George Washington's Graduate School of Business and School of Law. In less than four years, he'd earned both his

MBA and JD. His ambition paved the way for the creation of the company that *Ebony* had once named one of the "Most Distinguished Companies Owned by Young African-American Entrepreneurs." At one time marriage was understood for Manney and Amil. He knew Amil belonged to only him, and Amil knew that Manney barely had time for her let alone anyone else. Since common law marriages were recognized in the state of Tennessee, Amil had taken on Manney's last name primarily for business reasons. Dr. Amil Lindsay sounded much better than Dr. Amil Blake, and, more importantly, Amil's financial interest in the company was best protected that way.

Emanuel "Manney" Lindsay was one of the managing partners in Locke, Lindsay, and McKay. He and Rondell Locke invested all of their personal finances in the company and practically took over Beale Street—with the exception of the one property that they couldn't touch, Memphis' Best Barbecue Joint. To get their hands on that piece of real estate would mean letting go of some serious cash, and, tempting as it was, that was one sacrifice neither of the miserly two was greedy enough to make. "Let him keep that place. Soon he'll be begging us to buy it," Rondell said. "He's only a one-man show, and the heavy tourist traffic down there is going to run his customers off. Just give it time." Well, not long after that statement was made, Rondell ate those words—the restaurant was voted "Memphis's Best Barbecue Place" and held the title for three consecutive years. As quiet as it was kept, the only reason Rondell wanted the barbecue joint to stay open was because he was its most frequent customer. Manney was the strategist, the mastermind behind the company. However, his relationship with Amil only made everything half his. If the company split up for any reason, she got half of his cut. If she ever left Manney, or vice versa, she still got half. Rondell, on the other hand, was different. Although he had a fifty percent interest in the firm, he didn't do shit; he'd bootlegged his success from Manney and had inherited his financial assets from his deceased father. The only reason why he was a partner was because his money helped run the company's investments. Rondell couldn't tell you what an investment was if it'd slapped him in the face, but to make him feel like more of an active participant in the company's affairs, Manney suggested that Rondell get his real estate license. In case they ever desired to sell any of their properties everything could be done in house. And that's exactly what Rondell did. He signed up for the class, bought the books, paid off the instructor, and then paid someone to take the test for him. After Manney discovered what Rondell had done, Cecil McKay, a licensed real estate attorney from Michigan, was brought in as a silent partner to keep the company out of any shit that might arise from Rondell's ignorance. His brief attention span kept Rondell out of meetings, and his ignorance kept him out of important business negotiations. So Manney ran the company and had a sometimes-strained relationship at home with Amil to prove it.

Upon arriving in Memphis several months before, Manney set his eyes on living in Downtown Memphis. He got Amil's approval to buy something for little or nothing, and then later renovate it. Manney found and soon purchased a warehouse on the south end of Main Street. Over 9,000 square feet of the warehouse was devoted to living space with another 1,500 square feet committed to a media center and recreation area. The building's roof had been converted into a sunroom with a retractable roof.

Rondell didn't have the good business sense that Manney possessed, but let him draw you some lines, squares, circles and shit? Hmph! Although he had no formal training, Rondell knew enough about buildings to hook some shit up, and that's exactly what he did to Amil and Manney's house. The first floor boasted an atrium that opened up to the second and third floors, and it also housed two private offices: one for Amil and the other for Manney. Italian ceramic tiles, carefully chosen on one of their excursions to Europe, covered the floors throughout the bottom level. They had compromised and used only vibrant colors to accentuate their zest for life. The walls of Amil's office were covered with a faux-finished coating of Ralph Lauren's Lifevest Orange, and the ceilings, painted the same color, were outlined in white crown molding. Her genuine cherry office furniture had been custom-designed by Drexel Heritage, and the interior was abundant with African-American art and sculptures. She'd met the eccentric but talented Selma Glass at an American Bar Association convention that she'd attended with Manney, and from that moment, whatever Selma created Amil got the first artist proof of it. There was a sitting area that opened up to a bay window that had a beautiful view of the river, and sometimes, after a long session of IMs with CreolSista, she'd curl up on the loveseat with a glass of wine and watch the barges pass by. In the winter she'd light the antique fireplace she'd purchased from an estate sale at an old, abandoned mansion on Central Avenue and give her Gateway desktop computer a break by logging on to her laptop. At the beginning of their friendship, Amil spent hours on that laptop talking to CreolSista and quickly made their virtual meetings part of her day. CreolSista, an apparently astute individual, had unmasked, and been able to dissect, Amil's personality and understood their communication but made sure that their conversation remained respectful.

Once they'd said their goodnights, Amil retreated to

her lavish all-white bedroom accessible by a spiral staircase located near the center of the bay window in her office. Climbing into bed with Manney used to be a welcome event at the end of a long day, but now that was an over-rated activity. By the time she got under the covers, he was already asleep. She thought maybe he'd sense her movement and automatically roll over to embrace her in his lap; hold her in the muscularly manicured arms in which he prided himself. Sadly though, Amil was lucky if Manney even moved over to her side of the bed. He used to do that...before there was ever a law degree; before there was ever a law practice; before he knew anything about real estate; before he had it in his mind to buy every abandoned building and turn it into an apartment building. There was a time when no day was complete without a kiss from Manney at bedtime. But now for Amil, no day was complete without talking with CreolSista.

Over a period of ten years, Manney and Amil had thrown themselves into their respective professions, leaving little room for social lives or children. The friends that they did have were equally as busy, and just like Amil and Manney, often rewarded themselves with lavish trips abroad. The most recent trip had been a four-week stay in Paris. In addition to spending quality time with Amil, Manney did have some business to take care of while there. The property he'd seen advertised on the Internet was a cluster of apartment buildings that he wanted his company to purchase and redevelop for student housing. Trying to get a meeting with the Vice President of Admissions for American Students had taken up way too much of his time, though. Manney hadn't been told until the last of his numerous visits to the school that the staff person he was in search of was out of town on vacation for two months, but that two months was supposed to end on the coming Monday. "I don't really know what to tell you, Monsieur. I know she'd love to talk with you," the secretary said.

"Well, my flight leaves tonight. I was finna go back to my hotel room, and I thought I'd stop by one more time before I left. I guess this will give me a reason to have to come back to Paris." Manney smiled as he headed for the door.

"Pardon moi, Monsieur." The secretary's English was good enough to ask easy questions. "Are you, errr, from Memphis?"

Manney was shocked. He didn't recall telling her that. "Well, yes, I am. Not originally but I live there now. How'd you know that?"

She laughed. "Errr, Mademoiselle—my boss—sometimes says, errr, finna just like you just did, and she's from Memphis."

"Getthefuckouttahere! I mean, really? She is?"

"Oui. Uh, that's where she is now. Hold on, I can..."

"No, no, don't disturb her," he suggested. "I'll give her a call next week. Besides, Memphis is so small that I probably already know someone that she knows," he joked.

"Very well, then."

"Thanks for all your help." Manney wanted to leave just a little of an impression on the young lady, so before turning to head out the door, he said, "Je m'appelle Emanuel Lindsay."

"I will tell her. Au revoir."

Every time Manney left the hotel room Amil jumped on the phone. Amil had often imagined hearing this sexy, raspy voice that was attached to someone who was able to define herself in only a word or two. And that's exactly what happened. CreolSista's voice was unforgettable on the answering machine. Amil thought about those many nights when their chatting went beyond being friendly and shifted briefly to something sensual and compassionate. She imagined that voice whispering in her ear. She caressed herself when her imagination allowed her to feel CreolSista's touch and send her into complete ecstasy. CreolSista, in an effort to always look out for her own feelings, kept those times limited, for she saw an opportunity to have a friend that she could love without the sex and one that she could touch without ever being physical. Being in love with someone that you couldn't have had been hard, and CreolSista was determined to respect Amil's relationship by being what Amil seemed to need most... a friend. During the entire time she'd been in town, all Amil had reached was an answering machine with a message in English and a message in French. Although leaving a message was an option, Amil chose not to do so simply because it would have taken away the intrigue. She left a series of hang-ups and extended pauses...enough to piss off anybody returning from a long trip and coming home to find ten messages turning out to be absolutely no one.

As a last resort, Amil decided to sign online with hopes of seeing her girl online. No such luck. Nearly two months had passed since they'd last spoken, and there was a lot that Amil had on her mind. Their last conversation had given her plenty to think about. It seemed that she'd started holding back her feelings when, at one point, they'd flowed so freely. Amil knew that CreolSista loved her even though she'd never laid eyes on her. Their chatting had become this nightly ritual, and the only thing that kept them from it was when CreolSista was out of town on extended trips like this one. It was okay that they led their professional lives privately and never shared more than asked. It was also okay that CreolSista had admitted being gay but was still fond of the companionship and conversation with Amil—a straight woman that kept CreolSista in touch with her femininity and occasional need for girlfriend-to-girlfriend talk. It was becoming increasingly okay with Amil that a gay woman was interested in being friends with her, straying away from her own kind; it gave her the attention that Manney had so often taken away. The words, "You're beautiful," had taken on a new meaning, for CreolSista reminded Amil of the inner beauty that was so often masked by her physical obligation to Manney. It had become ever so important to finally put a face with the same love and compassion that Amil felt while she was on the computer. Their last conversation, however, had been so disheartening that Amil didn't even know if all her attempts to reach her friend had been in vain. She wanted and needed to finally tell CreolSista that she loved her. But, as Manney came bursting into the room announcing that their cab was downstairs, Amil regretfully realized that wasn't going to happen on this trip. Disappointedly, she turned off her laptop and packed it up with the rest of her things. It was going to be a long flight home.

LORD, TAKE THIS WOMAN

Iysha was nervous as hell. She had been in the bathroom for over twenty minutes, and, between the shits and tears, there was no telling when she was coming out. For almost two weeks, Iysha and her parents had been in constant disagreements about the fucked-up choices she had been making. And to make matters worse, Iysha had run the phone bill up trying to find Chris in Paris. At hundreds of pennies per minute, she was in debt to both parents for over $500 for their phone bills. Message after message had been left on her sister's answering machine but no return calls. Chris had a way of disappearing without a trace and only resurfacing on holidays, birthdays, and maybe a special occasion. Her calls were brief but joyous.

The last time Chris was in Memphis she went into auto-bitch mode on the whole family. Everybody claimed to be concerned about Chris's daughters, Chelsea and Gaylon. They thought it "proper" to have let the babies remain in the states for a good upbringing. "Those babies need to be around family," they kept saying.

"They need some stability." Chris went from room to room trying to escape undesired rehabilitation attempts. If it weren't Uncle Jarvis, then it was Aunt Lilly. Finally, after hours of relentless lectures with no reprieve, Chris exploded. "Have any of you ever wondered what life would be like if you just minded your business for just five minutes? I mean, damn, my kids aren't starving! They speak languages other than broken English, and, most importantly, they're happy! So what I fuck women! Those women have taken better care of me and my babies than any of you have ever offered to. This is one of the very reasons I try to keep them away from you!"

With that said, Chris grabbed her girls and was out the door. Iysha's sister and nieces hadn't been back in over three years, but, on this day, Iysha needed her big sister. She needed Chris's openness and her candid advice. She needed someone to tell her in a non-parental way that she was making a big mistake. Despite their history, Iysha sometimes valued her sister's warped opinions even though she had never told her so. She respected the fact that Chris had that "just live" attitude, and she instilled that same principle in her children. Chris and Iysha grew up in a house where their mother's useless boyfriend was crowned man of the house. Pete didn't have a job because he didn't want one. He didn't take care of his kids from his previous marriage because he didn't want to. He never filed taxes because it would alert the government that he wasn't dead in a ditch somewhere and would be deemed able to take care of those nine children he had. The government would take that money and send it to the mother of those babies regardless of what she eventually chose to do with the cash. Pete had no love for life, so why would he—how could he, have any love for anyone, or anything else? Ms. Desmereaux had given him shelter and food during a time when she and her children themselves were needy. She, most importantly, had a need for love. So, for twenty years, Ora Desmereaux loved a man whose only needs were a home and something to eat. He had no morals, no class, and no education. He wasn't suitable for this beautiful, independent woman, and it took her all of those twenty years to realize that. But now, at the age of 50, Ora was unhappy but content, and it was that contentment which drove Iysha to her wedding day. It was also one of the motivating forces that kept Chris on the path of success, determined to not ever need love or support from anyone other than herself.

"Damn, I hate this!" Chris yelled as she slammed on brakes in the airport tunnel. Looking at the traffic jam from just over the tunnel's hill, Chris could see that she and the girls would be there for hours.

"Mommy, don't say that!" The little girls giggled in the backseat.

"Oh, I'm sorry, sweeties. Mommy's in a really, really big hurry."

"But you don't have to say those bad words," Chelsea said.

"You're right, and I apologize." Chris sighed as she watched a fire truck, rescue team, and an ambulance speed by. She'd retrieved all of Iysha's messages and was trying desperately to make it to Harbor Town for the wedding. No one in Chris's family knew that she had been back in town for almost two months. Still maintaining a residence in Paris, Chris had purchased a condo in her hometown and had managed to keep it a secret from her family.

"Mommy, where's that fire truck going?" Gaylon asked. When Chris moved to Paris after completing grad school in Philly, Chelsea had just turned three, and Gaylon was getting ready to turn two. Each of them had developed a cute Northern brogue, but once they got to France, that changed. Now five and four, respectively, Chelsea and Gaylon picked up the French language rather quickly, especially after their mother had hired a private tutor. "Is somebody hurt?"

"I don't know, baby. Looks like it's going the same way that we're trying to go." *Shit.* By that time, another ambulance was passing by. Surprising Iysha at her wedding was now definitely out of the question.

❧♥❧

Harbor Town was such a prestigious address that most people were too intimidated to ride through and sightsee. Security would be on your ass so fast that it'd make your head spin. The houses seemed to be built so close together that privacy was a foreign amenity. Overlooking the Mississippi River, the development accommodated doctors, lawyers, architects, and recently a couple of Black families that had come across some money that they didn't know how to spend.

One family, the Townsends, was the recipient of Tunica County's largest jackpot ever. Jessie Townsend had just gotten out of jail one Friday afternoon and borrowed five dollars from his neighbor. Longtime residents of the Scutterfield housing project, Jessie and his sister Camille stayed in trouble. She was often at 201 Poplar (Shelby County Jail) for food stamp fraud, and his most recent arrest was for nonpayment of child support. Ever the smooth talker, he had managed to convince his son's mother to drop the charges so that he could get out of jail and look for a job. But instead of going straight to the unemployment office, Jessie bummed a ride with his cousin, Stick, who was on his way to work at the casino. "Man, should you be goin' down there? You just got out of jail."

"Fuck them, muthafuckas. I go where I wanna go.

Besides I can get a few drinks while I'm gettin' my slot machine thang on. I ain't got but five dollars no way. I'll be back home befo' the sun goes down good. Nobody'll miss me."

"All I gotta say is that you need to keep a low profile. They'll lock yo' ass back up in a New York minute. They don't mess around with that child support shit." Stick dropped Jessie off at the entrance to the Tropicana Paradise Casino and Resort and went on to work at the adjacent casino, the Aztec.

The Tropicana was reminiscent of the Caribbean with its waterfall, palm trees, and vibrant colors. Foliage draped the entrance, the windows, and even some of the machines. Instead of wearing the traditional bow ties and cummerbunds, bow ties and vests, the dealers and slot hosts wore navy blue nautical hats and neon orange polo shirts. The attire was different, but it was a welcomed change from tradition. "Something to drink?" the waitress asked.

Jessie put a dollar in the machine and pulled the handle. Nothing. "Yeah, brang me a Jack Daniel," he ordered as he pulled the handle again, never pausing to look up. And again...nothing. "Damn, c'mon, now." This time he pushed the spin button. A little variety might help. Still nothing.

"Here's your drink, sir," the waitress said, leaning on the adjacent machine waiting for a tip.

Jessie looked up at her. "I got two dollars left, and that's it. And I ain't giving none of it to you. Now if you really want a tip, gone on and brang me another drink without me having to ask twice. And make it snappy."

The waitress angrily stomped off grumbling, "Sometimes you gotta give a little to get a little." She never did come back.

"Bitches, just gold diggahs." Jessie pushed the spin button one more time. *Click. Click. Click.* The sirens, whistles, and musical choruses went off louder than they ever had. "Goddamn! I hit this muthafucka!" Jessie screamed as he realized that he had just landed the biggest jackpot in Tunica County history…for $15 million dollars. As the cameras flashed and as the crowd cheered, Jessie kicked over the stool he was sitting on as he jumped up and down and pumped his fists in the air, yelling loudly for all to hear, "Who da man?! Who da man?! Yeah, ba-bay! I'm a celebrity now! Kiss my ass, CJC! I'm rich!"

Those folks at the Criminal Justice Complex that Jessie had so boldly told to kiss his ass were knocking on his door at 1:00 the next morning. Jessie was back in jail by 3 a.m. for violating his probation by going outside the city limits and for being in a casino. The few hundreds of thousands of dollars that Jessie was allowed to keep was spent on a home for his family and on retaining an attorney to keep him out of trouble. In a last-minute plea, he agreed to set up a trust fund for his children with the remaining winnings. For actually wanting to take care of his kids, the judge granted Jessie fifteen years probation and 2,000 hours of community service instead of ten years in jail.

The other family, the Maxwells, genuinely had a little money but, because of the casino, they had some issues with spending as well. Gunther Maxwell was the founder and owner of Memphis' Best Barbecue Joint. In less than ten years, he had won four International Barbecue Cooking Contests during Memphis in May and was worth close to three million dollars. Precious, Gunther's wife, ran the business while her husband "traveled." He was also the coach of the men's basketball team at West Tennessee University. Throughout the collegiate basketball season, Gunther was in and out of town a lot, rumored to be accompanied by a young co-ed who "didn't play no games." Gunther's manhood kept him in trouble a lot more than he'd wished. Precious always told him, "If you leave this house going to get liverwurst, then your ass better smell like liverwurst when you get back." She paid the bills out of Gunther's coaching salary, and most of the money they'd made in the restaurant was put on the blackjack tables in Tunica. Their mini-fortune was comprised solely of the land that the restaurant sat on. Gunther bought it on Third Street ten years before anybody ever thought about redeveloping Beale Street. He got the building and the strip of land beside it for less than $50,000. When the new developers—Locke, Lindsay, and McKay—came through, the city offered Gunther close to a million dollars for his property, and he cleverly declined the offer. Now, some fifteen years later, the property's worth, with the building and all, was estimated at a couple of cool millions.

Gunther and Precious didn't have any children of their own and took great interest in their nieces and nephews. Thus they offered to host the wedding and reception of Precious's often-needy nephew, Nathaniel.

The setting was simple. Some flowers here, a ribbon or two there. Nothing elaborate. Ms. Desmereaux, crying the whole time, used up ten of the twenty napkins that were allotted for guests. The only major expense seemed to be the cake. It had Seessel's bakery written all over it, and next to it sat Mr. Desmereaux and his second wife—the other Mrs. Desmereaux. Since this wedding was BYOB, he had, just like everyone else, brought his own liquor. The sole exception was the champagne that the bride and groom were to share. That's the way that their nephew wanted it. Simple but elegant.

"Do you, Nathaniel, take Iysha to be your lawfully wedded wife?" Rev. Edmonds asked.

"I do."

"And do you, Iysha Desmereaux, take Nathaniel Chamberlain Alexander to be your lawfully wedded husband?"

"I do."

The kiss was so quick that if you'd blinked, you would have missed it.

❧♥❧

As Chris approached the accident scene, she watched the paramedics wheel a bagged body to the back of the coroner's van. Chris recognized the officer directing traffic. His name was Brandon, and they had gone to high school together. He was the chunky boy who always sat in the bleachers and ate up all his candy during the candy drive. It was a damn shame that somebody could sit and eat a case of M&Ms in one sitting. His frail behind won that candy drive every year. A huge goofball during high school, no one would have ever guessed that Brandon would become a police officer. "Hey, Brandon. How you doing?"

The buff, uniformed officer looked in the window and immediately recognized the face that hadn't changed in over ten years. Chris was still gorgeous as the day she was voted "Most Attractive" by her high school classmates. He smiled. "Chris Desmereaux."

"Yes, it's me," she said, leaning her head out of the window to kiss him on the cheek.

"Damn, you still look good! Still smellin' all good, too."

"How have you been, Brandon?" She smiled.

"I've been doing okay. Out here trying to help out."

"What happened?"

"Well, a couple of my officers are out today. So, as their commanding officer, I had to come down here to lend a hand."

"Commanding officer?"

"Yeah, baby, I run with the big dawgs now. I am a Sergeant."

"You go, boy. So what's the deal with the traffic?"

"Pull over here for a minute and let the other cars by." Chris pulled her car into the median. She watched Brandon from her rear-view mirror. His ass was tight, and his pants hugged every inch of it. "Hell, I might be gay, but I ain't dead!" she mumbled to herself. "Damn, he looks too good!"

After telling his partner to take over for a few minutes, Brandon walked over to Chris's car to give her the low-down. "Well, it's kinda crazy. The paramedics just wheeled a body to the back of the coroner's van. One car flipped upside-down, ejected its passengers on impact. Not sure how that happened. A second vehicle, traveling north and seemingly out of control, flipped down the embankment and crushed one of the ejected passengers from the first car. I think that was who was in the body bag."

"Wow. Where did the fire come from?"

"That's where it gets a little more interesting. In that second car were two women. From what witnesses say, the car was already ablaze on impact. One was dead at the scene, and the other was airlifted to the Memphis General over half-hour ago. An off-duty fireman who just happened to be passing by had a fire extinguisher in his car and put enough of the fire out so that they could get to her. Then someone else pulled her from the car. She's burned pretty bad. Why the car was on fire is still a mystery. The only person who can tell us what happened is in that helicopter."

Chris's cell phone rang. Only two people had that number, and one of those was her boss who knew not to call while Chris was on vacation. The other was her ex-girlfriend's mother, Sadie. "Excuse me for a minute, Brandon." Puzzled by the ringing of a phone that usually never rang, she answered, "Hello." But the voice on the other end was breaking up. "Hello-o-o." The signal died.

"You're not likely to get any reception out here with all these radios," Brandon offered. "So how's Paris? Your Momma brags to everyone she sees about her baby working for the University of Paris. What do you do over there?"

"I'm the Vice President of Admissions for American Students. I'm working on my Ph.D. in International Business, too, since it's free."

"Impressive. We all knew that you were gonna amount

to something one day. A real go-getter. So, how long you in town for? I mean, wanna get a bite to eat or something?"

People had started getting out of their cars and walking toward the scene of the accident. There wasn't shit to see; everybody was just being nosy. "I will be here only through the weekend, but here's my number in Paris. And don't worry; I'm giving you a toll-free number that goes through the school's switchboard." She smiled. "If I could get out of this madness, I just might make it to my sister's wedding."

"Why didn't you say so? I can get you through here. You take care, and look to hear from me soon."

"Okay, Brandon. I will, and it was nice to see you after all these years." Brandon guided Chris off the median, through the traffic and onto the Airport Parkway. The best that Chris would be able to do was to make it to the reception. As she entered the I-240 ramp, the cell phone rang again. "Hello."

"Hi, Chris."

"Sadie?"

"Yes, it's me." Her voice was shaking. "How are you?"

"I'm okay. What's wrong, honey? Was that you just trying to call me?"

"Yes." Sadie gave a huge sigh. "Can you come home to Memphis?"

"Actually, I'm already in Memphis. I've been here for a few weeks. What's wrong?"

"It's Gayle. She's in the hospital. Can you come to Memphis General? I really think that you should come down here."

"Sadie, I'm on my way to Iysha's reception since I missed the wedding. I was stuck in traffic for over an hour. Hopefully, I'll make it there in time for some cake."

Sadie's tone was somber, and words were scarce. "Okay, just make it if you can. Ask for the ER's Chief of Staff."

"I will. I'll try my best to get there." Chris hung the phone up and considered her options. She wouldn't have to stay at the reception too long because it was probably almost over anyway. After making sure that she got a piece of the cake and that the girls would be taken care of, she would head over to Memphis General.

❧♥❧

By the time Chris got to Harbor Town, most of her family was still there. She dreaded having to see them because she knew that if they caught wind of the fact that she'd been in town for nearly two months, they'd hit the roof. No one knew about her condo…yet.

"Can I help you?" a man in a gray suit asked.

"I'm looking for Iysha."

"Does she know you?"

"Yes, I'm her sister." At that exact moment, Chris

laid eyes on her baby sister. "Never mind, I see her." Dressed in a simple but elegant ivory pantsuit, Iysha looked absolutely beautiful as she stood next to her parents. Rushing past the other guests, Chris grabbed her sister from behind. "You just couldn't wait for me to get here, could you?" she whispered in Iysha's ear.

"Ahhhhh! Where did you come from?" Iysha squealed as she turned around and hugged her sister. "I guess you got my messages."

Chris laughed. "All fifty of them."

"My baby!" Ms. Desmereaux screamed. She looked behind Chris and saw Chelsea and Gaylon. "All of my babies! Look at you!" The girls jumped in their grandmother's arms. "How Granny's babies been doin'?"

"Fine," they said in unison. After being drenched with kisses on the cheeks and forehead, the girls dashed for their grandfather who had made his way to the skimpy buffet table and the punch bowl with his whisky flask in tow. Chelsea and Gaylon followed his every move asking for a little bit of everything that he had on his plate.

"Hey, Momma," Chris said, hugging her mother. "You look good."

"Thank you, baby. When did you get here? You missed the wedding."

"I know. I got stuck in traffic at the airport, and..."

Cutting Chris off, "Don't worry about that," she said. "I'm just glad you're here."

Chris looked around. "Where's my new brother-in-law?"

Ms. Desmereaux answered, "He's outside talking with the minister."

Iysha pulled Chris from her mother. "I need to talk to you right now."

"Okay. Okay. What's up?" Chris looked down at Iysha's stomach. "Well, I see one thing that you need to tell me."

Iysha rubbed her stomach. "Can you tell?"

"Hell, yes. How far along?"

"Three months."

"And you're this big?"

"Twins." Iysha smiled. "I'm going to have twins."

"Twinzes? Well, congratulations! I'm finally going to be an auntie. Do you know what they are yet?"

"Nathaniel wants girls. Speaking of which, here he is." Iysha's face didn't light up the way a new bride's face should when her new husband walks into a room. He came from behind Chris. "Chris, this is your new brother-in-law, Nathaniel Alexander."

When Nathaniel took his place beside Iysha, it was déjà vu for Chris. And as fate would have it, she couldn't, for the life of her, place his face. "Hi," he said flamingly... pleasantly. That one word did it. The voice was unmistakable as was the demeanor. Chris's new brother-in-law looked just like...*No way*...Chris figured that it couldn't be the Menagerie's grandest drag queen. "I don't know if I should shake your hand or give you a hug?" Nathaniel wasn't fooling Chris. She realized that he knew that she was aware of whom he was.

Chris was flabbergasted. "I guess since we're family, a hug would be in order." They embraced. Chris wanted to faint. At a loss for words, Chris tried desperately to regain her composure. Her knees were wobbly, and she felt a slight hot flash coming on. She had to be mistaken. Maybe it was just a coincidence. It had to be just a coincidence.

"Are you all right?" Nathaniel asked as he tried to comfort Chris. "You need some water or something?"

Chris casually shook off his kind gestures. "No, I'm okay. It's probably this champagne. It's my second glass on an empty stomach."

"Oh, okay, then," he said. "Iysha has told me so much about you. We were thinking about coming to Paris for our honeymoon, but..."

"Iysha, um, you know what?" Chris interjected. "I need to talk to you about something. Come out on the terrace with me."

Afraid that Chris was going to blow everything, Nathaniel interrupted, "Well, Chris, we need to cut the cake first before the two of you disappear."

Ewww. The sound of his voice made Chris's flesh crawl. As odd as it were, Chris wasn't that fond of gay men. She thought they were rude, confused, loud, and most of all, nasty. "We'll be right back, Nathaniel," Iysha said calmly.

"I know," said Nathaniel firmly. "But the photographer needs to get these last pictures before he leaves." Chris sensed that all was not right and told Iysha that she would catch her later. While standing on the terrace, Chris spotted the Maxwell's neighbor, Jessie, as he waxed and buffed his new Lexus LS400. Chris knew that she had been away for a while, but she also knew that she was not that far behind in culture and style. This man, with his nappy-haired gut sagging over the top of a pair of too-tight cut-off shorts, was styling and profiling in front of this Lexus that had an 8-inch high spoiler on the back and 20-inch rims on all four tires. It also had a gold kit on all the emblems, and there were even gold plates above the tires and gold trim around the doors. Windows tinted jet black, script initials stuck on all the back passenger windows, and lastly, the neon undercarriage reminded Chris that she was home. Some of those lavish signs of new money could have been forgiven until Jessie opened the back door of the car where the back seat used to be. It had been taken out and replaced with $3,000 worth of speakers. *Oh, the comforts of being back at home.* Chris sighed.

An hour passed, and Chris found an opportunity to leave. She had promised Sadie that she would come to the hospital. "Momma, Iysha, I've got an errand to run."

"How the hell do you have an errand to run when you haven't been in town but a couple of hours?" Ms. Desmereaux asked.

Chris blurted out, "I've been here for almost two months, Momma. Taking care of some business. Be pissed at me if you want to." Gulping down a glass of champagne, she continued, "Please don't ask me any questions about it right now because I got to leave. But before I go, I need to ask you a favor."

Ms. Desmereaux knew what was up. "Leave them, Chris. I'll take the girls on home with me."

❧♥❧

Despite the fact that it was a world-renowned research hospital, Chris had always felt that Memphis General was among the filthiest places she had ever seen. It turned away no one. Sometimes there were such influxes of patients that there was no time to properly clean. Drops of blood were everywhere. Kids were crying and running all over the place, some with runny noses, one or two with broken limbs, and many with high fevers. In the bathrooms, homeless people looked for empty stalls to take refuge from the night. The security guards were too busy flaunting their horrible attitudes to be concerned about the traffic in the ER. That was the job of the Emergency Room's Chief of Staff, and that was whom Chris had been told to ask for when she arrived.

"Excuse me," she said to the security guard. "I am looking for the person in charge of the ER."

"Oh, the new girl. She's right there at the counter. Dr. Lindsay is her name," the guard said.

"Thank you." Chris walked to the counter and noticed that, in front of her, stood the woman of her dreams. Dr. Lindsay, a well-endowed and seemingly refined woman, was handling business. People were running every direction at her command. That kind of shit turned Chris on. Dr. Lindsay had light brown eyes and white chocolate skin gently kissed by the sun. Yes, it was the ER, but Dr. Lindsay was wearing heels with matching toe and finger nail polish. Her hair barely brushed the shoulder of her coat. In comparison to previous pieces of booty, this was the first real GIRL that had ever caught Chris's attention. No, she wasn't sure if the good doctor were gay (sometimes it's easy to tell when a straight woman has thought about getting her kat licked by another woman, but you've got to be gay yourself to recognize the signs. If you're wrong, then you've lost nothing but might've gained a possible good fuck if liquor ever gets involved. But, if you're right? Then, congratulations and bring on the U-Haul!) Her mannerisms, the movement of her hands, the.... *Woo-woo!* "Dr. Lindsay?"

"Yes," the woman replied. "May I help you?"

"I'm Chris Desmereaux. Sadie..."

"Oh, yes, yes. I've been waiting for you." She came around from behind the counter and offered her hand to Chris. "I'm Dr. Lindsay." And then she hesitated for an instant, too.

"Nice to meet you." By this time Chris wanted to know what the hell was going on. "Do you by any chance know what is going on here?" Chris panned the doctor's entire body from head to toe. *This couldn't be.* There was something amiss.

"Let's find some privacy," she said, leading Chris to the lounge. "Do you know Gayle Evans?"

"Yes, I do. She's Sadie's daughter and an acquaintance of mine. What's wrong?"

"The family wanted me to talk with you about Ms. Evans's accident."

"Accident?"

"Yes, I don't know if you've heard about it by now, but it had traffic tied up really bad around the airport." Dr. Lindsay gave Chris the same inspection that she'd just unknowingly received. A woman with even a little Creole in her was sometimes easy to spot.

Chris thought back to her conversation with Brandon. She remembered that only one person had survived the crash.

"Wait a minute," she gasped. "Was Gayle airlifted here?"

Dr. Lindsay paused. "Yes, she was. She has extensive internal injuries, but it's the burns that concern me. We attempted to do emergency skin grafting, but she said no."

"What do you mean she said no? She's awake?"

"Barely. She's alert enough to make her own decisions, and, per policy, we have to respect those decisions. All we can do is keep her comfortable."

Chris was dumbfounded. "Wait a minute; you're telling me that you're through?"

"If she'd been unconscious when they brought her in, then it would have been up to her family. They weren't called until after she got here. Her emergency contact information was found in her purse along with this picture." Smiling, Dr. Lindsay handed it to Chris. "Those babies look just like you." It was a picture of Gaylon and Chelsea that Gayle had taken from Sadie. "Did you know that she had you listed as a secondary contact person in case of an emergency?"

"No, I didn't," Chris said. She couldn't think of much to say. It was like a freight train had run her over. "How's Sadie?"

"Well, I've explained to her what will happen next. We've done everything that we can. Gayle is painfully conscious right now, and I can't tell you when she'll go into cardiac arrest."

Chris was on the verge of shock. She and Gayle hadn't

spoken in a couple of years, but Chris had remained in contact with Sadie. Chris knew that Gayle had been living with Monica off and on, and she also knew that Gayle hadn't been happy either. "Dr. Lindsay?"

"Yes."

"So, you're basically telling me that she's going to die."

"Chris, if I may, Gayle was apparently set on fire. Her story is that the girl who was riding with her poured kerosene on the floor of the car. Gayle had been thinking that it was beer the whole time since the girl had it wrapped in a brown paper bag. Some words were exchanged, and the young lady proceeded to toss a match toward the driver's side of the car. The flame caught Gayle's pants leg that was apparently already saturated with kerosene. The car went off the road and over the embankment. The other passenger was killed instantly."

"I know most of what happened." Chris sighed.

"How do you know that?"

As her eyes welled with tears, Chris spoke, "I was stuck in that tie-up for over an hour, and a friend of mine was directing traffic. I saw the fire from the road, but I had no idea what was going on. Then Sadie called me just as I was passing through the scene, and I told her that I would get here as quickly as I could. I wish that she had told me what was wrong over the phone."

Chris began sobbing, and Dr. Lindsay provided her temporary solitude with a comforting hug and some consoling words.

❧♥❧

Gayle lie on the gurney in excruciating pain despite the fact that she was receiving morphine at its maximum dosage limit. In and out of consciousness, Gayle had decided that she wasn't going to fight a losing battle. All she wanted to know was if someone had gotten hold of Chris. The last time they'd spoken wasn't pleasant, but, today, on her deathbed, Chris was whom she wanted to see.

While Chris lived in Philly, Gayle had come to see her twice. The first time, Chris was a sight for sore eyes, but Gayle never told her that. She'd quickly found that the grass wasn't always greener on the other side. Making matters worse, Monica had a drug problem: one that had nearly cost Gayle her life on more than one occasion. Monica had told her dope dealer friends that Gayle would pay them their money. But when Gayle didn't pay, it was she who had gotten her ass beat, and it was she who had to come up with hundreds of dollars in order to keep her family and friends out of it and alive. Everyone knew that Monica didn't have an ounce of love for Gayle, and, given the amount of attention that Gayle almost demanded during her visit, Chris knew it, too.

The next time Gayle visited the City of Brotherly Love things were so bad that Gayle needed money, and, feeling that it was owed to her, she wanted it from Chris. While together, Chris had allowed Gayle to claim Gaylon on her taxes along with some other women's children that Chris knew nothing about. Gayle's tax return was almost $6,000.

Once she'd had an opportunity to completely heal from the drama of the years before, Chris told her best friend Darcy the whole sordid story of her relationship with Gayle. When all the shit hit the fan concerning Gayle's deception toward Chris, Darcy's mouth was like that of a low-rent hooker that had stolen from the mob. It couldn't stop running. She told the IRS that Gayle had used those other kids on her tax return, and what she nor Chris knew was that Gayle had done it three times before. "Chris, you are not going to let that woman make a complete ass out of you." Gayle had taken that year's inflated return and paid off Monica's drug debts. By the time Darcy got through singing her stories, Gayle had to pay back almost $20,000 to the IRS.

Turning angrily on Chris, Gayle demanded, "Don't you think that you should help me pay that money back? You helped spend some of it, too."

What's fair is fair, Chris decided. She did help spend

the money. As a matter of fact, she helped spend the hell out of it. They bought brand-new furniture for the house and took a couple of mini-vacations. When Chris started her job, Gayle bought her a new wardrobe and got Coach purses for Iysha and Ora. "Okay, I'll help you repay it, but I'll send it in myself. I don't trust you."

Naturally, Gayle was furious. "No, that ain't happenin'. I'll turn it in myself. Who's to say that you won't change your mind the second I turn around and walk out that door?"

"You know, Gayle. It's a matter of trust. Apparently, you don't trust me like I don't trust you. I'm just trying to do what I believe to be the right thing. If you want my help, then tell me where to send it. If not, fuck you, kiss my ass, and all that good shit. Just remember that the IRS is looking for *you*—the person whose name was on the check and not the bitches that helped you spend it!" The IRS never got its money, and the two hadn't spoken since.

"She has burns all the way up to her mid-section. The odds are not in her favor. If she were to live, there would be lots of surgery, possible infections. Then she has internal injuries." Dr. Lindsay hesitated. "Is she a friend of yours or something? I heard you say that she was an acquaintance."

Chris didn't know how to classify Gayle. They had never been friends, but they once were lovers. "I'm just a friend of the family." And she turned and walked toward the trauma unit.

Gayle had been moved into isolation. She wasn't connected to any machines. Her mother was standing beside her bed watching the RN shoot morphine into her eldest child's veins like some junkie looking for a quick fix. When Sadie caught a glimpse of Chris at the nurse's station, she leaned over and whispered to Gayle that Chris had arrived. Despite the pain, Gayle asked to have her head raised so that she might be able to see Chris walk toward her once more before she died.

Tears were pouring so fast from Chris's eyes that there was no way for her to wipe them all. When she got to Gayle's bedside, Chris reached for the hand of the one woman who had been able to bring out the ugliest parts of her personality. On any given day, however, Gayle was the one that Chris would respectfully call her first love. "What have you gotten yourself into this time, Ms. Evans?" she asked as she rubbed Gayle's forehead with her other hand. Gayle's strength was almost gone, but she still managed to squeeze Chris's hand.

Gayle whispered as tears slid down from the corners of her eyes. "Something that you can't get me out of. That bitch kept telling me that she was gonna kill me."

Sniffling, Chris whimpered. "Why didn't you just leave?"

Gayle tried to snicker, but the pain was too great.

She tried to clear her throat, but the scratchiness only became worse. "You know how I am when it comes to pussy." The hair on Sadie's back stood straight up. Ordinarily, she would have left the room, but there were no more secrets to hide. Her quest for acceptance of Gayle's lifestyle was too little, too late. It didn't matter what was said; a tornado wouldn't be able to move Sadie from that room. "I've missed you, Chris. I've wanted to call you so many times, but I just knew that you hated me."

Weeping, Chris said, "If I hated you, I wouldn't be here."

"Why didn't you come back for me, Chris? I would've straightened up. We could've been happy together," she struggled.

"Gayle, we don't need to talk about all of that right now. Is there anything I can get for you while I'm here?"

"No, Chris. There's nothing that you or anyone else can do," she whimpered. "There is one thing, though. Something that I need to know."

"And what is that?"

"How do you feel about me?"

"Don't do this to me, Gayle. Not now."

"Please, Chris. I need to know."

Chris had harbored so many ill feelings toward Gayle that she wouldn't even know where to begin. But in order to see the woman who had once been able to make her smile and who had also been able to love her and to provide for her and her kids, happy for one last time, the only thing to do was to tell the truth. "I will always love you, Gayle. You were my first real lover, and you know that's always special. But I won't regret turning my back on you when I did. We caused each other too much pain. The fights. The deception. I couldn't live like that. Then you were abusive toward the kids. You had so much anger in you that you destroyed everything you touched. You needed to be with someone who would give you a taste of your own medicine, or, even better still, you needed to be by yourself. Sometimes I hate that I allowed myself to give so much of me to you. I did a lot of crazy shit when I was with you, and I hate myself for that. I really do. But it was all a learning experience. I have used that part of my life as a stepping-stone. And so far, it's been all uphill for me. The best thing that came out of my relationship with you was Gaylon. It took me months to bond with her, but I'm glad that I finally did. I realized that I owed so much to both of my children and that I had missed some milestones in their lives trying to keep up with you. Thinking back on our time together, there was a lot of love going on. It was just going in the wrong direction."

Gayle lay there. No movement. So still, Chris thought that she was dead. But then, Gayle said, "Damn, you really know how to hurt a sistah. But I guess that I deserve it. I know I hurt you, and I'm sorry." She swallowed.

"Don't be down on yourself, honey. I do love you. But like I said, I just couldn't be with you. Please don't leave here thinking that I don't care. Because I do. I just chose to take a different path. I will admit not a day goes by that I don't think of you. I simply came to a point where that negative energy needed to be turned into something positive."

Gayle still loved Chris and wanted to know one more thing. "So you still doin' women?"

Chris chuckled. "Not too much. I don't really have a lot of time for that. You want me to slide in bed next to you?"

Gayle smiled and started pulling her hand away from Chris. The pain was far worse than it'd ever been. She just wanted to be quiet. "No, I don't want you to get into the bed with me. A kiss would be just fine." Chris leaned over and gave Gayle a heartfelt kiss on her lips.

"You still wearing that strawberry shit on your lips, I see."

Gayle nodded her head slowly. "I'm through with you, Chris. You can go now. I just wanted to see your face."

"What did you say?"

"You can leave. I'll always love you, Chris. I like the way you turned out. Over the last few hours, I have been thinking about my life, and I haven't been pleased with too many of the memories. Right now, I'm just tired. Tired, Chris," she moaned. "When you leave, take Sadie with you. I got some things to talk over with God."

"Gayle, let us stay with you," Chris wept.

"God is not going to let me die alone. The Lord is gonna take me with Him when He leaves this room. Now get out of here. That's the last and best thing that you could ever do for me."

Gayle's heart stopped within ten minutes of Chris and Sadie leaving the room. While Chris and Gayle had been saying their good-byes, Sadie was on the phone making preparations with the funeral home. She didn't see Gayle take her last breath, but she felt it as any other mother would have. "Chris, the funeral home is coming to pick her up in half an hour."

Chris didn't respond.

"Chris, baby. Are you gonna be all right?"

"I'm okay, Sadie. This shouldn't have happened." Devastated, Chris's emotions that evening had gone from joy to bewilderment and then from pain to sorrow. There was so much already going on with Chris that the best thing for her was to leave but not without first offering her assistance. "How are you going to pay for the funeral?" she asked.

"I don't know. I haven't even thought about that. I was gonna call her daddy when I got home to tell him that she's gone."

Chris listened while Sadie talked, but she also watched all the hustle and bustle of the ER as if it were a busy street intersection complete with all the lights, noise, and constant movement. She was that pedestrian who didn't know when it was time to cross the street. The one who waits for the "Walk" sign to flash even though there are no cars, and, if it changes to "Don't Walk" before she is halfway through the crosswalk, then she turns around and returns to the curb. Rather than get caught in the crosswalk again, she decided to go another way. "Sadie, I'll pay for the funeral, but I won't be there. I can't be there."

"Oh, Chris. You don't have to do this. I got..."

"There's nothing you can say to change my mind." Reaching in her purse, Chris found a pen and her checkbook. "Here's a blank check. Use whatever you need."

Sadie was speechless. After all that Gayle had put Chris through, love seemed to have prevailed. Sadie knew that Chris had unconditionally given Gayle the love that she struggled so hard to reciprocate. "You really loved her, didn't you?"

Chris put her purse back on her shoulder. "Sadie, some things just go without saying." Kissing Sadie on the cheek, she turned and meandered toward the exit.

As it seemed that one chapter in her life was ending, Chris sensed that another was about to begin. Leaning over the security guard's desk was the gorgeous Dr.

Lindsay. Chris was careful to not let anyone see her gawking at the doctor, but she just couldn't help it. Passing by, Chris overheard the doctor and the security guard talking about her recent trip to Paris. "I really enjoyed it. We're going to have to go back over there in a few months. Manney still has some business to attend to," she said.

Hmmm. Maybe that would explain the hang-ups on Chris's answering machine. Chris scrambled to the waiting area to find some paper to write on. Digging profusely, she couldn't find shit. No gum wrappers, no Kleenex. She snatched a postcard from a nearby magazine and started scribbling on it. Could it be that "MOCHAMD," was within forty feet of her? If so, then she was everything that Chris, the "CreolSista," had imagined.

Keep the note short and sweet but meaningful.

But what if it wasn't her? Damn, she'd be embarrassed for life! Nonetheless, it was a chance Chris was willing to take. When she'd laid eyes on Dr. Lindsay, she got those same butterflies that the two of them had always talked about. The tone of her voice echoed the words so often communicated on the computer screen and slightly resembled the voice that Chris had briefly chatted with over the phone. The energy around this woman was phenomenal, and there was no mistaking it. "Excuse me, nurse?" Chris summoned the lady with the name "Sharon" on her ID badge as she folded the postcard.

"Yes."

Chris had second thoughts. "Can you answer a question for me?"

"I'll try."

"Do you know a Dr. Blake?"

The nurse stopped and thought for a minute. "No, I don't, but then again, I don't know all the doctors on staff. You might want to check with personnel on Monday."

"Okay, thank you." *On second thought, forget the note.* Chris made her way through the exit doors, preparing to take her emotions back on a plane to Paris.

❧♥❧

"Oui, Oui, Dr. Lindsay, and all that other stuff," Sharon teased. "How was the trip? I heard you'd be back today."

"It was beautiful. We're already making plans to go back. How's it been going with you?"

"Okay. I was just heading outside for a breath of fresh air. Oh, um, do we have a Dr. Blake on staff?"

Amil paused for a minute. "Well, yes, Blake is my maiden name. Was someone asking for me?" she inquired, trying to hide her curiosity behind a chart.

"That woman that was here with that family in the ER was asking me."

What! Amil's heart was thumping! "Where'd she go?"

"She left here in a bit of a hurry after I told her that I didn't know of anyone by that name."

Damn! There was only person who knew Amil as Dr. Blake, but she didn't want to draw any undue attention to herself. "Okay, then. Don't worry about it." Amil sighed. "Did the funeral home ever get here?"

"Yeah, they came right on."

"How was the mother?"

"Holding her own. She wanted to see them roll her out of here. She was humming 'God Will Take Care of You' like nobody's bidness. It sounded like Aretha herself was walkin' through here. So sad. So, so sad."

Amil was curious. Without seeming insensitive, she wanted to know about the other woman that might have been down there, too. "Was she alone?"

"Yeah, she was. Why?"

"Just wondering." Scanning the ER, Amil noticed the dinginess of the floors and the rest of the surroundings. "We need to get on the job of getting this place cleaned up. It looks like a pigsty in here."

"Yes, ma'am. I'll get the building engineer right on it."

"Okay, thank you. I'll be in my office if anyone needs me."

"This place must be a morgue compared to the hospital in D.C.?" Sharon interjected.

Amil laughed. "Kinda, but I could get used to it."

Heading for the elevator, she scoped the entire ER looking for the woman who had piqued her interest earlier...the only person in the world who knew to call her Dr. Blake.

TIME WILL REVEAL

Nathaniel was bullshitting about going to Paris for their honeymoon, but Iysha believed it to be heartfelt in spite of the fact that she thought he was just making small talk with his new sister-in-law. But Nathaniel knew what he was doing, and Chris appeared to know as well.

Iysha had accepted some time earlier that life with Nathaniel wasn't going to be easy. He was a neat freak—everything had its place…in the house, in the car, right on down to his clothes. His taste in designer clothes was impeccable, and he wanted Iysha to be the same way. "Buy this, wear that," he instructed. Money was never an object when it came to clothes and to decorating the house. It was all in the "appearance" of things that mattered most to him. Although she came from a background of strong women, Iysha allowed Nathaniel to control her every move and her every dollar. Once it was discovered she was pregnant with twins, the doctor asked her to cut back on her hours at work because she needed to rest as much as she could.

Just prior to the wedding, Iysha had agreed to give Nathaniel her paychecks so he could pay *his* bills. The only benefit she got from doing that was a new suit or two when they went shopping or maybe even something new for the babies. All of this before anybody had said, "I do." Iysha had grown accustomed to Nathaniel's sometimes-shitty attitude and attributed it to him being spoiled and used to getting his way. The sex was good. She gave it to him when he wanted, where he wanted, and how he wanted. Usually, they were a step or two short starring in their own porn movie. Every once in a while, though, this really nasty side of him would come through.

It all started once they were in the limo after the wedding reception. "That was rude of you," Nathaniel said. "Other people were in the room," he commented as he glared out the window.

Taken aback, Iysha asked, "What are you talking about?"

As he took of a sip of orange juice, Nathaniel responded, "Trying to steal time away to talk to your sister. Hangin' all over her like you were needing to kiss her ass or something."

"Nathaniel, I hadn't seen or talked to my sister in months, and you're gonna sit here and give me grief over being happy to see her and my nieces?"

"I'm just saying, Iysha, a marriage is about love and

respect. You disrespected me back there in front of all those people."

Iysha had to get a grip before she went completely off. "If I recall, it was you who interrupted my conversation with Chris. It wouldn't have taken but a minute to talk to her."

"Why you on her side after all she's done to you?"

"That stuff's old, Nathaniel. Sibling rivalry stuff. She hasn't done anything to me that I didn't let her do. She's got herself together now, and I just want us all to be a family."

Nathaniel's problem wasn't Iysha disrespecting him. He had issues with Chris because he knew that Chris knew folks that knew Miss Nay. The more time Chris had with Iysha the more likely something was going to come out. Nathaniel saw the way Chris looked at him. He saw how startled Chris was when he spoke his first words to her. "I'm just saying. You've always said that she treated you unfairly and never cared about anyone but herself."

"She's changed. Chris finally got it all together, and now she would do anything she could to help me."

Nathaniel nipped that in the bud quick. "We don't need anything from her, and don't ever let me know that you've even asked. I don't want her in our business."

"But..."

"Iysha, what did we just discuss? A woman's place is

behind her husband...not beside him." Nathaniel started preaching that religious doctrine that he'd been taught in church. As part of her initiation into the family, Iysha had to be baptized again and had to attend hours of marriage counseling. She was being made to believe that her husband was the sole breadwinner. A wife listens to her husband and never refutes him. A wife's place is in the home with the children. "You know, Pastor Edmonds has newlywed counseling every Monday night. I think that we should start going."

This new church home for Iysha was not what she'd been used to. Women were not allowed to pray or step foot in the pulpit. There was no choir—only hymns sung by the thirty-member congregation. "Are we still going to visit my mother's church for Christmas and on Mother's Day? We promised her, remember?"

"I doubt it. We need to spend time in our own surroundings. If we don't get to go, she'll just have to get over it."

Iysha didn't know what had come over Nathaniel. Had she sacrificed her friendship with him for marriage? Ever since the day before the wedding, he'd been different, but Iysha couldn't put her hand on just what the change was. Their limo missed its turn onto I-240 from Sam Cooper Expressway. "Where are we going?"

Nathaniel looked through the window and too noticed that they'd missed their turn. "I don't know. Maybe he's taking the scenic route to Embassy Suites." After saying that, Nathaniel took Iysha's hand and placed it on his crotch. "Well, then, now we have a little more time for celebrating." He grinned as he stroked himself with her hand.

Iysha really wanted this marriage to work. Her parents' marriage didn't work, and she was determined to not make the same mistakes they had. "And what does Daddy want me to do for him?" Iysha taunted. Gesturing with his eyes that he wanted his new wife to give him a hand job, Nathaniel merely smiled. "Do I have to ask?"

As the limo rode through Shelby Farms Park, Iysha took Nathaniel's rock-hard dick from his underwear and groped it gently. She played with it and stroked the width of it just before tickling its tip with her tongue. Inhaling...exhaling...seemingly both at the same time and sensuously sucking through his teeth, Nathaniel's eyes rolled in the back of his head as she filled her mouth with him. In a matter of an instant, Iysha came down with a sudden episode of nausea and pulled up. She hurriedly jerked herself away and threw up in the ice bucket. "Nathaniel, I really don't feel too good right now."

"You always sick," he snapped, putting his dick back in his pants.

Surprised at his disinterest, Iysha painfully apologized. "I need a little bit of ginger ale, and this will pass.

I probably just ate too much at the reception. Can you get me a..." The limo pulled up to the front door of the hotel.

Before she knew it, Nathaniel had jumped out of the car and had stormed to the front desk to check in. He never asked Iysha if she needed anything, nor did he try to help his wife regain her composure. Nathaniel was selfish like that sometimes. When they got to their room, Nathaniel made his way to the bathroom and closed the door. Iysha didn't hear him as he moaned and stroked himself into sexual bliss.

The only thing that Iysha had the strength to do was to get a glass of water and lie down.

REVELATIONS

The flight back to Paris departed at 3 p.m., so Chris had very little time for socializing with Ora once she'd arrived to pick up the girls. Time had to be allotted for customs, and the entire process could take anywhere from fifteen minutes to two hours. The only thing on her mind, though, was that she talk to Iysha before leaving. Something had to be going on. There had been a dire need on Iysha's part to talk to Chris about some things, but they couldn't get any privacy at the reception. For once Chris regretted not having told anyone that she was in town.

It was 6:45 when Chris pulled up in her mother's driveway. She knew that Ora wasn't going to be pissed about her being gone all night since she hadn't seen the girls in so long. Chris was also quite certain that, by now, Chelsea and Gaylon had informed their grandmother that they had been in town for weeks. Chris's key to the front door still worked, but she rarely used it. She would freak the hell out if she'd ever walked in on Pete and her mother taking care of business. "Why don't you ever use your key instead of ringing that damn doorbell?" her mother snapped through the window as she fumbled with the deadbolt.

"I couldn't find it," Chris teased.

"Yeah, right. Where have you been all night? I started to worry, but I figured that you could handle yourself. So..."

"Momma, Gayle died last night."

Ora held her head in her hands. "I know. It's all over the front page of the newspaper. Was that why you left in such a hurry last night?"

Sitting down on the sofa, Chris fought back tears. "I was trying to get to the wedding, but I got caught in the traffic jam that the accident caused. Sadie called me on my cell phone and asked if I could come to the hospital. I told her that I had to make it to Iysha before it was too late, and she understood that. So I agreed to stop by as soon as I could get away. That's why I left the reception."

Ora, as usual, only heard what she wanted to hear. "You got a cell phone, and I don't even have the number?"

"You do have my cell phone number...just not this one."

"Oh." Ms. Desmereaux had already starting cooking breakfast for Pete, and Chris saw that some things were never changed. "I would offer you something, but this is Pete's stuff. You know how he likes a big breakfast on Sundays."

Chris couldn't believe her ears. But then again, yes, she could. It was the same old shit; just a different day. "Don't worry about it. We can eat at home."

"You're gonna wait to eat until you get all the way back to Paris?"

The time was finally right. Walking into in the kitchen and removing a key from her key ring, Chris slid the extra copy of her condo key across the counter to her mother and said, "Actually, right now home is my condo across town. Just a small one for impromptu visits here."

"So you're planning to move back to Memphis?" Ora inquired as she picked the key up and slid it into the pocket of her bathrobe.

"Nope. Paris is still home for the moment. I've had some loose ends to deal with. And the way things are going I'll probably be in and out of town, off and on, for a while. Some other things have come up."

"I can't believe you, Chris. You've had these babies here all this time, and you didn't tell me. You know how much they mean to me."

"Didn't you hear anything I just said?"

"I did, but..."

"But what, Momma?'

"You know how much I love my grandbabies. It just hurts..."

"This is not about hurting you. It's about me being

my own person and doing my own thing. The girls go wherever I go. I just didn't want to go through all of this emotional bullshit every time I come to town. Everybody always has something to say, always wanting to be heard."

"Iysha needed you, and you turned your back on her."

"No, I didn't. Until the last two or three, all of her messages were vague. I had no idea that she was going to marry..."

Ora had her reservations about Nathaniel, too, but she didn't dare say anything about them. "Go on, say it, but I'm not touching it."

Shaking her head, Chris wasn't in the mood. "I can't do this this morning. My plane leaves in a few hours, and I need to get the house in order before I leave. Where are the girls?"

"In the back. They're still asleep." Ora knew her older daughter quite well and was confident that Chris was hiding something. She took a break from cooking and sat down next to Chris. "Before we wake up the girls, let me ask you something."

Chris started digging through her purse to make sure that she had the plane tickets. She didn't want anything to prevent her from getting to the airport on time. "What is it?"

"What do you think of your brother-in-law?"

Chris belted a hearty "HA!" and said to her mother, "Don't get me started."

"I can sense that you know a little more than I do, and it almost seems that you know more than your sister does."

"How did she meet him?"

"They were in a class together over at West Tennessee. I know that they went to the same high school but hung out with different crowds. He left for some reason, and the two of them met up again in college. Next thing I know he's over here all the time. Then they stayed in the malls. He's got credit cards up the ass. Somehow he managed to get Iysha that job working for the post office. I don't ever remember them going out on dates much 'cause he worked nights. But they were constantly on the phone."

"Did he propose before or after she got pregnant?"

"I don't think he ever really did. They just did it. I mean, she came home one day, moved the rest of her things out, and said that they decided to get married. There was never an engagement ring or anything. But let me tell you, he went out and bought himself a bad-ass wedding band. Now, your daddy and I had thought that the boy was a punk, but I guess we were wrong about him."

No, you weren't, Chris thought. "Is Iysha happy?"

"You want me to tell the truth?"

"Of course."

"I think that she did what she did to get out of here. I know that you two don't like Pete, and I sometimes think that his being here ran you off. I also think that she'll deal with whatever just to keep from coming back home. She mentioned having a big wedding, but he said no. My baby is sacrificing all of her dreams just because she wasn't happy at home with me."

"Don't beat yourself up about it, Momma. We're grown now. You've done your job." Chris noticed the time. "Look, as much as I would like to chat, I've to get these little women up. Our plane leaves in a few hours." She walked to the back bedroom and found the girls still sleeping. Chris woke them, gathered their things, and dashed for the front door. In the twenty years that Pete had been around, Chris had never spoken to him, and this time was no exception.

"Wait a minute, Chris," Ora said, flagging Chris down in the driveway. "I almost forgot to tell you."

"What is it, Momma?" she asked, getting in the car.

Leaning through the driver's side window, Ora sniggled. "Your grandmother asked me if you were a sissy."

Chris jokingly banged her head against the steering wheel. "What?"

"I don't know what came over her. She just blurted it out the other day when I was sitting on the porch with her. You know how that medication makes her act."

"And what did you say?"

"Nothing as usual. What do you want me to say?"

Chris smiled. "Next time tell her that boys are called sissies. I wish I had time to stop by to see her."

"Well, before I get started with my day, I've got to take her some Ida-motion."

"Some what?"

"Imodium A-D, honey. You know how your grandmother is. Making up her own words and shit."

"That's your mother. We're gone. Love ya! Bye-bye!" Chris put the car in reverse and sped toward Shelby Drive.

After making it to church to catch the 9 o'clock "come as you are" service, Chris realized she still hadn't fed the girls. As they approached the boarding gate at the airport, Chris's youngest yanked her mother's purse strap. "Mommy, I'm hungry," Gaylon whined. "My tummy's growling." Chris knew that the baby had seen the Krispy Kreme stand as had she. There was no way that any of them would be able to sit still on the plane with those doughnuts on their stomachs. Gaylon would have to shit thirty minutes into the flight.

"Wait until we get on the plane. We'll get something then."

"But, Mommy, my tummy is making funny noises. You know like it does when I ain't had nothing to eat."

"First of all, it's 'when I *haven't* had anything to eat.' You know better than that. Second, you're going to have to wait until we get on the plane like I said a few minutes ago. We don't have time to go over there, stand in line, and all that fun stuff." Just then someone stuck a hot glazed doughnut in Chris's face. Gaylon snatched at one half of it as Chelsea reached for the other half. "What the hell?" Chris snapped around and saw a face that she hadn't seen in years.

"You sure can tell those are your babies. Greedy as hell and would beat somebody's ass in a heartbeat over a Krispy Kreme doughnut!"

"Rudy!" Chris screamed. Her purse and bags hit the floor in the excitement. "What are you doing here? Of all the bitches to see, I run into you!"

"Just getting in from North Carolina. Had some business to tend to. Are you getting ready to leave?" As soon as Rudy closed her mouth, the intercom came on, and pre-boarding was beginning.

"Yeah, I've been here for a few weeks and need to get back home today. I've been on vacation for a while and go back to work tomorrow. I tried to call you when I first got here, and the message said that you were out of town. I really needed to talk to you, especially last night," Chris said nervously. Tears streamed down her cheeks.

"What's wrong, honey?" Rudy asked as she reached for a tissue and handed it to Chris. "Why the tears? Miss me that much?"

Wiping her eyes, Chris whispered, "Gayle died early this morning. She was in a car wreck last night with Mimi."

"Oh-ma-God, Chris," Rudy said warmly as she hugged Chris.

"Mimi was thrown from the car. It's all over the front page of the newspaper today."

"Well, you know, Gayle always liked to be in the middle of shit and was never shamed of having her business all in the streets. I guess she died as she lived… always caught up in shit."

"Rudy, please. I don't want you to do that to her."

"Do what?"

"Disrespect her. I mean, I know that she did some pretty shitty things to me, but I really did love her. Before she died, we made peace with that."

"Wait a minute. You were there?"

"Yes, I was, and I think that what happened needs to remain in that hospital room. So don't be tryin' to get nosy." Scrambling to get the kids on the plane, Chris reached in her pocket and pulled out a business card. "Here, take this," she said, placing the card in Rudy's hand. "I have got to get my butt on this plane. Call me if you need me for anything, and I mean *anything.*"

"Ain't it about $100 a minute to call France?" Rudy joked.

"Yeah, but you can afford it." Chris laughed as she handed the gate attendant her boarding passes. "You can call collect if you need to." She and the girls with their sugar-glazed faces waved to Rudy as they descended onto the ramp. When she got to the entrance of the plane, she remembered that Rudy knew everything about anybody on the gay scene in Memphis because, at some point or another, they came to the club...whether they danced, drank or hung out in the bathroom. Chris asked the flight attendant to seat the girls while she ran back to the gate. "I need about two minutes to find her."

"Ma'am, you're lucky because the bag handlers have to shift the luggage around to balance the weight on the plane. It's going to take them a few minutes to do it. Please hurry."

"Thank you so much. It'll only take a minute." Chris dashed up the jetway and stopped just short of the boarding area. The crowd had thinned considerably after the final boarding call, but Chris knew that Rudy couldn't have gotten far that quickly. "Rudy! Rudy!" she called into the airport. The gate attendant saw Chris frantically calling out Rudy's name.

"Excuse me, Miss. Are you looking for that lady you were talking to earlier?

"Yes, I am. Have you seen her?"

"She went into the ladies' room."

"Thank you." As she hurried past the attendant, Chris spotted Rudy coming out of the restroom. "Rudy!"

"Damn, girl! What you want? I heard you calling me, but I was trying to pull up my pantyhose. Got a damn run, thanks to you."

"Real quick. You remember Miss Nay that used to dance at the club?"

"Girl, do I? Got the nerve to be perpetrating a fraud."

"What you mean?"

"Oh, Ms. Gurl. She done rehabilitated herself. Back to callin' herself 'him' and thangs. Patty really fucked that queen's head up."

"Stop with the dumb shit and tell me what's up."

"Why?"

"Rudy!"

"He was freaking on some girl last I heard. As a matter of fact, they was supposed to be getting married sometime this month, but you ain't heard that from me."

"That's what I thought," Chris whispered to herself.

"And she's a pretty girl, I heard. Just hope she ain't finna be no fool."

"So that was that muthafucka." Chris saw the flight attendant flagging her down. "I gotta go, Rudy, but I'll be in touch soon." She leaned over and kissed Rudy on the cheek. "Keep me posted about that, okay? Just promise me that you will do that."

"Okay, I will."

❧♥❧

Yet another Sunday and Pete was lying up on his ass in Ora's rice bed. His Paul Bunyan breakfast, complete with a mayonnaise jar full of orange juice, had been brought to him, yet again, on a serving tray. Inside of ten minutes, he'd cleaned his plate and set it aside for Ora to pick up on her way back to the kitchen. "Brang me some wauda, Ora," he asked when she picked up the tray. "Put lotsa ize in it." She quietly returned with his mayonnaise jar full of ice water and sat it on the nightstand. He was watching NASCAR on ESPN and never uttered a "thank you, cow, bitch, or dog" to his girlfriend of almost twenty years.

Later in the afternoon, Pete, still resting on his ass, ordered Ora to call Pizza Hut. "I wanna Super Supreme with extra meat and cheese, and get a Meat Lover's, too, with extra meat." He never gave her a dime.

Ora sat on the sofa and waited patiently for the pizza deliveryman. For twenty years, she had been this man's sex slave, his maid, his launderer, his cook, and maybe sometimes his friend, but Ora realized that she had never been his lover. There had been no flowers or cards; no candy or fine clothes; no candlelit dinners or weekend getaways. When her job with the airport phased out, one would've thought that Pete would've gotten a job. Nope. He continued hanging out with his friends and would periodically check in with Ora to see if her unemployment check had been deposited into the bank. When it seemed that Ora had developed a slight gambling problem running back and forth from the casino twice a day, one would've thought that he would've stepped in and cautioned her about such behavior. Nope. He sat on the stool right next to her begging for quarters to put in the slot machine. While all of her other friends bragged about their husbands taking them out to dinner and a movie, Ora simply smiled and did her best to change the subject. Pete felt that finding another job was Ora's problem and not his. He adamantly made it understood that he wasn't going to get a job; therefore, he had no need to look for one. Ora finally could see that he didn't get this way just last week. She finally realized that he had been this way for twenty years. It was then, at that very moment, that Pete had an odor: an odor that the rest of the world knew he had from day one. Ora got up from the sofa and sprayed Lysol all around the house.

A little black 1987 Honda Prelude pulled in the driveway exactly as the clock ticked into the 45th minute. To hell with giving the customer a discount; time was money. When she opened the door, Ora stood there and tried not to stare at the one-armed delivery boy. The most heartwarming part was that this boy was loving his job and was taking it seriously. *That's it!*

"Pete, your pizza's here," Ora snapped as she put the pizzas on the stove.

"Brang it t-me, Ora. I'm watching the game right now," he yelled from the back.

She didn't say anything. She'd had it. Heading for the bedroom, Ora braced herself and made up her mind that no matter what happened, this man had to go TODAY. "Get the fuck out, Pete." She was calm.

Pete never looked up. "Woman, brang me my food and quit playin'."

"I ain't playin', Pete. I'm tired of this. You gotta go."

"What you talkin' 'bout?"

"You don't wanna work. You don't wanna do anything that would make you look better in the eyes of other people. You don't even wanna do anything to make yourself look better for me. My daughters left because I let you in here, and when it was most likely the worst time to do so, I ignored them for five minutes trying to give a lifetime to you. And then, just now, that delivery boy did it for me. He had one damn arm and was working. Yo' ass got all yo' damn limbs and won't even cut the damn grass let alone get a job. It's over. Get your shit, and get the hell out." She was still calm.

Pete sat up for the first time all day. "C'mon, baby, what's wrong wit-chu? That time of the month again? If this is about me not cutting the grass, then I'll cut the damn grass after I eat."

"No, it's not just about the grass. I need you to leave." Ora broke a smile, and Pete immediately thought this was a joke and got back in the bed.

"You a trip, Ora. Could you get my food, please?"

Little did he know, Ora was in control, and that's

why she was smiling. She went back up front and got the hedge clippers from the utility closet. Violence was never her thing, but at this point, whatever it took. "Pete, if you don't get your shit and get out of here, I'm gonna snip yo' dick off! I mean it!" He reached for his pants and shoes and started for the bathroom. "Don't go in there. Put yo' shit on right here, and leave. If you got to take a shit, do it at yo' boys' house."

"You done lost yo' mind, Ora!"

"No, I didn't. I found it, Pete," she declared. "I found it."

There was no use arguing with Ora about anything. She'd obviously made up her mind. "You gonna throw away twenty years just like dat?"

"Yep."

"You gonna put me out with nowhere to go?"

"Yep, and you know what? If you even try to set one foot back on my property or in my house, I'll call the police and tell them that there's a warrant out for you for nonpayment of child support." She knew that would keep his ass away for life. By the time he got to the front of the house, he realized what Ora had been so busy doing all morning and afternoon. All of his shit was packed and sitting by the front door. It was time for Pete to change his address, and for Ora, it was time to live.

LOVE AND HAPPINESS

Fatherhood did wonders for Nathaniel. Iysha gave birth to twin girls, Erica and Jessica, five months after she and Nathaniel were married. It was a difficult birth, but, as any proud father, Nathaniel was there the entire time. He'd bought layettes from Dillard's and had run up the credit cards buying clothes and diapers. Once home from the hospital, Iysha had plenty of time to herself because Nathaniel fed, bathed, and clothed the girls.

Two weeks after Iysha's six-week check-up, Nathaniel surprised his wife with a trip to Washington, D.C. He'd made child care arrangements, and, while she'd slept, he'd packed Iysha's clothes a little bit at a time. It was going to be the honeymoon they'd never had. The first two days they went sightseeing and dined at Paolo's in Georgetown a couple of times. As a late wedding gift to Iysha, Nathaniel took Iysha shopping at Tysons Corner and at some of the boutiques in Georgetown Square. The sky was the limit for his wife. Every time she said, "I like…," he got it for her.

On their way back to the hotel, Nathaniel decided

that taking the subway would be a romantic adventure for the two of them. As the train crossed into D.C. from Maryland, the passengers became a little more diverse, and, by the time they reached the Dupont Circle stop, there was a plethora of riders on the train. Nathaniel cut his eyes at a gay couple seated up a row and across the aisle from him and Iysha. Busy looking over the map of the Metro system, Iysha paid the couple no attention. Nathaniel, however, glanced over at them long enough to catch the two men rubbing each other's thighs. Their girlish laughs locked them in their own little world with neither of them caring who saw or heard them. Nathaniel shifted in his seat, placed his arm around his wife but still couldn't take his eyes off the couple. One of the men caught Nathaniel staring at them and gave him a wink. Quickly turning his head, Nathaniel asked Iysha if she wanted to change trains so they could go to Pentagon City. Thankfully, she agreed, and he rushed to help her out of her seat and gentlemanly escorted her off the train.

Once they returned to the hotel, Nathaniel went in to the bathroom to run a hot bath for the two of them. While seated on the side of the tub, Nathaniel watched his wife undress. In his mind, Iysha was beautiful. He'd found comfort in someone who loved him first as a friend and later as a lover. Their friendship was priceless. They'd laughed together and cried together. They'd eaten at all the posh restaurants in East Memphis. They'd hit the malls like best girlfriends, and Iysha quickly found herself with a taste for the finer things in life but lacked the finances to acquire them. On one income, Nathaniel didn't care about living beyond his means. He was only concerned with "appearances," making sure he never missed a beat.

As Iysha raised her blouse and pulled it over her head, Nathaniel reflected on the first time he'd seen all of her bare skin. It was two months after Patty had broken off their relationship. Iysha had come over for dinner and was preparing to tell Nathaniel about her day at work when he, all of a sudden, without warning, grabbed her in his arms and kissed her. That whole day had been about missing Patty and all the times he'd been made to feel like a woman. Nathaniel then took that energy and passed it on to Iysha, making her feel like the woman she truly was. From there, the relationship started and swiftly moved beyond just friends.

Its hanger still dangling from the closet doorknob, Iysha's blouse was returned to its original place in the closet next to Iysha's other outfits. Nathaniel didn't care if they were going to walk to the corner to get a Slurpee; he wanted Iysha to look her best. As she walked back to the dressing area, she reached behind her to unsnap her bra. It was then that Nathaniel turned off the bath water and walked over to her to provide some assistance. "Let me help," he asked, kissing her from the nape of her neck to the small of her back. Each impression made the hair on Iysha's back stand straight up. She hung her head in ecstasy while he unzipped her slacks. Sliding her pants down to her ankles, Nathaniel kissed every inch of Iysha's front side…first the tips of her nipples, then the top of her waist, and the flow of her navel. The closer he got to her hairline, the more she shivered. "Please don't stop," she requested. Slowly she turned around, feeling wood just below her buttock. Moaning in sheer pleasure, Iysha bent over as Nathaniel gently tried to enter. In one swift thrust, he made his way into the depth of his wife's soul making love to her in his own way…in his own time. They enjoyed each other for hours that night, and, while sitting on the plane, Nathaniel held his wife's hand intermittently kissing it to remind the world she was his.

Two weeks later there was no mistake in Iysha's mind that she was pregnant. That taste in her mouth. The look of food when she was starving, the smell when she wanted to throw up. "Iysha, I thought you were taking something," Chris asked from Paris. "The twins aren't even three months old yet."

"What am I gonna take somethin' for? I'm married, remember?"

Chris recalled when she first saw Nathaniel with her sister. "Does my brother-in-law know?"

"I'm planning to tell him when he comes home." Iysha had taken the twins to her mother's house for the evening so she could break the news to him in peace.

"I think you should reconsider this because you two are still newlyweds with newborns at home. You're not working, and he still spends money like he's a bachelor without children."

That conversation in the limo after the reception hit home. Iysha now saw why her husband insisted that she not discuss their personal lives with Chris. Before she knew it, Iysha blurted, "Mind your business, Chris. You're gonna let me and my husband have our moment."

"Ain't nobody trying to take shit from you and your…" Chris refrained from disrespecting Nathaniel. "Look, I'm not trying to interfere, Iysha, but you don't need to have another baby so soon."

"Chris, please don't take offense when I ask you to stay out of it. You haven't been concerned about me in the past, so why start now?"

Thumbing through her appointments for the day, Chris replied tersely, "You know what? You're right. So do what you want to do. I've got to go." She slammed the phone down and went on about her day.

Nathaniel insisted that he get the mail. His excuse was that he didn't want to lose his manhood by letting Iysha take control of the finances by looking at the bills and complaining about them. But he wasn't much better. When he got the credit card bills, he stuck them in his pocket or tore them up. Today was no different. He glanced over the Visa bill and saw that his monthly payment had increased to almost $224. Then he opened the American Express bill, and $1,536.00 was "due upon receipt." Lord & Taylor, which didn't even have a store in Memphis, wanted $100. The phone bill was astronomical because Iysha called her sister and talked for over an hour twice a week. He'd asked Iysha to call after 11 p.m., but she complained that by the time she got the twins to bed, the last thing she wanted to do was talk on the phone. Finally, there was Memphis Light, Gas and Water (MLG&W). The good thing about them was that they'd take a payment arrangement in a heartbeat. You could always go "sit in the chairs" and count on someone to empathize with you. The "chairs" was the step before total disconnection, and Nathaniel did everything he could to keep from having to go there. After skimming through the entire stack, he placed them all in his coat pocket. He'd by now made up in his mind which one he would discuss with his wife.

"Hey, baby," Iysha said, greeting him with a warm hug and a wet kiss on the lips. Nathaniel put down his bags after returning Iysha's affections. "Hey, yourself." He panned the room for the babies. "Where are the kids?"

"With Momma. I wanted to spend some time with just you tonight."

"I see. That works out perfectly because I need to talk to you about something anyway." Nathaniel took a seat at the kitchen table where Iysha had placed his dinner, piping hot from the stove. Taking his napkin and placing it across his lap, he grabbed his fork and stabbed at the filet mignon. "I got the phone bill today. It was $400 and some change," he said calmly.

Iysha froze as she stood with the refrigerator door wide open. She knew she was in trouble. There was at least one time last month when she had talked to Chris for two hours in the middle of the day. Taking a deep breath, she replied, "Okay, I can give you some money on it."

Nathaniel stopped chewing and inquired, "Where did you get money from?"

"Oh, Momma gave me some last week just to put in my pocket for emergencies."

"So you stashing on me?"

She knew it. *Here it come*s. "No, I'm not, Nathaniel. It was just $100 in case I needed to get something for the babies. I mean, what's wrong with that?"

"It makes me look like I can't take care of my family."

"Nathaniel, my mother has always given us money to put in our pockets. It ain't nothing new. Hell, she still sends money to Chris even though she already makes a killing in child support and salary."

"Speaking of your sister. Those calls are gonna have

to stop. If I wasn't spending so much money on phone bills, I could have extra money to give you. She makes enough money. Let her call you if she wants to talk."

What Nathaniel didn't know was that Chris did call. She called every day, especially when she hadn't already heard from her sister. It was Chris who initiated the three-way calls amongst her, Ora, and Iysha. "You're telling me I can't call my sister when I want to? You're out spending two and three hundred dollars on suits, but I can't call my sister?"

Nathaniel was almost willing to compromise until she said it like that. "Tell you what. Don't put any more long distance phone calls on the phone, especially none to your sister. If you want to call her, take your ass over to your momma's house and make the call."

"I said I'd pay for the call."

Nathaniel snapped, "What are you not getting? No long distance calls."

Iysha didn't want to argue. "Okay, Nathaniel. Whatever you say."

Sipping from his water goblet, Nathaniel was ready to move on to something else. He looked at her plate and realized she was hardly eating her dinner. "So I guess you've got an attitude now."

"Actually, I don't. I'm pregnant."

"What!"

"I'm pregnant. I went to the doctor today. Seems that we brought home a little souvenir from D.C."

Over $2,000 in debt and here she comes with this shit. "How could you let this happen?"

Confused, Iysha responded, "I can't believe you would ask me something like that."

Getting up from the table, Nathaniel removed his empty plate from the table and walked over to the sink. Scraping his plate, he complained, "Iysha, we can't afford to feed another mouth around here."

"I'll get a job. It's not like I'm not able to."

"Who's going to take care of the kids, cook the meals, and keep the house clean? You sure can't if you get a job."

"I don't understand you. You don't think I know we have a mountain of bills? Even if I weren't pregnant, I'd want to work to be able to help you out."

"Do you realize how much child care would cost if you got a job? I ain't about having somebody take advantage of me because I have two, now three, kids."

Pouting, Iysha, removing her dishes from the table, asked, "Do you want me to get rid of it?"

Abortions weren't right…at least that was what he believed. He figured that perhaps if he wished for it hard enough or prayed for it long enough something would happen, and the pregnancy would end on its own. "No, I don't want you to do that. We'll be all right."

Leaving his wife to wonder why he had such a quick change of heart, Nathaniel went to the bedroom and undressed. He never removed the bills from his coat pocket because he was fully aware of what and to whom he owed. In order for him to maintain the lifestyle that he so desired, Nathaniel mentally prepared himself to find a part-time job.

SAVING MISS RUDY

Rudy was up to her ass in debt. Every valuable thing in her apartment was in the pawnshop. Fortunately, she gave really good head and was able to influence the shop manager to extend some of her loans without paying any money. Her services, however, were not frequent enough to cause him to forget the loans altogether. "That," Mr. Fenton said, "would be bad for business." Rudy had changed her phone number so many times that the phone company finally gave up on trying to collect money from her. She'd used her father's name, her mother's name, her sister's name, and even her old name to acquire phone service.

"May I speak to Rudolph?" the caller would ask. Rudy knew that it was a bill collector by the interim beeps and pauses she heard in the background, and, when she glanced at the Caller ID, it displayed "Out of Area."

"You have the wrong number." And Rudy would abruptly hang up the phone. The calls came day in and day out. One afternoon while she was watching *The Young and the Restless* she got a phone call from a collection agency. Unusually pleasant, the caller said,

"Good afternoon, Ma'am. How are you doing today?"

"Just fine," Rudy replied. "And yourself?"

"I'm good," the woman asked. "I was trying to reach Rudolph Harris."

"Uh-hmm," Rudy said. "May I ask who's calling?"

"This is Samantha, and I need to speak with him about a personal business matter."

"I see."

"Is he available?"

"No, he's not."

"Do you know where I can reach him?"

"No, I do not."

The initially pleasant voice was surging from the demeanor of a field mouse to the fierce combat of a dragon. She went from zero to bitch in a matter of seconds. "Well, who am I speaking with?"

Whoops! That did it. First of all, this bitch was interrupting the soaps. Then, she had an attitude, and lastly, she had gotten a little too nosy. Rudy recognized the voice because apparently Samantha had been assigned *Rudolph's* credit file. She called every day at about the same time asking for Rudolph, and it was really a shame that this person was so dense. After weeks of trying, she should have picked up by then that she was never going to talk to Rudolph. "Look," Rudy snapped. "Rudolph is not here."

"I can't believe that. He's never home. You mean, he never comes home?"

"Well, if you'd let me finish my statement, then maybe..."

"This is just unacceptable! I'm going to recommend that this case..."

"Wait a minute, Susie, Susanna—or whatever your name is. It amazes me! You go on and on and on about Rudolph. Putting his business all in the streets. And I just sit here and listen every day at the same time listening to your ranting and raving about needing to speak to him. Well, here's a bit of information for you, and I think that you will find it beneficial as it will allow you to concentrate more on your public relations skills and good customer service skills, and even more so, it will give you a chance to re-evaluate your career choice because how can you possibly sit there and enjoy being cussed out on an almost daily basis?"

On the other end of the phone, Samantha's face had to have been blood-red by now. She was unhappy with her job, but the money was excellent, and it paid the bills. She swallowed and calmly continued, "What information do you have, Ma'am?"

"Rudolph," Rudy cried, "is out at the penal farm doing triple life sentences. That boy ain't coming home! But, I will gladly give him the message that you called. I don't think, though, that he'll even give a damn."

"Thank you for your time." And the call was disconnected. The only reprieve for Rudy was that she never received those kind of calls at the club because that phone was listed in her grandmother's name. Mamanin bitched tough at Rudy for even asking to do such a thing. "You're just irresponsible, girl! This don't make no sense! Don't let me ever get a call that you didn't pay this bill. I'll have that shit cut off so quick that it'll make your head spin! Better yet, you better pay it before it even gets to you! And I ain't putting no long distance on it either!" Rudy made sure to pay that bill even if she paid none of the others. All of the income from the club was put back into payroll, maintenance, and supplies. The assistant manager, Dallas, was good at hiring and firing people until the day he fired the bartender, Greg.

"Why did you fire Greg, Dallas?" Rudy had asked. "He was one of the most reliable people in here."

Dallas quickly snapped, "He had too much drama around him. His baby's mama was always calling, and then one day the bitch came up here and showed out! I can't have that kinda shit goin' on around this place, and you know that. He always seemed paranoid about shit."

"His ass might have been paranoid, Dallas, but he did his job. All you had to do was talk to him."

"I tried to, but he just… Never mind. What do you want me to do?"

"I hope your impulsive actions don't come back to haunt you. Business hasn't been what it used to be. And,

Lord knows, I can't afford to have disgruntled employees running around, coming back to shoot up the place. Fortunately for your behind, I think I gotta plan."

In an effort to attract more customers, Rudy opened the club during regular operating hours and solicited everybody, both gay and straight. Exotic coffees, fresh bagels, and Krispy Kreme donuts were served until 11 a.m., and, going into the mid-day, deli sandwiches and hot wings were sold to famished lunchtime patrons. By 3:00, Rudy was strapped for help and often had to make drinks herself and even wait on tables. Beer and coolers were all that the Alcoholic Beverage Commission would allow the establishment to sell despite the constant demand for mixed drinks and hard liquor. The $30,000 Rudy needed for the liquor license was too far from reality. Thus she served the stuff that the wannabe winos drank. The tips sucked, but it kept her in business for a minute. Rudy's opinion was that God didn't put her on this earth to be a servant, but He did put her here to be served.

The first three interviews for the bartending job were horrible. Dallas had major personality conflicts with them for one reason or another and had gotten to the point where anyone would do. "I have one more interview this afternoon, but I have an errand that I need to run. Is there any way that you can do it for me?"

"Hell, no," Rudy said. "This is your job to do. It's your

damn fault that we're in this predicament anyway. Besides I have an appointment myself that I can't miss. Just hire whomever the hell it is that's coming in and tell 'em to start tonight."

Dallas interrupted, "You don't want to talk to him?"

"I didn't need to talk to the last muthafucka you hired, did I? And I liked him. I still don't know why you let him go. At least his ass was here when he was supposed to be, and he kept this bar packed. And the best thing was that my ass didn't have to be in here waiting on people. So, unless your ass is looking to be out of work, you need to get somebody in here, and I mean today!" Rudy snapped Dallas up, popped her head to the right, and switched her butt out the door. At the next interview, Dallas took one look at the guy and hired him on the spot. Fortunately the new guy was able to start immediately.

❧♥❧

701 Jefferson Place was a sleek contemporary building with black tinted windows and was also the most beautiful office building in downtown Memphis. Located at the north end of Third Street, its glamour and prestige were in the process of being replaced by Peabody Plaza at the south end of Third Street. Many of the attorneys who had offices at 701 Jefferson Place snubbed Peabody

Plaza's developers when approached about relocating their offices to the new digs. To attract the best of the best, rental rates were temporarily lowered, and the offices were state of the art; but, for most of the attorneys, the building was too close to Beale Street and offered too much distance between the law offices and the courthouses. Behind the windows of this structure, though, sat seasoned bankruptcy attorneys who relished the fact that the bankruptcy court was located in the same building. Some had only to travel a couple of floors to get to the courtroom, and there were an elite few who only needed to walk a few feet outside of their offices. Rudy's attorney, Tristan Noel, was on the ninth floor.

"May I help you?" the receptionist said as she greeted Rudy at the door.

"Yes, my name is Rudy Harris, and I have an appointment with Ms. Noel?"

The receptionist smiled. "It's Mr. Noel."

"I'm sorry."

"Don't worry about it. He's been called worse." She laughed. "Take this clipboard, and fill out everything on the front and the back. Make sure that you sign the last sheet. That's for your credit report. Tristan will be with you in a moment."

It took Rudy almost half an hour to complete the forms. She had so many bills to list that she finally pulled them all out of her purse and wrote "see attached" on all the lines and clipped them to the clipboard. Many of them she had never opened, and some held postmarks over six years old. Since her operation, the hospital and doctor bills had piled up considerably. Six thousand here, three thousand there. There was no way that Rudy would ever pay those bills.

Even if she could pay them, she wouldn't. That was just the type of person Rudy was. No kids, no bills, no lovers...nothing. Her heart and soul had been put into the nightclub, and, saving it was all that she cared about. The last thing that she ever wanted was to have bill collectors calling or coming by the club. That's why she kept Dallas in the forefront.

Mr. Tristan Noel must have already known how long it would take Rudy to complete the forms because his entrance was like clockwork. He came in just after she had signed her name. Tall and cocoa brown, Tristan was fine with all of his degrees plastered on the office walls. Yale, Vanderbilt, and some other pieces of ego paper made him one of the most respected Black lawyers in town. He came highly recommended by one of Rudy's customers. "He's a good guy that knows a thing or two if you know what I mean. He gets things done, and it's done fast. Not a lot of questions either. Down-to-earth, and he ain't trying to make a dollar like the rest of them. You can trust Tristan," the guy told Rudy. With her landlady threatening to put out the few things that

Rudy did own and with the mailman having to wrap her bills up in a rubber band because there were so many of them, Tristan Noel was Rudy's only hope.

"Ms. Harris?"

"Yes," Rudy replied.

"Tristan Noel," he offered as he extended his hand.

"Nice to meet you."

"Come in, please, and make yourself comfortable. Can I get you something to drink?"

"No, thanks." Rudy walked past Mr. Noel and took a seat across from the attorney's beautiful cherry desk. The entire office was decked out in cherry and was accessorized with Italian marble fixtures and brass. Gorgeous African sculpture and vivid artwork by Charles Bibbs and Terry and Jerry Lynn adorned the credenzas and walls and spoke volumes about Tristan's culture.

"How may I help you today?" he asked as he perused Rudy's intake form.

"I would like to file bankruptcy, Mr. Noel."

"Oh, please. I am no different from you. Call me Tristan."

"Okay, Tristan. I need to file bankruptcy."

Tristan adjusted his chair and leaned across his desk, resting on his elbows. "Rudy, no one needs to file bankruptcy. There are other options that I wish more of us would consider."

"Such as?"

"Well, let's take credit counseling, for instance. Did you ever think about doing that?"

Rudy paused for a minute before answering. "I think that my situation is beyond that kinda help. I have some loans that I've gotta repay. And I just don't have the money. And, regardless, there's still gonna be a bill."

"Okay, have you thought about calling the credit bureaus?"

"For?"

"Well, for starters, you can get them to send you a copy of your credit report."

"Oh, I did that. They shipped it to me in a big brown envelope. UPS delivered it. It was just that damn thick."

Tristan smiled. "I see."

"Besides, Tristan, calling the credit bureau, in my opinion, would open up a can of worms that I simply don't have time to be bothered with. Any more suggestions?"

"All righty then. Forget about that." He then asked, "Do you have any student loans?"

"Yes, I have three."

"I can't do anything about those, you know, if you are filing a Chapter 7. But if you are doing a wage earner, Chapter 13, then I can get those taken care of on a payment plan. You could put the loans under what we call a wage earner plan with your other secured debt and could possibly put the rest under a Chapter 7. It just depends on how your creditors are going to react."

"What do you mean?"

"Some creditors want equal treatment, especially if it looks like another creditor is going to get even a portion of what's owed to them. If you're going to pay one creditor under a wage earner plan, then they may all want to get a piece of the pie."

"Well, what happens under Chapter 7?" Rudy asked.

"That's easy. All of your unsecured debt is gone. You don't have to pay it back." Flipping through Rudy's pile of bills, he added, "It seems that most of what you have is unsecured debt. You have an awful lot of hospital and doctor bills. Were you sick?"

Rudy smirked. "Not really. I had some adjustments made. Let's just leave it at that."

"Whatever you say. Do you still have the merchandise you bought with these credit cards?"

"Not all of it."

"They may or may not want their stuff back. You need to be prepared to return the merchandise if necessary."

"Who's going to want some old funky dresses and run-over shoes?"

"You never know, Rudy. Let me ask you this. Do you have any property like real estate or a car that's paid for?"

Rudy was afraid to answer. "Why?"

"Because if you do, you need to get rid of it if you're going to file Chapter 7. It is considered a liquid asset and can be sold so that your creditors can get their money. Your only option would then be Chapter 13." Rudy hesitantly explained that she owned the Menagerie and that it was her only source of income. "Well, your check can't be garnished if you're self-employed. That's a good thing, I guess. But you'll have to come down here and make your payments for the wage earner plan."

"That's not a big problem."

"But I would still look into getting rid of that building. You could end up with nothing after this is over. When filing bankruptcy, that's what you're basically saying. You want a fresh start, and the court wants to make sure that you do exactly that. With all of this debt, how is it that you own this building?"

"You're a lawyer, and you still have to ask me that? Look in front of you. I haven't paid shit in over six years so I could own that building!"

Tristan noticed that Rudy owed several months' rent to a couple of property management companies and was currently living in another apartment. "Are you still living in this apartment?"

"Yes, but I owe this month's rent." Rudy had included three months in back rent at her current address in her anticipated bankruptcy claim.

Tristan's legal advice was plain and simple. "Okay, well then, you need to move."

"What?"

"You need to move in with a relative or something. You're not going to be able to find an apartment with a bankruptcy on your credit. So many apartment complexes have tightened up on people who've filed bankruptcy that it's a shame. And if you did find anything, it'd most likely be somewhere you wouldn't want to live. You don't have money to pay three or four months in advance, so you may want to look up those relatives or a really good friend."

"Tristan, give me some advice as to what to do. I can't lose this club. I have put everything I own into that place."

"Well, bankruptcy is definitely your best bet. I don't think that it's wise, however, to have any property in your name. I'd take care of that before I filed. The trustees office is going to do a title search, and you will show up as the property owner. The judge could order the property sold to collect your debt, or he could deny your bankruptcy claim based on the fact that you didn't disclose this property in the first place. Then you're back where you started. May I ask you a question?"

"Yes." Rudy smiled.

"Who is Rudolph? Most of these bills are in Rudolph Harrison's name."

"Well, I might as well be honest with you. Rudolph is whom I used to be, if you know what I mean. That's why I owe those doctors and hospitals out the ass."

Blushing, Tristan responded, shaking his head, "Oh, I see. Well, let me tell you they did an excellent job! So whose name is the club in?"

"Rudy Harris."

"Is your new identity legally recorded anywhere?"

"North Carolina."

"I'm not trying to be nosy, but the Court pays people to investigate stuff like this. They do cross-references, medical record verification, all of that. You know that, right?"

"I kinda figured they might."

Tristan hesitated for a minute before he finished. Memphis ranked third on the nation's list of cities with high bankruptcy claims and often toggled between first and second. Cars were easy to come by after filing a claim because finance companies provided third and sometimes fourth chance credit. If you had a job, that was your credit. Car sales were particularly high during income tax season since folks had lump sums of money from inflated refunds—claiming kids and shit that they didn't even have. It didn't matter too much because, by the time the payments reached $400 and $500 for a Hyundai, people were back where they had started. Memphis' economy catered to the bankrupt and corrupt, and the people who benefited from it the most were the attorneys. It had become so easy to file a bankruptcy claim that everybody was doing it. If you didn't have to put any money down on the case, then it was worked into your plan. If you did put any money down, the balance of it was worked into your plan. Either way the attorneys got their money even if no one else did. Some people took advantage of the fact that you could even file more than once. So what, your credit would be fucked up for ten years? Hell, the average repossession stayed on your credit for five to seven years depending on what had been repossessed, and some collection activity stayed on just as long. You couldn't get shit anyway! And least, you weren't supposed to. Life for many was better while in bankruptcy than it had ever been. Life was simpler.

During his first years as a lawyer, Tristan promised himself that he would do whatever he could to promote the Black agenda. From listening to Rudy, Tristan realized that the Menagerie had tremendous potential, but Rudy needed help with it. The best thing he could do was to make some valuable suggestions while inquiring about Rudy's business and industry contacts. "Look, I know some things that you could do to save your business, but, for professional reasons, I won't tell you here. If the wrong person heard me, I could get into a lot of trouble." They agreed to meet later at the club so that Tristan could discuss those other options with Rudy.

When Rudy returned to the club that evening, Dallas was emptying the trash and stopped her as she came through the alley heading to the back entrance. "I hired that guy who came by after you left. He's inside."

"Good. At least you're following instructions. By the way, a man is coming by here a little later to take a look at the building and to meet with me."

"What for?"

"There you go again being nosy. Just make sure that shit is up to par, and let me know when he gets here."

"Okay, boss lady." Dallas returned through the front door by the bar while Rudy went through the back. The new guy was completing the last of the paperwork that Dallas had to give to Rudy. "Will you be able to work overtime?" Dallas asked. "Sometimes on Fridays we may need a little extra help after midnight."

"Sure, I don't have a problem with that," the new bartender replied.

"Good," Dallas said, glancing down at the application.

"Nathaniel, it'll be great to have you. I wanted the owner to meet you, but she's busy right now. You can do that some other time. Just make yourself at home and let me know if you need anything else." Seeing that Nathaniel was comfortably fitting in, Dallas went back to his office to tidy up and prepare for Rudy's guest.

❧♥❧

By the time Rudy closed up the club it was after two in the morning. She had given instructions to Dallas about picking up a U-haul truck and to meet her at her apartment by 3 a.m. She had planned to call Mitchell and Sons Moving Service because they specialized in those after-midnight moves. Their motto, *"Don't let your neighbors know your payments are slow. We get you outta the house quiet as a mouse."* But, her good and reliable employee, Dallas, had convinced her to save that money by letting him do it. With all the traffic in and out of the club, Rudy hadn't found the time to introduce herself to the new bartender. The employment papers had been shoved in her briefcase with her hotel room confirmation and other effects. Thanks to her play-brother, Juan, who worked at the Radisson, Rudy had a suite for a week. Before checking in, though, Rudy needed to let Dallas into her apartment so that he could begin moving her things out. Relocating in the middle of the night was trifling, but it kept her neighbors out of her business. "Under no circumstances," Rudy said to Dallas, "are you to go through the front door. The troll fairy's apartment is right on the front. I think she sleeps sitting up in that damn rocking chair. She sees everything. Park the truck in the back and back it all the way up to the door. That way you won't have to use that loud ass ramp." Rudy's landlady, Mrs. Crenshaw, had been threatening to come down to the club with a picket sign demanding payment of Rudy's rent. Now, that she was sneaking out in the middle of the night, Rudy knew that the decrepit old lady would get much pleasure in taking the handicap bus over to The Menagerie. With her future entrusted to the advice of Tristan Noel, however, Rudy wouldn't have to worry about that. If everything went as planned, she would finally be on her way and free to leave all of the drama of unpaid bills behind her.

The only reason why Rudy never pawned her Coach leather chairs and big-screen TV was that they were too heavy to pick up. As she watched Dallas go from room to room, Rudy contemplated her next moves. "Don't drop my shit, Dallas!" she haughtily commanded as he struggled to balance two stacks of shoeboxes in his lanky arms.

"Why do you keep all of these boxes? It'd be easier to just take these shoes out of the individual boxes and put them all in one big box."

It was like Dallas had suggested she donate possessions to charity. Each pair of shoes had a box. Rudy knew where each one had come from. Consistency and neatness were a must. "Dallas, don't fuck with my shoes. All your ass has to do is put that shit on the truck. I don't care how you do it just as long as when I see my shoes again they're in those boxes. You should've brought some help with you. You know damn well I don't do manual labor."

"Rudy, it's after three in the morning! I wouldn't have been able to get anybody this late."

Plopping down in the chair that Dallas was about to move, she said, "Well, it seems like you've got your work cut out for you. Be a little quieter, please, while you're moving shit. I've got to make a long distance call before they cut this phone off." That call was a $4 per minute phone call to Paris.

"Allo."

"Allo? Don't try that French shit with me, bitch. This is Rudy. Get yo' tired ass up!"

Chris was hysterical with laughter. "It's after ten in the morning here, Rudy. What's up with you?"

"Nothing, girl. How have you been?"

"Fine."

"And those girls?"

"Growing like weeds. We're all doing just fine."

"You still working?"

"Yes, I don't go in until noon. This is my half-day."

"Oh, okay. I see that you still don't do mornings." Rudy laughed.

"Girl, with these kids, I have no choice. I've been up since six. Gaylon had to be at school by seven and Chelsea at eight. This is usually my quiet time." Chris poured herself a glass of wine and went out on the balcony to sit down. "What's going on, Rudy. I can tell that something is up. You know I know you better than anybody."

"I need a favor." Rudy just jumped right in. She knew Chris hated beating around the bush. "Be straightforward and to the point," she always said. "I'm either going to say yes or no." Rudy went on to tell Chris about her plans to file bankruptcy and about the information Tristan had disclosed to her. "So that's it in a nutshell. I'm fucked."

❧♥❧

Recalling all the times that Rudy had saved her ass, Chris didn't say anything at first. While they were in college, Rudy made a killing dancing at the Gurlz Club in Dupont Circle on Friday and Saturday, easily bringing home over a thousand dollars in tips nightly. At the dorm on Sundays while everyone else was playing bid whist and spades, she did $5 perms with customers lined up at least ten deep. Pretty soon, business got to be so good that Rudy gave appointments and made you pay even if you didn't show.

Rudy and Chris had met in chemistry class during the fall of Chris's junior year. Wanting to pledge AKA, Chris needed to make at least a C in this four-credit course in order to maintain her 2.5 GPA. Rudy, a whiz at mixing up shit—from perms to colors to chemicals to mixed drinks, made sure she and Chris were lab partners. Secretly, Rudy fantasized about pledging a sorority, especially Alpha Kappa Alpha because she could "skee-wee" with the best of them when wearing pink and green, and twenty pearls definitely complemented her style.

Chris was gorgeous and seemed to have it all together until the day she came to class in tears. "What's wrong, girl?" Rudy had asked.

Chris didn't know that Rudy had seen her numerous times in Dupont Circle hanging out at the coffee shops and bookstores. Nor did she know that Rudy had also seen her kissing Trey on the cheek and holding his hand while the two of them were on the yard. Rudy couldn't be fooled. She knew her folks. To the contrary, Chris knew nothing about Rudy except that she wore an awful lot of make-up even in 95-degree heat. Still, there was a certain level of comfort that Chris felt whenever Rudy was around. It was like Rudy knew what Chris had been feeling, and she knew how to fix it. "Are you going to make me ask you a second time?" Rudy inquired sarcastically as she passed Chris a piece of Kleenex.

Chris took the tissue and in turn asked, "Are you going to make me answer you while we're in here?" Wiping her running mascara and glistening nose, she continued, "That would seem so beneath you."

Rudy abruptly turned off the Bunsen burner and packed up her bags. With their station in the back of the lab, they were easily able to sneak out the back door. "You want to get something to eat?"

"I don't have any money for food. My financial aid hasn't come through, and my parents have already sent me all they were able to come up with. I don't get paid until next week, and..." Chris started sobbing.

"What about your boyfriend? Will he help you?"

"I get so tired of mooching off him. Besides, he's part of the problem."

"He is? I see the two of you all the time hugged up on each other." Not saying anything else, Chris sat down on the steps next to the Chemistry Building and bawled.

"I tell you what. Let's go get something to eat. I'll take care of you. Don't worry about the money."

"I can't leave. I have Rush this evening." As quickly as the tears fell, Chris wiped them away. "I have got to go buy something to wear."

"You just said that you didn't have any money."

"I don't have any money for food. I've been saving to buy something nice for tonight. I have $100 for a suit, and I have $5 for a box of perm. I'll buy some food with what's left."

"So why are you crying then?"

"I'm going to this thing tonight knowing that I am going to fail chemistry. I have already made two Fs on my tests. Thanks to you, I have an A in practicum."

"That will come out to be a C, Chris. Chemistry is not your problem, is it?"

"Walk with me, Rudy." The two of them walked and talked for hours. Before they knew it, they had walked down to the Mall, which was about six miles from campus. Chris needed the company, and Rudy provided the unbiased point of view. "I know that you know about me," Chris said. "I've seen you at Dupont Circle a few times, and a couple of those times I caught you looking at me."

"So now that we have established the obvious, we can move on to what we need to do to make you feel better. I don't know you from Eve, but I like you. And for some strange reason, I trust you. The first thing that I am going to do is to give you what you need to get validated so you can finally feel like a real student. Next, I am going to take you to Hecht's and get you the baddest suit we can find. Then, it's on to the shoe department. After that, we're going to the make-up counter for some real stuff 'cause that Wet-n-Wild shit ain't gonna cut it. When we get back to the dorm, I'm giving your ass a fierce makeover from head to toe. If those bitches don't choose you on looks alone, then at least they'll know that you have what it takes to be chosen the next time."

"What do you mean next time? I need to do this, Rudy. I want to belong to something. Do you know what it feels like to not belong?"

"More than you know."

"Whatever. You don't know what it's like. You're gorgeous, you've got…"

Rudy grabbed Chris by the hand. "Don't be deceived

by what's on the outside. You could be looking at anyone or anything when you look at me. The same way that you don't know what that group of girls is like. They could be some of the most treacherous bitches on campus, and right now, the worst thing that could happen to you is that this group of girls tells you that you don't belong. It would be devastating for you."

"You don't know that."

"Chris, I watch you more than you realize I do. The way you move, the way you speak. Why would you need a group of girls to define who you are when you have yet to even define yourself?"

Chris glared down the Mall at the Lincoln Memorial. She knew what Rudy was telling her, but her stomach was starting to growl. On the other side of the street was a hot dog stand. "Want to get a hot dog? I can afford that." Chris laughed.

"Hell, no! That shit ain't nothing but mystery meat with mystery sauce they been passin' off as chili. Tourists buy that mess 'cause it's cheap. By the time they get through running through these over-priced museum cafeterias, they'll eat anything. We'll go get some real food on the way back to the dorm."

"Okay." Chris winced.

"Now, back to what I was saying. I don't know when or if you're ever going to accept the fact that you're gay. That's why you're so unhappy."

The sunglasses had only hidden her red, swollen eyes from the sun. The tears were still her responsibility, and, by now, Chris had smeared all of her make-up onto her coat sleeve. "I can't leave him. He's so nice to me, Rudy. Nicer than any man has ever been to me."

"You know what's going to happen if you carry on with him?"

"No, what?"

"You're going to hurt him so bad because he is not what you really want. You're going to continue to be abusive toward him, and eventually he's not going to be able to stand you. Do you actually want that?"

"I am not going to leave him. It would almost kill him. I'd rather be okay with him leaving me."

"I hope that you know what you're doing."

"Look enough about me. I want to know more about you."

Rudy started walking toward Metro Center and pulled Chris alongside her. "Honey, we'll have a lifetime for you to get to know me." By the time they reached the dorm, Chris had decided to withdraw from her chemistry class and had concluded that pledging was not such a good idea. But Rudy gave her a makeover anyway to make her feel better and the next day took a check to the Bursar's office to pay the remaining balance of Chris's tuition. When Chris had the money to repay Rudy for her kind gesture, she refused to take it. The favor was hopefully done for a lifelong friend, and it was. For her generosity, compassion, friendship, and love, Chris owed much to Rudy. Years went by without them seeing or talking to each other. Rudy had wanted to get in touch with Chris after the Gayle episode, but it was best that Chris go through that alone. Rudy would have tried to fuck Gayle up for hurting Chris, and Chris would have gotten tired of hearing Rudy's *I told you so's about messing around with gutter-rat women.* "Those bitches ain't got shit to lose, so leave them alone. Never, ever, fuck around with somebody who has nothing to lose because you could wind up losing everything. You got too much class back there behind those 36DDs, and you don't need to waste it on gutter-rat trash." Thanks to Rudy's wisdom, Chris was able to reach back and pull out that classy lady and mix her in with the bitchiness that had become her trademark. As the best of friends, Chris and Rudy were always able to pick up their friendship where they'd left off.

❧♥❧

"Rudy, you know that I would do anything for you," Chris chimed in as she peered over her balcony at the fresh produce stand.

"I know that this whole thing sounds crazy, but it's the only thing that I can do. Do you know what quit-claim is?"

"Yeah, I do. It's when you transfer property to someone with no strings attached. Basically, you're signing the club over to me. I'm responsible for the taxes and shit like that." Chris thought she was dreaming. She'd always wanted a club but at the time simply could not afford to take such a big financial risk. Now, money wasn't the issue. Chris, who had become such a devoted mother, would have to, at some point or another, put her daughters second, and she wasn't having that. She'd have no time for them and that would have left her wide open for a barrage of unwanted criticism. The worst part was that she would have to move back to Memphis. "How long do you have before you go to court?"

"Well, I haven't filed yet. I wanted to talk to you first. If you decide to do this, then I will go tomorrow and sign the papers."

"And that's it?"

"Hmmm. Well, not exactly."

"What the hell does that mean?"

Rudy knew how much Chris hated being in Memphis, but the only way that the quitclaim could be done was if Chris was present. "You're going to have to come here to sign the deed."

"What!"

"I know you don't want to come here, but I need you to do this for me, Chris. When was the last time you were here?"

"Shit, the last time you saw me."

"That was over four years ago! Have you been here since then?"

"I came to see my new nephew. Iysha had another baby by that fucka she's married to. Speaking of which, you remember when I asked you about Miss Nay?"

"Yeah, you and the girls were running to catch your plane. I told you that he had gotten married."

"Rudy, he married Iysha."

"What?"

"You heard me. He and Iysha got married."

"Chris, how could you..."

"By the time I laid eyes on him, they were already married. I recognized him immediately even though he wasn't in drag. I think he knows who I am, too."

"What makes you say that?"

"We exchanged words when I was there last time, and I also heard that he was at Gayle's funeral.

"You know what? Now that I think about it he was there. He came with Patty and some more folks from Gayle's church. That had to be a few days after his wedding."

"It was. He wasn't even there when Iysha had Max. Had his ass out in Santa Monica."

"I heard about that. Heard he was no joke while he was there."

"Say what?"

"Oh, honey, Mr. Nathaniel was getting down. Was the biggest ho on the Strip. I guess he was tryna be a movie star and shit."

"I hope he didn't bring any of that shit home. You know what I mean?"

"Are you going to tell Iysha?"

"I want to, and I need to. But it's not my business, Rudy."

"Chris, you know his reputation. You have got to tell your sister."

"I can't do it. Iysha would hate me for it. He's already blocked the long distance at their house so Iysha can't call me. She has to sneak and use the calling card I got her." Chris knew that Miss Nay had really gotten around, and, of course, whatever Miss Nay had, so did Nathaniel. And then to top it off, his ass had been to California where even the biggest hustlers get hustled. Chris knew that Rudy had spent time in Santa Monica one summer while they were in college. And she also recalled the sleazy stories about the Strip. "Rudy, I'll try to be home in a week or less. The kids will be out of school for a break soon, and I'll take some time off then. Hopefully by that time, one of us will come up with something. In the meantime, call my daddy at this number and tell him that you need to talk to Mr. Tolley."

"Mr. who?

"Mr. Tolley. T-o-l-l-e-y. He's a contractor who specializes in nightclubs. I can afford to put some money into renovations. Let him come by and take a look at the place. Then go downtown to the State Office Building and pick up a liquor license application. To get business moving, we're going to need to sell more than just beer, malt liquor and wine coolers."

"Chris, that costs $30,000!"

"I know." Now was the perfect time to tell Rudy about her settlement. "Rudy, you remember when I worked for that company in Philly a couple of years ago? The one that I left after being there for only six months?"

"Vaguely."

"Well, I sued them. The long and short of it is that I got a $750,000 settlement."

"DAMN! What did you sue them for?"

"Discrimination based on sexual orientation. My boss was a homophobic bitch who also hated Black folks. It would've been too hard to prove racial discrimination since over seventy percent of the staff was Black, but she was the only person in the building who knew that I was gay. My attorney and I both thought she was on a mission to make my life hell. Sexual orientation discrimination was a path the company didn't want to go down. It ended up being a piece of cake."

Rudy chuckled. "Did you try to flirt with her, Chris?"

"Nope. She was White, and you know how I feel about White women. That was problem number one. Besides, I was all up in my beautiful, chocolate big-booty lawyer."

"Oh, so your love life ain't so boring after all?" Rudy giggled.

"Now that's a story for another time. I'll tell you

about it when I see you. I'll call Mr. Tolley myself later on in the week and discuss designs and stuff. I'll also talk to his wife. She's an accountant, and she knows her shit. We'll let her do payroll from now on, and, Rudy?"

"What?"

"When the time is right, we're changing the name."

"To what?"

"Don't know yet, but it'll be fitting."

"Run thangs, then, Ms. Gurl! I guess I need to get off this phone and haul ass over to the mall when it opens. I need to run these cards up before I go bankrupt. That's how the White folks do. Let me give you my number at the hotel."

"You're staying in a hotel?" Chris asked as she put on her suit jacket. She'd managed to dress herself while chatting with Rudy.

"It's not a big deal. Juan hooked me up."

"Uh-unh, go to my momma's house and get the key to my condo. You can stay there until you get yourself together. Don't worry about the utilities. They are already taken care of."

"Thanks, Chris."

"Now, get your ass off this phone 'cause I know you ain't paying the bill. I've been standing here eyeing the fruit stand on the corner. I want to get down there and get some bananas before they're all gone. The kids love them, and I need to keep up this gorgeous figure of mine."

"Handle yo' bidness, and I'll be in touch."

After rushing Rudy off the line, Chris picked up her briefcase and headed for the fruit stand and then to work.

❧♥❧

A week had passed before Rudy was able to meet the new bartender, and just as anybody else would have known, there was no mistaking a drag queen…even when he wasn't in drag. Nathaniel knew Rudy as "Miss Rudi"—the cross dresser—and not Rudy, the new and improved all woman. After her extensively transforming surgery, there wasn't a trace of manhood. Thanks to hormone pills, there was no longer any facial hair, and the chest that was once covered by frilly, padded Miracle bras, was now graced with 38C cup breasts. Nathaniel quietly recognized *Rudy—you know your own*—but, since the club was no longer a strictly gay club, he didn't realize that Rudy still owned—or, for that matter, appeared to own it. He didn't offer much in the way of conversation, nor did Rudy ever say anything to him. She just let him come and go like the rest of the employees. Whenever he had been asked to stay over on Friday nights, he obliged. Nathaniel had no idea that it was a business move to let straight people in the club for light meals and drinks during the day; however, once Chris got to town, things were definitely going to change. Rudy had decided to let Chris in on the news about Nathaniel working at the club once she arrived in town—catch her fresh while she had nothing pressing on her mind. This kinda shit you didn't tell someone over the phone. Insisting that it stay a secret, no one knew about Chris and the coming change in management. Dallas had retained the responsibility of handling all personnel matters, and any problems with Dallas were submitted in writing to the owner, which Dallas hand-delivered to Rudy. The only reprimand for him was a good cussing out.

Dallas was instructed to be lenient with Nathaniel but to keep a close eye on him. One evening Nathaniel overheard some of the customers talking about the shows on Saturday nights. Despite the renovations, the place was still packed, and tips were plentiful. Rudy graciously acquiesced—through Dallas of course—when Nathaniel finally asked if he could work extra hours on Friday and Saturday nights…with the rest of the drag queens.

At home, Nathaniel was having trouble sleeping at night, waking up in cold sweats, pacing the hallway until dawn. After a few weekends of serving drinks to gay customers and watching the midnight shows, Nathaniel could no longer resist temptation. Throwing open the doors to Iysha's closet, he gently caressed the silken and cotton fabrics, choosing only the most luxurious outfits and shoes in his wife's collection. Strolling sensuously to the bathroom, he retrieved her MAC make-up and sat down to work on his image with the alluring colors and matte finishes. *Lovely.* Amazing how it all comes back. Gazing at his reflection and kissing the results in the mirror, with hips sensuously swaying and arms lithely waving, Nathaniel poised himself to make a comeback...for now. Once a queen always a queen. But this one was headed for exile. *This shit was gettin' good!*

A HOUSE IS NOT A HOME

Manney came in from the office and put his briefcase on the table. The house was quiet. There was no mail on the coffee table, so he knew that Amil hadn't been home. He looked at his watch, realizing that he might be able to catch Chris in her office. During the course of their professional relationship, they'd only met once in person. Manney had taken a trip to Paris, without Amil, and relished in Chris's uncompromising demeanor. Although he'd come across many women in his career, this was the first who knew how to not be so serious all the time. There was an attraction to her that he couldn't really define. She was pleasant but aloof; wise but cynical: an intriguing combination. In another time, Manney felt that maybe they could have had a chance. But that was what *he* felt.

Chris treated Manney just as she did the rest of her colleagues. She was charming but alert when hanging in unfamiliar circles; astute with a sharp business acumen. As far as she was concerned, Manney was just another "brotha" with skills reaching for the brass ring in the corporate game. Yes, she'd walk the walk and talk the talk with the best of them, but she didn't appreciate a lot of bullshit which exactly described their first meeting.

That day the meeting was tense. Chris was irritated that Manney had chased her down like some wild beast when there were other people he could have spoken with at the office. It seemed that whenever someone Black found out through the grapevine that Chris was a "sistah," the rules changed. Corporate structure was out the window. Most automatically assumed Chris's blackness would make her more lenient and much easier to deal with. By the time those calling upon her expertise reached her office, they had been hipped to the game that Chris was no joke—you either had to come correct or not at all. She was a woman about business. Chris gave credence to Manney's business proposal only because she needed something to boost her image in the eyes of her French counterparts. Now, well into its fourth year, the renovations were going according to schedule. Once Manney discovered that Chris was from Memphis, he took the down-home approach and invited her to dinner the next time she was in town. No one imagined it would be four years later.

Before Manney had left the office, Rondell mentioned that he would be hanging around downtown kind of late and would be available to talk if Manney wanted. They had been trying to hook up for days, but their schedules wouldn't allow for any one-on-one time. So Rondell stopped by the house. "What's up, Manney?" Rondell asked when Manney opened the door.

"Nothing, man. Come on in. You must've gotten my email." Manney smiled.

"Yeah, I did. I was planning to come by here anyway. What's going on? Something bothering you?" Rondell definitely wasn't the brightest light bulb in the bucket, but he knew when something was wrong with his partner. "You ain't been yourself lately."

Manney poured himself a glass of Perrier. "You want something to drink?"

Rondell perked up. Manney *always* had good stuff to drink. "Yes, I believe I will. Got any chocolate milk?"

Shaking his head as he reached in the cabinet for the NestleQuik chocolate milk powder, Manney wondered what wisdom this man could ever offer him. "It's Amil, man."

As Rondell sat there with a chocolate milk mustache, he said, "Look, I don't know what's about to come out of your mouth, but I do know this."

"And what's that?" Manney asked.

"You need to either shit or get off the pot," Rondell stated as he gulped his last swallow of chocolate milk. He took his straw and scraped the chocolate mix from the bottom of the glass and stuck the tip of the straw in his mouth.

"What are you talking about?"

"Man, y'all been engaged since I first met you. This common law shit is for the birds, and, on top of that, Amil is a fine-ass woman. She definitely don't need to be out there legally unattached."

Walking over to the patio window, Manney folded his arms and gazed at the mighty Mississippi spanning across the horizon. "Something's distracting her. I haven't been able to get her attention for a couple of years now."

"You think she's having an affair?"

"When? How? She barely has time for herself let alone someone else. The hospital has her hopping almost 24-7."

Manney was right. Amil's time at the hospital made it close to impossible for her to see anyone else. For three years, she had worked double shifts because of the nursing shortage. By now, she'd grown accustomed to it and spent most of her day doing something at the hospital.

Rondell paused for a second before he asked Manney anything else. He wanted to make sure he was ready for the answer. "Is there some reason why you haven't married her yet? You've been doing everything else with her."

Scratching his head, Manney replied, "No, there really isn't. I guess I've just taken her for granted all this time."

"Well, you see. That's the problem. Right now, she *ain't* obligated to do shit for you. She *ain't* got to be here when you get home. She *ain't* got to cook, and she *ain't* got to clean. I'm surprised you had it good for as long as you did."

"Rondell, Amil is a strong woman with a strong mind. That's why I love her."

"Man, didn't you tell me that one time you made her perm the hair on her pussy to make her look like one of those girls at the strip club?"

"Yes, but that was a dare. I didn't expect her to do that, nor did I think the hair was going to fall out."

"But she did. And what about the whole thing with the fake big toe nail? That wasn't a dare." For a little while in their relationship, Manney had this fascination with fake, big toe nails and had convinced Amil that getting one would make her sexier.

Manney chuckled. "That was all my fault. She got a fungus because of it. It actually made her kinda sick. I admit I was wrong for that."

"Don't sound like no strong woman to me. You need to make that move. Do it up, too."

After years of waiting on Manney, Amil had stopped asking when they were going to get married. She had figured it would happen when it was time. Until recently, Manney had felt that everything was cool like it was. He'd never expected Amil to be so casual about their relationship. He knew the perfect solution. "I'll surprise her with a wedding in Paris this spring."

Rondell's eyes lit up. "Dayum! I wasn't expecting that!"

"And she won't either. It is so beautiful there in the spring. I'll pay for all of our friends to come and will arrange the whole thing myself."

"Now that's what I'm talking about. Don't discuss the obvious with her anymore. Just tell her when and where it's going to happen."

Suddenly, it occurred to Manney. "What if she up and says no?"

"You aren't giving her the opportunity to say no. What woman in her right mind would turn down a Paris wedding in the spring?"

"I guess you're right. I'd actually talked with Chris about it once."

An eyebrow went up. Rondell interjected, "Wait a minute, wait a minute. You sure talk to Chris an awful lot. What's going on between you two?"

Manney burst out laughing. "Man, it ain't even that kinda party with her. She's just really cool people. I don't talk much about Amil with her, but when I've been in a jam about like what to get her for Valentine's Day or Christmas, she seems to always have the perfect solution. She never gets too inquisitive about my personal life. If she'd been digging on me, then there's a whole lot she could've asked by now."

"Yeah, I know when I've talked to her she seemed pretty down-to-earth. Do you know if she's got a man?"

"Wouldn't be surprised, but like I said, she's pretty much to herself. Never mumbled a word about her personal life. When she gets here, I'll ask her for some suggestions. She's supposed to have dinner with me the last Friday that she's here. Can you come?"

Rondell's Friday nights were reserved for the casino and the all-you-can-eat buffet. "Naw, man, I can't do that. Why don't you take Amil with you?"

"She might have to work. And her birthday's that same weekend, too."

Heading toward the kitchen to get an apple, Rondell asked, "You've got that covered, right?"

"Oh, yeah, yeah. Always do."

"Aight, then." Rondell nodded. "Just tell her what you gonna do. I bet she's gonna be all right with it."

❧♥❧

"Dr. Lindsay, HR wants to talk to you about the Internet policy," Sharon stated. "They've been asking everybody to sign this agreement about not abusing the new system."

Amil was exhausted. She'd gotten a cot set up in the ER to take a nap whenever she had a chance, and the last thing on her mind was a policy about the Internet. She'd given up trying to talk to CreolSista. It was like she had fallen off the face of the earth. None of Amil's emails had been answered, and she couldn't get through to her at work. "Is there something I need to know about it? I mean, why is it such a big deal all of a sudden?"

"Oh, it's no big deal. They want to put Instant Messaging on our computers to help with floor-to-floor communication. I think it'd be great. It'd be much easier for me to be able to contact someone in an Instant Message instead of having to wait for them to check their email. I think the only problem they're looking at is being able to filter the outside from getting in."

"So we'd be able to use our personal email accounts?" Amil inquired.

"Yes, you can hook it up if you want. You can use any Instant Messaging you want. They're just saying it's okay to do it."

That wasn't such a good idea. Amil had weaned herself from Instant Messaging. The one thing that had been constant in her life was gone...with no warning... nothing. She managed to spend that empty time with Manney—for what it was worth. Their conversations were never anything of real substance. It was merely enough to show that they could still hold one another's interest. The only thing she'd requested was that Manney keep work at work and she would do the same. At this point, she had no knowledge of his business associates in Paris. "I don't see a problem with IMs at work. Might really save time down the road. I'll call them when I wake up. Don't let me sleep more than thirty minutes."

"Okay, I won't."

Thirty minutes later Amil went to HR and told them how efficient IMs would be. By the time she got back to her office, the Technology Department had already installed AOL on the server. All she had to do was import her Buddy List, and it was done. For the first time in nearly four years, she saw that CreolSista was online. She quickly reached for her Palm, and within a matter of seconds, her IM was sent.

MOCHAMD: Hi

MOCHAMD: Hi

MOCHAMD: How are you?

Amil waited for a couple minutes and saw that she wasn't going to get a response.

MOCHAMD: I guess you're still mad at me.

Another five minutes passed, and there was still no answer.

MOCHAMD: Sorry to bother you.

CreolSista: You're not bothering me. I was away from the computer.

MOCHAMD: I see. So how have you been?

CreolSista: Busy as ever. What about you?

MOCHAMD: Pretty much the same. I'm here at work most of the time.

CreolSista: I hear you. You're IMing me while you're at work?

MOCHAMD: Yes, but I'm on my Palm. I'd just signed on

to my desktop to import my Buddy List and saw you here.

CreolSista: I see. Well, I'm off. I'm on my way out of town.

MOCHAMD: You were on your way out of town the last time we talked.

CreolSista: Damn, your memory is good. I sure was.

Amil was asking for it. The best thing to do was to let it go. There was no telling what was going to come out of CreolSista's mouth.

MOCHAMD: You don't have a couple of minutes for a friend?

Some minutes passed.

MOCHAMD: I know you're still there.

CreolSista: Reluctantly, what did you need?

MOCHAMD: Nothing in particular. We haven't talked in a long while.

CreolSista: And you know why that is?

MOCHAMD: Please tell me.

CreolSista: I did us both a favor. We were getting caught up, and I don't think either of us was ready for that. You were looking for a friend, and I gave that to you. Anything else needed to be avoided. You don't realize what you were getting yourself into.

MOCHAMD: You don't know that.

CreolSista: You've got who you're going to be with for the rest of your life right there with you. I don't. It made no sense to me to get further emotionally attached to someone and something I would never have. You feel me?

MOCHAMD: Yes I do, but he doesn't make me feel like you do.

CreolSista: I miss you terribly, but if you want to go back to where we were, I can't. We can be the best of friends again, but we have to keep things above-board.

MOCHAMD: I understand.

CreolSista: Now, I really have to go. The girls and I have a plane to catch. I'll try to contact you later on in the month, Birthday Girl.

MOCHAMD: You remembered.

CreolSista: I've always remembered. Bye.

After putting her Palm away, Amil's heart was full again. The line of communication with CreolSista had been re-established, and for Amil, it meant that her lifeline was reconnected.

❧♥❧

Maxwell Theron Alexander had the most beautiful, innocent spirit that anybody in the Desmereaux family had ever known. With sleepy, brown eyes and eyelashes that stretched to just below his eyebrows, Max was a heartbreaker. At three and a half years old, as he never hesitated to remind you, he was energetic, smart, alive with love, and the apple of his aunt's eye.

Born two months premature, at twenty-eight weeks, Max was a survivor from day one. Every time the nurses pricked a part of his body to draw blood, his risks for infection and death increased. To minimize the likelihood of contamination from the many transfusions to come, the neonatalogist suggested a blood donor be found within the family. Nathaniel, away in Santa Monica on business, put an abrupt end to his trip and rushed to his wife's side. After two days of testing, only one member of the family ended up being a perfect match.

Everyone except Nathaniel appeared happy about the new addition to the family. He didn't hold Max like he did the girls, nor did he make endless purchases for his layette. Chris and Ora bought nearly everything Max owned...his toys, his clothes, his diapers. Iysha lied on a WIC application and was able to get milk for him because Nathaniel never had enough money after he'd paid the bills. She was too ashamed to reveal that information to her family. They already had their own opinions of her husband, and some of them didn't need to be repeated. As Max grew older, Nathaniel became more distant, and when he was around, all he did was yell at him. Iysha mentioned to her husband that he needed to spend more time with Max, but he quickly reminded her of his increasing responsibilities as man of the house. He had to work. He had to work. He had to work. Those were his three priorities. All of the household duties, including raising the children, belonged to Iysha. It was what he demanded.

Nathaniel's hours at the club had increased... tremendously. He now worked on Friday and Saturday nights and brought home thousands of dollars in tips on Sunday mornings. Ten percent went to the church, and the rest he spent on clothes for the twins and himself. Money from his day job paid the household bills. MLG&W had been by once to turn the lights off, but Iysha wrote a bad check to the technician to keep them on. Nathaniel was too proud to sit in the chairs. She got the money to cover the check from her mother and knew she'd be killed for it if Nathaniel ever found out. He and Iysha didn't talk anymore. No matter how compromising their conversation was it always turned into an argument.

Privately, Iysha couldn't wait to see her sister. They'd have a whole month to talk and hang out. The kids would have a chance to spend time together, and maybe, just maybe, Chris could give Iysha some insight as to how to make things better at home. It was no secret that Nathaniel didn't want Chris in his business, and, out of respect for her sister, Chris stayed away. It became clear to her when Ora told Chris that Iysha couldn't make any more long distance calls from home. Nathaniel didn't just ask her to stop making calls. He went a step further and placed a long distance block on the phone; Iysha couldn't even dial an 800 number.

The house she and Nathaniel had built together was

no longer a home. For almost four years, he'd been, at times, a stranger she didn't know. The only thing she could do was to love him for being the father of her children and to be there for him when and however he needed her to be.

HAPPY BIRTHDAY

It seemed like every damn kid in Memphis was in Chuck E. Cheese's on Max's birthday. Iysha figured that having Max's party on the same day that Libertyland was having its Kool-Aid Day celebration would cut down on the traffic at Chuck E. Cheese's. No one took into account two months before that it might actually rain on that day and cause every child in Hickory Hood, formerly known as Hickory Hill, to take the fun indoors. Just ten years before, Hickory Hill was a nesting spot for trendy shops, fine furniture, great dining, and fabulous shopping. Every other backyard had a pool surrounded by well-kept pine privacy fences, and the front lawns were meticulously manicured. Black families were abundant, but they took care of what they had. It was important to "mix" and get a decent piece of better living.

But then something happened. First, T.J. Maxx moved, followed by Jennifer Convertibles. Then low-end furniture stores, where your job was your credit, replaced them. Inside the mall, many brand-name stores struggled financially. It wasn't appealing to have your merchandise chained to the rack, so they closed. But Victoria's Secret's business was booming because everybody wanted to look and smell nice underneath. Pear Glacée and Vanilla Lace had become so played from overuse that their soothing aromas had lost their appeal. The worst thing anybody could do was to mix those fragrances with that not-so-fresh feeling. To certify this transition, the ultimate newcomer, the Dollar Store, did more business than any other store in the strip mall. And those backyards? Some of the pools were maintained—for a while. The wood from the privacy fences had rotted so badly that the fences leaned and often had missing or broken boards. You could tell when it was income tax time because everyone exploded with a sudden burst of "home improvements."

Cars were parked across the lawns. Where there used to be grass, bald spots and cheap folding chairs had replaced it. Property values went down instead of up. What White people had paid nearly $100,000 for, Black people paid only $75,000. The Black community feasted on the crumbs of the pie the White community had left behind. On the other side of town, little townships like Cordova and Collierville became the Hickory Hills of the 21st century.

Chris's children hadn't seen a Chuck E. Cheese's since before they'd left for Paris. Iysha hated the place, Chris loathed it, and Nathaniel didn't bother to show up, claiming that he was exhausted and needed the quiet time to sleep. His hours at the nightclub had become longer while his time at home had become shorter. There were lines to do everything: the tickets in the skeeball game were jammed; the fishing pole to the Bass Fishing Game was broken; the puck to the air hockey game was missing; and some trifling ass child had taken the time to throw every single ball out of the ball pool. "Iysha, you wanna go somewhere else?" Chris asked. "We can't even sit down in here. Didn't you reserve two tables?"

Iysha stood there amazed at all the children. There was no way that she could give her son a birthday party when the place was already an apparent fire hazard. "Chris, I reserved this two months ago. I don't know what's going on."

"All well, hell, you ain't said nothing but a word. I'll be right back." Chris turned her back and walked over to the counter and requested to see a manager. Iysha knew that Chris could and would perform if she had to. The bad part about it was not knowing who would be the unlucky recipient. That girl had a crazy chip in her. With all her culture and intellect, Chris could get as ghetto-fied as they come when necessary. She adored Max and wanted his birthday to be perfect. "Excuse me, is there a manager here today?" The girl behind the counter looked into Chris's eyes and immediately knew that she wasn't in the mood for it. There were over two hundred kids in the place—running wild and unsupervised and many with parents who were pissed completely off. The air was out, and the poor girl had been asked to work an extra two hours when she had already been there for over seven hours.

"My name is Kia, Ma'am. How may I help you?"

Chris knew that she hadn't stuttered. "Is there a manager here today?"

In a high-pitched attitudinal voice, Kia reluctantly inquired, "What do you need, Ma'am?" She obviously wasn't giving up a manager and was determined not to be disturbed by Chris.

Calmly, Chris rolled her eyes and replied, "Look, we reserved this place two months ago for a birthday party. There are obviously no vacant tables or empty booths. What are we supposed to do?"

"Did you have a reservation?"

Chris just stood there and looked at her. "Yes," she snapped. She handed the reservation card to Kia. "If possible, can I see a manager?"

"He's making pizzas right now and can't come out here. You didn't see no empty spaces out there?"

"No."

"Did you look?" Before Kia could get that question out, Chris had gone behind the counter and into the kitchen where a short bald white man was making pizzas. He looked more like he didn't want to come out versus not being able to come out. Kia came running behind Chris, proclaiming, "Ma'am, you can't be back here."

"I'm already back here, so you go back out there and do your job." Chris pulled the reservation card from Kia's hand and passed it to the man with "Mr. Kendrick, Manager" on his nametag. "Is there not something that can be done about this? We've already paid for our space here."

Mr. Kendrick looked at the card and saw that a receipt was attached to the back of it. "I'm so sorry, Miss. Of course, we had no idea that Libertyland was gonna be rained out today. It was kinda an unofficial announcement that the event was to be moved here. We didn't coordinate that with anyone, but then again, who's complaining? We haven't had this much business all summer!"

"Look," Chris began. "This is my nephew's fourth birthday party, and he is so looking forward to it. Can you…" Mr. Kendrick stood there adjusting his pants as Chris went on and on.

"Wait a minute; let me stop you. Policy is policy no matter how green the money is. I'll be right back." The little man stepped into the wash area and cleaned his hands. "Go on back outside. Give me about ten minutes, and I will have this taken care of. I promise."

Before heading toward the back, Mr. Kendrick turned to Chris and said, "You know, I got a four-year-old grandson that I'd move heaven and hell for. I saw that in you when you stormed back here, and I know what it's like to break the heart of a child. And I just don't want that on my head today." Then he disappeared into the storeroom.

Looking into Max's eyes as she strode from behind the counter, Chris reached for her nephew as he took a running leap into her arms. "Tee-tee made this all right for you. It's gonna be all right," she whispered. Max was Chris's heart. But during the first two years of his life, Max wouldn't let Chris touch him. He'd snatch his hand away from her and turn his head whenever she tried to kiss him.

Nathaniel had been so hard on Max that Chris had once thought about turning him in to DHS. "Aw, that boy can handle it. Don't want him to grow up and be a sissy. He has to learn how to take shit like a man." Max was a baby, though, and didn't need to be concerned with taking shit like a man. Chris argued that point with Iysha day in and day out, but all Iysha ever said was to let Nathaniel raise his son the way he wanted to. It was bad enough that Chris and Nathaniel couldn't stand each other, and it was even worse when Chris tried to tell him how to raise his child.

Iysha walked over to Chris and rubbed Max's back.

She looked into the eye of the mighty tiger and regretfully asked what had happened. Chris smiled at her sister and told her that the manager was taking care of everything. Seconds later, kids started pouring out of the private party area, and the curtains were closed. All of the available staff—both of them—were called to the party area. Each of them carried boxes of party favors, plates, cups, and napkins. Mr. Kendrick hurried past them with two of four freshly made pizzas. "Damn," Iysha remarked. "What did you say to him?"

Chris smiled and said, "Nothing. He's just doing his job."

Mr. Kendrick pulled Chris by the arm and took her around the corner and gave her a brown paper bag. "We don't generally do this, but, since a great deal of the machines are malfunctioning at this point, I got you all some tickets." He gave Chris over 10,000 tickets for the kids to spend on prizes. "I hope he has a good day. Let me know if you need anything else." Chris was so overwhelmed by his gesture that she hugged Mr. Kendrick and then shook his hand.

Later that evening when everyone was leaving the party, Max caught Chris by the hand. "Wus wrong, Tee-tee? You look sad. Didn't you like my party?"

"Well, yes, I loved your party, sweetie," Chris replied. "But, I haven't given you your present yet."

Max's face lit up. Chris had told Iysha that she had

gotten Max a pure-bred cocker spaniel for his birthday. Having made sure that Iysha had cleared the air with Nathaniel before making such a purchase, Chris knew that Max was going to drop to the floor. "Are you sure that your bitch ass husband isn't going to say anything about this?"

"Girl, he's not home enough to give a damn. Max needs somebody to play with besides me and the girls," she said as they approached her sister's car.

"I know, Iysha. But that bastard took your last dog and..."

"Don't worry about it, Chris." Those words haunted Iysha, but this was for Max so what Nathaniel thought didn't matter.

As they were standing by the car, Max tugged at Chris's dress with a puzzled look on his face. "Tee-tee, do you hear dat noise?"

"What noise?"

"Dat noise."

Chris pretended that she didn't hear the puppy whining and scratching in its kennel. "I don't hear anything, baby."

"Tee-tee! Thar it is agin! It's in yo' car!" he screamed.

The window was down in the backseat. Chris reached in and unlocked the kennel. Ora had just dropped the puppy off, and she managed to get a pretty red bow around his neck. As Chris reached in, she reminded Max about a game that they used to play in his backyard. Max always said that he was the King of the Mountain and that someday a prince would come and take his place on the throne. For a child Max's concept of growing up was keener than most adults. It seemed as if he experienced life almost in fast-forward. Although only four, with his intellect he could pass for eight. "Max..." Chris smiled. "I want you to meet Prince."

If Max knew what fainting was, he probably would have done it. His eyes glistened as he pulled the puppy from his aunt's arms. "Thank you, Tee-tee. Oh, thank you so much for him."

"You're welcome, Max. Take care of him, okay?"

"I will. I promise! I can't wait to show Daddy!"

❦♥❦

Three weeks after Max's birthday, Iysha was preparing to celebrate hers. Nathaniel had already told her that he had to work and that they would have to celebrate on Sunday evening. It was the first time in a long while that Iysha's birthday had fallen on a Saturday.

Earlier that week, on Monday, Chris stopped by Iysha's to check on Max and Prince. Chris hated calling Iysha whenever Nathaniel was home because, despite the fact that his wife was on the phone with someone, he would always strike up a conversation with her. It was his rude way of saying *you aren't paying enough attention to me so get off the phone.* Stopping by in the middle of the day was the best way to avoid Nathaniel, so Chris made it a point to be at her sister's house by noon.

When Iysha came to the door, her words were harsh but loving. "Bitch, do you have my silk scarf that I just bought from Goldsmith's?"

"I love you, too." Chris breezed by Iysha.

"I take that as a yes."

"I wouldn't."

"Look, Chris, give me back my shit. All you had to do was ask."

"Iysha, I told you when you bought the scarf that it was hideous. Now why would I borrow it from you?"

Iysha sat down on her new leather sectional. Chris hadn't seen it before and stood there in amazement. "I don't know what's been happening to my things. I can't find my scarf or those new shoes I bought when I was with you. And you know that dress you brought me from Paris? It's disappeared and I was going to wear it this weekend."

Chris was mesmerized, standing in the family room with her mouth wide open looking at the sectional.

"Where the hell did this come from?"

"What?"

"Don't be no damn 'what.' You know what I'm talking about. That shit you're sitting on!"

"Don't be j—, honey. My man got this for us. Got it from Samuel's."

"I didn't know that bartending paid so well. He's been doing that every night?"

"Yeah, almost every night. You know, we got church on Tuesday nights now."

"I thought it was Wednesdays."

"We still do that, too. The manager at the bar has been asking Nathaniel to work overtime on Friday and Saturday nights until the other bartender gets back from his vacation."

"How long has this been going on?"

"For a while now. His tips are real good on those nights. Girl, my husband be bringin' home stacks of one and five dollah bills."

Chris, after having had a long conversation with Rudy, wanted to tell her sister so badly that she knew where her scarf, her shoes, and her dress were; but Chris promised herself that she would mind her business. "Have you talked to Momma today?"

"Yes, she came by here before she went to work. Dropped off my gift."

"Really? What'd you get?" Iysha flashed a check for a hundred dollars in front of Chris. "You better hold on to it. You never know what might happen."

"What do you mean?"

"Never mind. Just fucking with you." Chris looked around and noticed how quiet the house was. "Where's Max?"

"Honey, he's outside with Prince. Since you got him that dog, I can't keep him in here."

"Let me guess. Prince is not allowed in the house."

"You got it."

"Iysha, he's a house dog. You promised..."

"It's just gonna take him some time, Chris. Hell, now that we have this new sofa, he'll probably never get to come in here. We got him a really nice dog house, though."

"Whatever. I know that he's your husband, but I can't stand him. I really hate the way he treats Max. That boy thinks his daddy walks on water. Good thing he's not old enough to realize that his daddy spends more time buying dresses and lace socks for the girls than he does buying things for his own son. If it weren't for Momma and me, Max wouldn't have much of anything."

"Now, Chris, that's my man, and I'm not going to have you disrespecting him in his own house."

"Right. We wouldn't wanna upset Massa. Ize gon ta run out heh and speak ta Max and Prince befo' Massa git home. Ize knows dat you gotta heapa cookin' and cleanin' ta do," Chris said sarcastically as she curtsied and bowed out the back door.

"Tee-tee! Tee-tee!" Chris's heart pounded rhythms of joy whenever she heard that voice. Max ran to his aunt, jumped into her arms, and launched into his adventures with Prince, relating stories filled with a character called the Black Knight who often came in the dark to try to destroy the Prince. Although sometimes slow to the punch, it didn't take Chris but a minute to realize what Max was really trying to say.

On her way back to the car, Chris stopped in the house and asked Iysha what she had planned for her birthday. Iysha reminded her that Nathaniel had to work on that day, so, unless she found a babysitter, she would be at home. "Don't worry about all of that. I'll take care of it. Just the two of us out on the town. I want to show you some of the new stuff I've discovered around downtown."

"Now, wait a minute. Don't be taking me to one of those dyke clubs. You know I'm a woman of the Word."

"I promise. We won't go there. I've got a couple of places in mind. By the way, the girls and I are going back to Paris on Sunday. I've got to get the kids ready for school."

"So soon?"

"Damn, girl, we've been here far longer than I'd planned. I finished my paper weeks ago, and, by the end of the week, I will have finished up some other business." To keep from getting any deeper into the conversation, Chris cut it off quick. "I'll tell you all about it on Saturday. I need to get out of here. Got places to be and things to do."

That afternoon a summer storm moved in. It was one of those where the sky turns a half shade lighter than blue-black and the lightning bolts rip through the ground. When Nathaniel came in from work, he reminded Iysha that they had to attend a dinner party at their pastor's house. The wind was whistling through the swaying trees as Iysha studied the weather report on the television. The National Weather Service had issued a tornado warning because a funnel cloud had been spotted in Southaven. Frightened by the sudden change in the weather, Prince had been howling all evening. "Nathaniel?" Iysha asked.

"What?"

"I know that you don't want him in the house, but…"

"No."

"Nathaniel, they've issued a tornado warning."

"He'll be all right out there in his house."

"Please, honey. Anything could happen to him. Do it for Max, please. He'd be devastated if anything happened to Prince."

"He'll be okay even if something does happen to him. It's just a damn dog."

Iysha knew that she was losing this argument. There was only one thing that she could do. "Well, I'll stay here with him. It's not right to leave him here alone like that. Look at that sky."

There was no way that Nathaniel was going to allow himself to be upstaged by a dog. He had promised Pastor Edmonds that both he and Iysha would be at the party. "Bring him in the house, Iysha. You just better hope that he behaves."

Nathaniel was cheap no matter how expensive his clothes and tastes were. He left the house completely dark whenever they left the house, and, this time, with Prince on the inside, was no different. Prince howled right along with the wind, and, when the thunder clapped, he bounced off the furniture…all of it.

It was close to midnight when the family finally returned home. With the power out in the entire neighborhood, there was no need to deactivate the alarm. Max dashed past his parents, pushed on every tap light in his path, and headed for his room to see Prince. The battery-operated tap lights provided just enough illumination for Max as he made his way down the hall. Iysha had made Prince a little bed in the corner of Max's room and left all of his little toys that Chris had gotten for him in the corner, too. Max found Prince sleeping soundly on his blanket. Stroking his forehead, Max kissed Prince on the nose and scrambled to find his way to the bathroom to release a pee that he had been holding for almost an hour. Iysha's purchase of two introductory offers of tap lights had turned out to be a worthwhile investment.

In the kitchen, Iysha searched diligently for matches to light a few candles and to perhaps catch a rare romantic moment with her husband. Sex wasn't as frequent as it used to be since Nathaniel was always working. Before he took on that second job, he had been banging Iysha up her ass almost every night. Sometimes his sole preference was a blowjob. There was never any pleasure in it for Iysha. She felt that her satisfaction was secondary and most often not even necessary. Nathaniel never wanted Iysha on top of him. He complained that she had put on a few pounds when actually she had lost weight. Since Chris had been in town, Iysha stayed on the go trying to spend as much time as possible with her sister and nieces. The drawer next to the oven was always full of matches, but Iysha couldn't find any. "I am going to go outside and see if I have some in the truck."

"What do you need them for? We got those lights that you bought. The kids are already in their rooms anyway."

Iysha walked over and kissed Nathaniel on the cheek. She stroked the back of his neck the way she always did, but he yanked away. Shocked, Iysha stood there in disbelief. "I only wanted to spend some quiet time with you." She reached for his belt buckle, but Nathaniel smacked her hand away.

"It's late, Iysha. Maybe tomorrow."

"But we have church tomorrow night and the next. Then you have to work the rest of the week."

Nathaniel wasn't in the mood. He was tired and

wanted to do nothing but go to bed. If he had to sleep on the sofa to avoid Iysha's advances, he was prepared to do it. "I want to go to bed, Iysha. This foolishness..."

"Foolishness?"

Damn, Nathaniel thought. *Here we go*. "I didn't mean it like that. You're standing there pouting because I don't want to have sex. I'm tired, Iysha! Don't you get it?"

"Yeah, I get it." Iysha retired to her bedroom oblivious to the white fluffy matter strewn about the hallway. Reaching in her jacket pocket, she found a box of matches and lit the candle next to her bed. Her eyes closed, Iysha tearfully whispered a silent prayer. The man that the Church of Christ had brainwashed her to obey and to follow had hurt her feelings, once again. Torn between what her body yearned and what her mind and heart felt, Iysha pulled herself together and quickly got over it. Nathaniel didn't have time for another woman because he was either at work or at church. So Iysha didn't even want to think about going there with this confusion. Maybe he was really tired, and maybe she was being too insensitive. Emotionally and physically drained, she decided to run herself a bath. Nathaniel used to do it for her before he started working all the time. He had conditioned Iysha to believe that her baths were her refuge from the day, and he spent hundreds of dollars on bathroom amenities such as gels, brushes, soaps, candles, and other types of shit that really had no purpose. Hell, Nathaniel spent more time in the bathroom than she did, though. Showers were a thing of the past for him. He looked forward to the bubbles and the flowery scents. The associates at Victoria's Secret and Crabtree and Evelyn knew him on first-name basis. They believed that he was purchasing these items for his wife. Little did they know that most of it, Iysha never even got to see. But for Iysha, the bathroom had, too, become her sanctuary. As she sat on the side of the tub lighting candles, she glared at the floor and saw pieces of white foam insulation next to the toilet. Thinking that she was hearing the wind, Iysha mentally prepared herself for a stormy night alone, but, when she turned off the water, it was clear that what Iysha heard was not the wind. It was the wails of both Max and Prince. Guided by the illumination from the tap lights, Iysha sprinted up the hallway as the power popped back on and she discovered what she knew would be Prince's fate. In his fear during the storm, Prince had torn the pillows to the leather sectional to shreds, and Nathaniel was savagely beating him with a leather belt while Max looked on. Terrified of his father, Max dejectedly sat on the hearth and wept as the horrific scene played out before him. Nathaniel had wrapped his hand with the slack from the leash that was around Prince's neck and whipped the dog like a slave with the belt in the other hand.

"Nathaniel!" Iysha screamed. "Stop it! Please stop! Max is watching you." She caught the belt as it was about to come down on Prince's swollen body. "Look at what you're doing! You're hurting him!"

Pointing to the sofa and the foam strewn about the living room, Nathaniel yelled, "Look at what this bastard did to my sofa! Ain't even been in here a week! Now it's destroyed!"

"It's a damn couch, Nathaniel! That's a living thing!"

"It's just a fucking dog, Iysha. It's gotta go!" With that, Max's weeping turned into sobs. "I told you that I didn't want him in the house!" Nathaniel stared Max dead in his eyes and couldn't miss the pain he saw reflected there. But he didn't care. He lunged at Max with the belt as he dragged the injured puppy alongside him. "You want some of this, boy? Huh? You want some of this?"

Max's heart was beating so fast that you could see his shirt vibrating. An asthmatic, Max quietly mumbled, "No, sir."

"I didn't hear you!"

Max took a deep breath and said a little louder, "No, sir."

"Well, then take your ass to bed!" Nathaniel raised his belt again in a fury. He was going to strike Max with all his might. Iysha jumped in front of him and tearfully stared him down. Her blood boiled as she watched her husband trying to prove his manhood by destroying the character and integrity of her only son. "Must you break him down before he even has a chance to grow up?" she asked.

Nathaniel reached for his shirt with his free hand. "Leave me alone, Iysha. This is all your fault. I told you that dogs stay outside."

"I'm not talking about Prince right now. I'm talking about Max. What are you trying to prove?" Nathaniel slid his feet into his sandals and never uttered a word. He picked up his keys and headed for the door…with Prince under his arm. Iysha, in disbelief, grabbed the leash.

"Nathaniel, please don't do this again. He's Max's dog. Chris…"

"Don't even bring up that bitch's name right now!" he snapped.

"But what am I supposed to tell her about Prince?"

Nathaniel chuckled. "Tell her that shit happens."

Iysha held on tight to the leash as Nathaniel hurried through the carport. He let the door slam on her, but Iysha broke the force of it with her arm. She was determined to catch her husband but even more determined to save Prince. "Nathaniel, wait!"

"Let it go then!" he ordered.

"Please!" Iysha tripped over Erin and Erica's Barbie Jeep, but she still held the leash in her hand. At this point Iysha was on her back, but Nathaniel never turned around. Her shirt had come up past her bra, and her flesh was brutally scraping against the concrete. It stung, it burned, it ached, but Iysha was not letting go. The circulation in her arm had almost cut off because the leash was wrapped so tightly around her wrist. "Please don't do this, Nathaniel!"

When he got to the truck, Nathaniel opened the door and tossed Prince's limp body into the backseat. He slammed the door and looked down at Iysha. "Unless you want to ride like that, then I advise you to let the leash go." He stepped over her and went around to the other side of the truck. Exhausted and battered, Iysha let go. Nathaniel wheeled out of the driveway and burned rubber down the street. Inside, Max had picked up his Mickey Mouse phone and pushed the button that would speed dial his Tee-tee.

Ten minutes later, Chris pulled in the driveway and ordered Gaylon and Chelsea to stay inside. "What's wrong, Mom?" Chelsea asked. "Why is Auntie outside?"

Chris turned the headlights off to take the spotlight off of Iysha. Prepared for anything, Chris jumped out of the car and ran to her sister's side. Iysha was crying, and she winced when Chris tried to rub her back. "What's wrong, baby? Tell me what happened." Chris looked at the back of Iysha's T-shirt, which was now covered with holes and blood. "Iysha, c'mon, honey, tell me."

Praying seemed to calm her. She prayed to herself often, and this time that was all Iysha knew to do. She turned to her sister. "You need to get out of here before he gets back."

Chris was bewildered. "Where did he go?"

Iysha began sobbing. "He took Prince, Chris. He beat him, and then he took him."

"Oh, God. Where's Max?"

"He's probably in the house asleep by now. His daddy scared him so bad."

"I don't think that he's asleep. He called me a little while ago."

Iysha pulled herself to her feet. "If you love Max, Chris, and I know you do, leave, and leave now. There's no telling what Nathaniel will do if he sees you here when he gets back. I promise that I will call you in the morning after he leaves."

Tears streamed down Chris's face. She hated more than anything to leave her sister there, but it was what she was asked to do. "Well, at least put something on your back. It doesn't look too good."

"I will. Please go, Chris."

"All right, all right. But you promise to call me in the morning?"

"I will." As she walked away, Iysha turned to Chris. "One more thing."

"Anything."

"Please don't tell Momma and Daddy. I don't need that right now."

"Okay, I promise." Chris got back in the car and drove off.

Chelsea looked through the rear window hoping that Iysha had come to her senses and had decided to follow them home. Although only eight, she was very astute. She didn't care for her Uncle Nathaniel because he was always trying to tell her and her cousins how to play and what to play. And probably the biggest thing was that she hated how mean he often was to Max. "Mom, is Auntie gonna be all right?"

Chris rubbed Chelsea's thigh and said, "I hope so, honey. I really hope so."

The back roads of Mississippi were not the place for a Black man on any given night. Too many rednecks with too little to do on a Monday night was almost a given this time of year. Nathaniel didn't care, though. He only wanted to get to bed. In his opinion, the events of the evening had been unnecessary. As he drove, Nathaniel remembered that he had purchased a Protection Plan for the sofa. So it ended up that he was going to get everything his way...once again. A new sofa and no dog. If there hadn't been a dog in the first place, then, well, whatever. In the dead of night, Prince was picked up from the back seat and tossed from the truck. Nathaniel arrived back at home close to two in the morning. Iysha had gone to bed…in Max's room. *Good*…Nathaniel thought. *I can finally get some sleep.*

It was Wednesday before Iysha was able to talk to anybody because Nathaniel had taken off work. Iysha, knowing that Chris would be calling, unplugged the phone. There had been almost complete silence in the house. To make matters worse, each morning after she dropped the twins off at camp Nathaniel would be waiting for her in the shower. "I thought that you been wanting to do this." Iysha didn't want any more fighting. No more yelling. No more of anything. She just wanted her man back. Something had a hold of him, and it seemed that he didn't want to be let go. So Iysha let her husband love on her the way that he wanted to love on her. No passion, no love, no intimacy. Just a fuck. Thursday couldn't have come quick enough for her.

Like clockwork, the phone rang. "Well, it's about damn time," the voice said on the other end. It was Chris. "I guess he finally took his black ass to work."

"Yeah, he did."

"I am on my way."

"Wait. Not here. Meet me at Momma's house. After I put on Max's clothes, we'll be on."

"See you there." Chris didn't have a chance to tell Iysha that their mother was off from work that day.

Chris hated traveling down Shelby Drive, but, with all the construction on Interstate 240, it was the quickest way to her mother's house from her condo on Kirby Parkway. Ms. Desmereaux had bought herself a well-deserved new house in Cordova. It had three levels and gave the occupant of each floor lots of privacy. After she put her lazy ass boyfriend out, all she needed was enough space for her and her grandchildren when they visited. Each daughter was given a key and was welcome at any time. Today, however, only Chris knew that her mother had gone to the grocery store and was due back any moment. When she pulled into the driveway, Chris saw that Iysha had beat her there. The front door was still open, and Max was standing there with the saddest eyes. "Hi, Sweetie. Wanna give Tee-tee a hug?" Max put his arms around Chris's neck so tight that she could hardly turn her head. "That's a good boy. I've missed you so much," she whispered. "Where's Mommy?" Max pointed to the kitchen where Iysha was making coffee.

"I made you a cup and brought the girls some breakfast. Where are they anyway?"

"At a friend's. I needed to see how you were first. They were pretty shaken up after Monday night. Worried about their Auntie."

"I'm okay. Got thick skin like my daddy. I got some of that flavored creamer you like, too." Iysha's face was swollen from constant crying, and her voice was groggy from the lack of sleep. Clearing her throat, she commented, "Thanks for staying away these last couple of days. How did you know that he went to work today?"

"I called that nosy ass neighbor of yours. She's the only person in the whole damn neighborhood who has put chairs on the front lawn. And when did she get that big ass black barbecue grill?"

Iysha finally cracked a smile. "Girl, some man came by in a pick-up truck with a bunch of them on the back of it. Was selling them for $50. You know that Massa Alexander didn't want one."

Chris sat down across the table from Iysha and reached for her hands. "Am I going to have to ask?"

"He took Prince and dumped him, Chris. He beat that dog so badly that it hurt me to even look at him. I tried to stop him. That's how my back got so messed up."

"He just started beating him?"

"It was storming that night, and I had asked that he let Prince come in while we were going to be out. I guess that with the sirens and the wind that Prince became restless and frightened. He tore up the sectional."

"Was the damage really that bad?"

"Yeah, it was," Iysha said, staring at the sugar dish.

"Good. Serves that muthafucka right. Go on."

"Anyway, I walked in on him beating Prince and got in front of him when he got ready to start in on Max. The rest of it's self-explanatory." Iysha looked up and saw her mother standing there. She wasn't sure what her mother had heard. It was clear, though, that she had heard enough.

"Where's the dog now?" Ora asked.

"I don't know. He didn't tell me where he left him."

Ora knew that Nathaniel, one of the scariest men that she had ever known, wasn't going to go too far to dump Prince, especially if it was dark out. This idiot might, though, go somewhere that was slightly familiar to him. *You don't just find dirt roads at night unless you've been there during the day*, she thought. "Chris, what's the name of the road that you took us down that day you were looking for some land to buy?"

"I don't remember, Momma, but I know how to get there. What makes you think that Nathaniel took Prince over there?"

"Just a hunch. Don't too many people in the middle of the night go to places that they don't know about. He's been there before." She sat down next to Iysha. "Baby, this has got to stop."

"Momma, I know, but Prince tore stuff up in the house."

"I just know you aren't going to sit here and defend him, Iysha," said Chris. "He could have really hurt you and Max. I know that sofa can be replaced. Samuel's doesn't sell anything without a Payment Protection Plan. Nathaniel was just being low-down."

"He's my husband, Chris. I told you in the beginning that it might not be a good idea to get Max that puppy. Nathaniel hasn't been himself lately."

"I bet he hasn't," Chris mumbled. "Look, let's go and try to find Prince. Momma, if we find him, can Max keep him here?"

"You know the answer to that," she said, reaching for her keys. "Let's go."

The four of them looked for hours in the woods just off Holmes Road. The August sun had no mercy, so Chris put Max in the car with the motor running and the air conditioner on. She gave him some bottled water and wiped the sweat from his face. "Don't worry, honey. Tee-tee is going to find Prince. I promise."

"Okay," he whined as he drifted off to sleep in the back seat. Chris sat down for a minute and regrouped. She had to think about what survival instincts Prince might have. Her mother and Iysha were getting frustrated and feared the worst. "Chris, we might as well leave. He's not out here." Iysha sighed.

"Yes, he is. Just be patient."

Ora, whose silk blouse was sticking to every part of her upper body, looked at Chris. "What are you thinking over there? I see your brain smoking."

"Iysha, what kind of games did Prince and Max play?"

"They always played that King of the Mountain shit. Prince would sit on top of the sand hill while Max kicked sand and shit on him."

"Let's go. I saw some newly developed land when we first turned in. There's a lot of dirt over there...with hills." The three women got in the car and rode to where mounds of dirt had replaced the grass and weeds. "Momma, you go that way. Iysha, you go over there." By this time, Max had awakened. "And little man, you come with me." It took only ten minutes for them to find Prince. He was lying on top of a pile of dirt. Ordinarily, his beige fur coat would have blended right in with the dirt. But today he was motley.

"Prince!" Max called. "Prince!" The puppy's head raised up, but he was too weak to move. "I'm coming to save you!" It was a heart-wrenching scene. Max fell to his knees and held Prince in his arms. "We're here, now. Tee-tee and me are here." Chris picked up Prince and kissed his dingy coat. "Ewwww, Tee-tee, you kissed a dog. You said you don't kiss dogs."

"This one is different. Let's get him to the vet."

❧♥❧

The sun was making its way to the western sky when Iysha got back home. Fortunately, she had cleaned up before she had left that morning, but she still had to make sure that Nathaniel's food was piping hot when he entered the door from work. Nathaniel was a stickler for his attention. He told Iysha that she had all day to do for herself and the kids, to talk on the phone, and to run errands. When he got home, it was his time. He expected all of the ironing and cleaning to be done. Iysha made the mistake once of dusting off and shining his shoes. Now that, too, was expected of her. She didn't have time to talk with her sister or friends. She didn't even have time to devote to the children. By 5:45 p.m., Iysha had taken the last piece of chicken out of the frying pan, and, like proverbial clockwork, the red Toyota 4Runner pulled into the carport. Massa was home, and no sooner than the last bite of food was taken, the family was out the door on their way to church.

On Thursday nights, Iysha and the kids got a much-needed break. Nathaniel had to be at the bar by eight o'clock so there was plenty of time for socializing with Chris and her girls. The two decided to meet at Wolf Chase Mall to take in a movie and then go over to Bahama Breezes for drinks. "Do you think that Momma was pissed today?" Iysha asked as she sipped her Kahlua Colada.

"Yes, she was. Who wouldn't be, Iysha?"

"I wish y'all would understand."

"Understand what? He all but beat your ass in front of Max."

"He didn't hit me, Chris. I tripped and fell to the ground. It was my fault that I didn't let go of the leash."

"There you go again. Defending him." Chris was so pissed that she could barely swallow her drink. "I don't even want to talk about him. And you need to know that Daddy wants to talk to you."

"You told him?"

"Momma did. And you know what else I think? I think your husband is a bitch. A punk. One of the biggest queens I've ever seen if you ask me. He's got more sway in his ass than I do."

"Girl, please. Trust me, he ain't hardly no punk. I guarantee that."

"How much do you know about him, Iysha. You've been married to him for five years, and, as your sister, you've never told me anything about him."

"There's nothing to tell really. Born and raised in deep South Memphis. Down by Mississippi Street. Graduated from Central."

Chris knew more about Nathaniel than his own wife did. She knew that he had graduated from Central only because he got kicked out of Whitehaven for sucking some boy's dick in the locker room. She also knew that Nathaniel came from the part of South Memphis where the choir groupies and fag hags came from. She knew that nearly ten years before there were ever any children or a wife, on a Thursday much like this one, Nathaniel, then known as Miss Nay, made his debut at The Menagerie. Chris knew who Patrick had once been to Nathaniel. But most importantly, she saw a sadness in her sister's eyes that she could not dispel. Nathaniel had another life that contradicted the one he was perpetrating with Iysha.

Forcing a smile, Iysha continued, "You know I can't wait until this weekend. We're gonna have so much fun out."

Change the subject, Chris. "Tomorrow night I have a dinner meeting at that barbecue place on Beale."

"Memphis' Best?"

"Yeah, why?" Chris panicked. "Has it gone downhill already?"

"Nawww! Nathaniel's uncle owns that place. You know, the one that catered our wedding."

"Well, that explains the pork meat appetizers and the riblets at the reception," Chris joked.

"See, you ain't right. Tell them who you are. I'm sure they'll hook you up."

This was one time that Chris didn't want any favors, especially from anyone in Nathaniel's family. "I don't need no hook-ups. Anyway, he asked me to dinner."

Iysha's eyebrow raised in suspense. *"He?"*

"Don't go there," Chris stated emphatically. "You know I ain't even interested. Besides he's already got a woman."

"Damn!" Iysha shouted. "I guess I'll never be a Matron of Honor!"

Chris, taking the last sip of her drink with a reassuring, sly grin on her face, responded, "Guess not."

❧♥❧

Meeting Manney for dinner had not been in Chris's plans while in Memphis. She was trying to tie up loose ends with the club and was especially eager to get back to Paris. With Rudy anxious to finally get the entire club open, Chris was swamped with last minute details. Both Friday morning and afternoon were spent doing last-minute inspections to make sure all the codes had been met. Security had to be screened one final time. Chris didn't want everybody's best friend or homie coming up in the club free of charge. There was a very strict guest list, and any member of security caught letting someone slide in would be dismissed on the spot. On opening night, there was no room for error. No hook-ups, no passes, nothing. Following a final staff meeting with Rudy, Chris reluctantly set aside her Friday evening for a casual dinner with Manney at Memphis' Best Barbecue Joint.

❧♥❧

MOCHAMD: Hey, you.

CreolSista: Hi yourself, Birthday Girl! How goes it?

MOCHAMD: Actually, it's not until tomorrow.

CreolSista: Really? My sister's birthday is tomorrow, too. I told her that she should celebrate the whole month like I do. Makes it more exciting.

MOCHAMD: lol. I'll be sure to keep that in my mind for next year.

CreolSista: Any special plans?

MOCHAMD: Well, he always takes me to dinner at some new place that he'd like to try, but I have to work tomorrow night.

CreolSista: oic. Why not just take you tonight then?

MOCHAMD: Can't. He's already got plans with a client from out of town. We'll probably do something on Monday.

CreolSista: Sounds like fun ;(.

MOCHAMD: Please. I'm just going tonight to get me some ribs and a piece of sweet potato pie. This place we're going to is pretty good.

CreolSista: Hold up. Where are you?

MOCHAMD: Um, in Memphis actually. I didn't have a chance to tell you the last time we spoke. Remember, it's been years since we last chatted at length. I moved here about four years ago, and I haven't chatted with you since before you left for your two-month trip. You always seem to be in such a hurry.

CreolSista: I can't believe this. This can't be.

MOCHAMD: What's wrong?

CreolSista is currently not signed on.

She'd done it again. Amil was left hanging. CreolSista was notorious for signing off without saying good-bye. Amil was used to a certain level of attention from CreolSista, but she hadn't been getting it lately. Sure, a conversation, here and there, during the week, but nothing comparable to what it had once been. Their conversations were no longer personable, and neither of them was breaking her neck to get to the computer to say hello. CreolSista was merely making sure that she'd gotten an opportunity to wish MOCHAMD well on her birthday. They'd chatted the day before, and both of them had gotten so worked up emotionally that it was MOCHAMD who actually had signed off first. Nothing raunchy or disgusting. Just two friends desperately wanting and needing each other when the world had already said no to such a request. CreolSista was tired of a game that no one would ever win. She'd wanted MOCHAMD to have a wonderful birthday, but after that, CreolSista had decided that it was finally over. Amil felt the strain and had prepared herself for whatever the outcome was to be. Tempted to call CreolSista if only to hear her voice, Amil hesitated. She couldn't even call her real name since after all this time Amil had never asked what it was. Had she ever taken this seriously?

A few minutes later Manney stuck his head in the bedroom door, checking to see if Amil was ready. She was taking her time considering it was supposed to be a casual dinner meeting. Amil wasn't in the mood for glamorous attire and formal settings. Her life was lacking the luster that it had while she was in D.C. She was bored, and sometimes the smallest distraction was a welcomed one.

Chris really wasn't very hungry. She'd had three drinks at the club and had also sampled a small appetizer with Rudy. She sobered up walking along Beale Street trying to figure out what the hell was going on. Amil was in Memphis. How long had she been there? Manney now spoke often about his wife who was a doctor. Before, he'd remained extremely professional and never mentioned his personal life. Now that he and Chris had broken the ice by making it clear that they both understood the stakes involved in making their collaboration a success, each of them realized that they both were in the business of making money and making names for themselves. In all of their conversations, Chris had been so caught up in keeping things on a professional level that she completely ignored the mannerisms that had been explained to her so many times by MOCHAMD. As much as she wanted to be right—for it would mean finally laying eyes on the person who'd once added another positive dimension to her life, Chris so desperately wanted to be wrong. Something like this could cause a lot of people a lot of problems, and Chris was out of the business of creating drama.

❧♥❧

The smell of charred, grilled hog was a familiar aroma on Beale Street. The line to get into Hogs On Beale was nothing compared to the one that wrapped around the block to get into Memphis's Best Barbecue Joint. Featuring closely guarded family recipes, everything on the menu was homemade and always fresh. Sweet potato pies were put in the oven every half-hour, and any leftovers, which never existed, were either thrown out or given to the last customers of the evening. Since it was such a beautiful night out, Manney suggested that he and Amil walk to dinner. Ever the health fanatic, she didn't mind. It would give her some time to think about how miserable her life had been, and now, as she was a day from turning forty, she found herself being forced to go to a business meeting that had absolutely nothing to do with her. "I really hope that this doesn't take all night, Manney. I worked a fifteen-hour shift last night and want to go to bed."

"Why are you being such a party–pooper? I thought that you might want to get out of the house. All you do is stay on that damn computer all the time."

"I'm not on the computer all the time." She could defend herself this time because she really hadn't been on the computer. With the exception of last night, she and CreolSista barely said hello. What was important now, though, was that Manney noticed Amil was distracted. Something or somebody somewhere had a hold on her attention. "Does it bother you or something that I even use the computer?"

"Not at all. But what does concern me is that someone as intelligent as you finds comfort in watching that screen for hours at a time and holding conversations with complete strangers. You know how many people get killed as the result of meeting some fanatic on the net?"

Sarcastically, Amil replied, "No, Manney, I don't. I'm so caught up in being plain ol' intelligent, Amil, the doctor who doesn't have a life of her own, that I don't get to keep up with statistics like that. Sorry if I disappoint you." With that she walked off concentrating on keeping a decent pace ahead of him.

Bursting into a slow trot, Manney caught up with her just as she approached the door of the restaurant. "Wait a minute," he said, catching his breath. "I'm sorry. I didn't mean that. Forget I said it, okay?"

Amil wasn't going to forget, and she knew it. "Sure, no problem. Maybe I could stand to pay more attention to us." She was lying yet again. They'd go home and never mention anything else about it. That had been the routine for ten years. A routine? Was that what they were? Everything was always done the same way day in and day out. Amil had officially concluded that she was bored and had been so for nearly half their relationship. Every year they'd gone to a restaurant that he'd chosen—she never had a say in it. One year before she'd moved to Memphis, he flew her in and took her to Robinsonville, Mississippi where one of the casinos was having its grand opening. Never mind that she hadn't wanted to go because she had no interest in sticking her quarters into the slot of a one-armed bandit. He, however, had been looking forward to going ever since the advertisements for it had started airing. They had dinner and walked around for hours, to Amil's consternation. No doubt, with its tropical atmosphere, the casino was breathtaking. Amil, disgruntled with the thought of doing what Manney had wanted for *her* birthday, dismally went along with the evening and counted the hours before she'd return to Washington. To top off the evening, of course, no birthday was complete without him showing her to whom her pussy belonged.

"Hi," Manney greeted the hostess. "I reserved a table for tonight."

"You're Mr. Lindsay?" she inquired. Reservations were never required since everything was always first come, first served. Holding a table simply meant being isolated from the rest of the hustle and bustle of the other customers.

"Yes."

"Okay, come this way."

"Someone's meeting me here. Is she already here by any chance?"

"A woman, right?"

"Yes."

As the hostess placed the napkin-wrapped bundle on the table in their booth, the young lady chuckled. "She was here about ten minutes ago and told me to tell you that she'd be right back. She had to run an errand. She's a hoot!"

"She sure is. Not many of them like that around here anymore." He sighed. The petite young lady was watching Amil for a nonverbal—a nudge, a look, something. Amil didn't flinch. Manney continued, "Well, that's fine. I'll just go ahead and order a bottle of champagne for us."

Amil chimed in, "I really don't think you should order for her. She might not want..."

"Oh, she'll want a glass of bubbly. She's like that."

"Fine," Amil snapped. Manney, cutting his eyes at Amil, stubbornly ordered a bottle of Moet and a large order of pork potato skins.

Chris had parked her car in a nearby lot, and, upon arriving at the restaurant, she realized her phone had fallen from her purse and went back to retrieve it. There was no way she was going to be unreachable with the club set to open in less than twenty-four hours. She couldn't help but think, however, about the last thing that MOCHAMD had said to her. No matter what happened from this point on, Chris had to play it cool.

"Oh, you're back!" the hostess squealed. "Your party is here. You want me to show you to the table?"

"No, you don't have to. Just point me in the right direction." Chris took a deep breath and headed toward the back of the crowded room. The closer she got to the back she could see the top of Manney's receding hairline, but the view was obstructed by someone else, and it looked to be a woman. *Here we go.*

"There she is!" Manney exclaimed as he rose from the booth. He'd taken a seat next to Amil, leaving the other side totally vacant for Chris. Although a simple handshake would've looked better, he greeted Chris with a handshake and a kiss on the cheek. "Here, here, have a seat. This is my fiancée, Dr. Amil Blake Lindsay." He'd explained to Chris that he and Amil were common-law husband and wife and were planning to have a formal wedding when the time was right.

Then it clicked. Dr. Blake? That was all the affirmation she needed. "Good evening," Chris offered. "It's nice to meet you." Chris looked at Amil and was blown away. She'd finally come to face to face with the woman that had been a secret part of her life for so many years. But then she glanced at Amil again. This was the doctor from the hospital—the one that she'd met the night that Gayle died. "You seem so familiar to me," she lied, placing her cell phone on the table. "You work at a hospital or something?"

Amil slightly recalled Chris's face from her past but was having trouble placing it. "Yes, I do. But..." Suddenly, there was no longer a lapse in memory.

"Let me guess. Memphis General, right?"

Intrigued, Amil replied, "Well, yes." And then Chris flashed that gorgeous smile, and there it was. Amil remembered everything. "Wait a minute, I met you in the ER a few years back. A friend of yours..."

No trips down memory lane. Chris interrupted, "That's right. You're head of the ER or something like that, right?"

"Chief of Staff. Basically in charge of everything." She smiled.

"I ain't mad at-cha!"

The waitress arrived at the table with the champagne and three glasses. "What's this?" Chris questioned, looking perplexed.

Manney chuckled and gladly took credit for the selection. "Oh, I ordered us a bottle of champagne. You don't mind, do you?"

Chris was flabbergasted. "Champagne with ribs?"

Amil snickered, turning her head toward the wall. She'd tried to tell his ass.

Stumbling over every word, Manney struggled to smooth over his faux pas. "Um, well, I thought, uh, since, well, you know, since we..."

Chris signaled for the waitress. Manney was wasting time. "Excuse me, could you bring me a Corona with lime, please? Actually, you can bring a bucket of them. I don't think that the doctor is going to want champagne to wash these ribs down."

Manney, sitting there with the taste of shoe leather in the back of his throat, tried to make small talk. "So who's French in your family?"

"What?" Chris asked. She'd been staring.

"I mean, Desmereaux—isn't that a French name?"

"It is, but my family's got some Creole blood running through it. I've never traced my name to find out its origin. I just know that my father's mother is Creole." Suddenly, the evening was preparing to take a different turn.

Creole? Amil thought. Blushing, Amil instantly realized that the evening might not be so bad. For over an hour, she sat and listened as Manney and Chris talked business. She cared nothing about those buildings they were working to renovate. It was Chris that she was most interested in, and then Chris mentioned Paris. She mentioned the city in a way that only CreolSista would have. Her face lit up when she talked about the Eiffel Tower and her morning walks along the Seine. She had to interrupt. "Chris, if you don't mind me asking…" Manney's cell phone rang. He looked at the display and saw that it was Rondell. With all the noise inside, there was no way he was going to be able to hear.

Pulling up from the booth, he said, "Look, I need to take this somewhere I can hear. Excuse me, ladies." He got up and headed for the men's room.

Amil watched as he disappeared behind the artificial greenery along the outside aisle. She had no idea as to how she was supposed to handle this awkward yet welcomed moment.

Resting on her elbows, leaning in toward Amil, Chris quickly asked, "What kind of coincidence is this? I knew that was you that night."

"Well, why didn't you say something?" Amil wondered.

"Something like what? As I recall, you didn't say anything either. I simply followed your lead. Besides, the nurse said that there wasn't a Dr. Blake on staff, so I left it alone."

Embarrassed, Amil replied, "I don't go by Dr. Blake as Mr. Big Mouth just told you. I only use Dr. Blake when..."

Chris smirked. "When you're preying on people's emotions over the Internet. Trust me, I know the drill."

"That's not fair."

"Whatever."

"I see you're still slightly pissed with me. Your attitude in person is no better than it is online."

Chris didn't know what to do with this moment, and neither did Amil. CreolSista's stance had become crystal clear on her and MOCHAMD, and now that they'd finally met, it wasn't about to change. Although she loved her immensely, getting caught up with a married woman was a risk that Chris was not willing to take. "Look, let me tell you something," Chris whispered. "I've imagined this moment many times, and now that it's here, I don't know what to do with it. Part of me wants to take you in my arms and give you this big, compassionate hug. The other part of me wants to tell you to kiss my ass, so that I can get on with the rest of my life. There's this feeling I get whenever I talk to or see you online. Talking to you last night for the first time in years reminded me of that. When I saw you that night at the hospital, I didn't know what to do. Had I found out it was really you, I would've handled business right then. I'd actually written a note to you, but once I was told that there was no Dr. Blake, I said to hell with it. It was just this feeling that I got when I first laid eyes on you. I can't even describe it."

"No need because I felt the same way."

"Prior to that, I had been so full of you and me that... Well, never mind."

"I'm still trying to figure why you didn't say anything."

"Amil, despite what I did or didn't do then, I knew that the time would come again. I just never expected it to be like this." Chris was so overcome with emotion that her eyes filled with tears. "The question is what to do now."

In shock, Amil sat motionless with her eyes closed as she absorbed the presence of the person that had been her drink when she'd been thirsty and her food when she'd hungered for compassion. "Creol, I mean Chris, I've missed you." It was funny how the both of them were able to pick up right where they'd left off emotionally.

Chris, peeping around to see if Manney was coming back, took Amil by the hand. "He's going to be back soon. Do you think that maybe...just perhaps we could spend some time together?"

"I really can't say. Things are so different now." Amil didn't have the time to give to Chris, and it was killing her to have to tell her that. She hadn't had an opportunity to tell her that she and Manney were at a different place since she'd moved to Memphis. "My feelings..."

Time was short. Manney would be back any minute, and neither woman knew what was supposed to happen next. Chris was so busy with the club and her family that she knew she couldn't afford to take on another emotional circus. "Before he comes back, I have to tell you this."

"Tell me what?" Amil asked coyly.

"You're more beautiful than I thought you'd be."

Grinning from ear to ear, Amil replied, "Same here."

Within that last syllable, Manney returned to the table. "That was Rondell. He's got some blueprints that he'd like for you to see. How much longer are you going to be in town?" Reclining her body and taking a sip of her third Corona, Chris informed Manney that she and her daughters were leaving on Sunday; Rondell could FedEx the blueprints to her in Paris. As she made eye contact with Amil, Chris suggested that maybe she should plan another trip home. "It must be nice to have your own place while you're visiting. No need to worry about hotel rooms and stuff like that."

"Funny, you should mention that, Manney. It's nice having my own place here, but this time I didn't get to stay in it much. A friend of mine lives in it when I'm not here, and this is one of those times where a hotel room was a sight for sore eyes. I'm staying at the Adams Mark," she said, tossing a fleeting look at Amil. "The Peabody was booked for some convention, so I went out east."

"I heard that, then." Manney reached in his pocket to get his wallet. He looked through the bill section and boasted that all he had was hundreds. "Um, you think they could break one of these?"

Amil, shaking her head, pulled out her credit card and placed it on the table. "I'll pay for it." *Show-off.*

"Oh, well, okay then. I'll just leave the tip." He threw a five-dollar bill on the table and put his wallet back in his jean pocket. "You know, Chris. Tomorrow is Amil's birthday. She'll be the big 4-0!"

As she reached in her purse to pull out a twenty to put on the table, Chris saw her phone's voice mail light come on, but she ignored it. It was time to see if Manney really was the dud that Amil claimed he was. She knew what Amil had told her about his usual plans for her birthday. She had to see if the story was a ruse to get her attention. "So do you two have plans?"

Manney chuckled. "Well, I usually take her out to dinner, but she has to work, and Miss Thing never calls in. We're going to do something on Sunday."

Chris gathered her belongings but not without quietly letting Amil know that she hadn't forgotten about the two of them. "Well, I have got to run. I have a million and one things to do in my room and I haven't answered emails in days."

Manney rolled his eyes. "Hmph, Amil knows all about that damn computer. That's the first thing she does when she comes home from work. She goes straight to her office and jumps on it. You'd think she was having an affair or something with the way she carries on."

It was definitely time to go. "Leave her alone, Manney. That's just your imagination," Chris joked. "I spend a lot of time on the computer myself and even have a couple of really good friends that I talk to on a regular basis. There's no harm in it just as long as you're careful," she joked, winking at Amil.

"Well, I just don't understand it, but anyway..." His voice trailed off and then continued, "It was good seeing you. Don't be surprised if you see or hear from me in a couple of weeks."

Puzzled, Amil looked at Manney like he was crazy. "Manney! We haven't made any plans to go to Paris," she kidded.

"Shhhh, I'll talk to you about it later," he whispered as he assisted her from the booth.

"Okay, I'll be looking out for you. Oh, and by the way, it was nice meeting you, Amil."

After stopping by the club, Chris took the long way back to the hotel. She needed time to think. *Chris, you promised yourself that you were gonna let this shit go. Don't be stupid. Let it go. She ain't giving up her man for no woman. Just let it go.*

❧♥❧

The walk home was unusually quiet. Manney had a full stomach and wanted to do nothing but go to bed. Amil, on the other hand, couldn't wait to get to her computer. It was probably going to take Chris about twenty minutes to get back to the hotel. That's all it took to get anywhere in Memphis.

MOCHAMD: Hi.

CreolSista: Hey, yourself.

MOCHAMD: Can you believe this?

CreolSista: Not really. Having a lot of trouble digesting this whole thing. This changes a lot.

MOCHAMD: What do you mean?

CreolSista: Amil, this can't go on. I'm too uncomfortable with it, and you should be, too.

MOCHAMD: But I'm not. What's the big deal?

CreolSista: L

MOCHAMD: What?

CreolSista: Until a few hours ago, Manney was simply "he." Now "he" has a name that you've never bothered to call.

MOCHAMD: So what? That doesn't change anything as it relates to you and me and what we have. We haven't talked much in a while and obviously have some catching up to do.

CreolSista: Do you realize what could happen if he ever finds out about this?

MOCHAMD: Nothing will happen because he's never going to find out.

CreolSista: We can't continue to do this.

MOCHAMD: You're kidding, right?

CreolSista: No, I'm not.

MOCHAMD: You're willing to throw away everything we've shared just because, by coincidence, you and he are business partners?

CreolSista: First of all, "he" now has a name, as do you. Second, I have too much going on in my life right now, personally and professionally, to be caught up in this, and third, I don't even think that I feel the same as I used to about you and me. (She was lying through her teeth.)

MOCHAMD: So, once again, you're gonna throw it all away?

CreolSista: I'm not throwing it all away. I'm just walking away from it for my benefit.

MOCHAMD: And what about mine?

CreolSista: I think you should do the same. This has been nothing but a thing of convenience for you. When he pisses you off, you jump on here and cry the blues to me. "Creol, I think I'm in love with you," and all that bullshit. You love the thought of me because I'm not him. In the real world, "we" don't exist. I said the things I said to you tonight because I meant them.

I didn't need alcohol or anything else to make me spill my guts out to you, and now that you know, you should forget about it. You're afraid to let me give you what you deserve because you think I'll peep into what you really want and need.

MOCHAMD: Chris, I care about you so much. Finally getting to lay eyes on you was the best thing that has happened to me in a long time. This is stupid. Can I call you since you're right here instead of halfway around the world? lol

CreolSista: No.

MOCHAMD: ???

CreolSista: You really don't need to call me while he's there. As a matter of fact, you don't need to call me at all.

MOCHAMD: He's asleep.

CreolSista: You don't know that.

MOCHAMD: Chris, this house is big enough for me to find a quiet place to talk.

CreolSista: I said no.

MOCHAMD: Fine. Meany.

CreolSista: Why have you never mentioned anything if you thought that you saw me that night at the hospital?

MOCHAMD: Don't know. Could ask you the same.

CreolSista: Once I was told that there was no Dr. Blake, I just let it go. Had a lot of shit on my mind that night.

MOCHAMD: Oh.

CreolSista: Amil, I need to get off here. I have a busy day tomorrow, and now, I have something else to work through.

MOCHAMD: Will I see you on here tomorrow?

CreolSista: Doubt it.

CreolSista: We should probably take a break from this for a while before feelings get hurt.

MOCHAMD: That's not fair.

CreolSista is not currently signed on.

❧♥❧

Iysha was excited about her birthday. She had gone shopping and bought a new dress and shoes to match. By the time she returned home, Nathaniel had already left for work. He hadn't bought her flowers or cards for her special day, but he had taken time to remind her if she were going to be out all evening that she needed to make sure that everything was in order for church on Sunday.

Iysha had starched and ironed Nathaniel's and Max's shirts and had hung the girls' dresses on the top of the bedroom door. The week had been a tense one for the entire family, and getting out of the house was the only thing on her mind.

Chris had let a friend detail her car while she packed the last bit of luggage for her departure on Sunday. She was aware that after tonight she might not feel welcome in Memphis for a while. But it was her sister's birthday, and the foolishness had to come to an end. Lives would be destroyed, but, at least, the truth would finally be out. She pulled into Iysha's driveway promptly at nine o'clock. Their dinner reservations were not until ten. But when Iysha came to the car, she had a puzzled look on her face. "What's wrong with you, Birthday Girl? Got your face all frowned up on your big day. Did Momma pick up Max?"

"Yeah." Iysha seemed to not give up on looking for her new MAC lipstick. She'd only purchased it the day before. *I get so tired of losing my shit,* she thought. *And I know that I brought that shawl home from the cleaners.*

"You okay?"

"Yeah, I'm fine. So where are we off to?"

"We have reservations at the Peabody for dinner, and after that, we're going to hit a club or two."

"Sounds great! Let's go!" Chris put the top down on her BMW, turned over the engine and pedaled the gas as she and her sister roared off for a night of enlightening adventure in downtown Memphis.

The lines at The Closet, previously known as The

Menagerie, were extraordinarily long for a Saturday. The marquee out front read, "Lady Champaign's Revue." The long lines meant nothing to Chris. She walked up to the front and pinched the butt of the bouncer who was talking to someone inside the club. "Gotta lot of junk in that trunk." She smiled. Nelson, the head of The Closet's security team, turned around ready to fight until he saw whom it was. He was over seven feet tall and weighed more than 400 pounds.

"Hey, Bay-By! I thought I smelled your perfume."

"Oh, you're such a liar." Chris smiled. "How's everything? Got quite a bit of folks to stuff in here."

"You should see inside. I don't know where they all are gonna go. Rudy's got your table set up. Is this your sister?"

"How'd you know?"

"Rudy told me to be expecting the two of you." He leaned over and whispered in her ear. "Still ain't into men, huh?"

"Fraid not, honey." She giggled. "We'll talk. By the way, you've got job security if all goes well tonight."

"Don't worry; I'm handlin' thangs," he boasted.

Chris turned to her sister. "Iysha, this is Nelson. He's just a big ol' teddy bear."

"Hello. It's nice to meet you. What's the big occasion?"

"Got a lot of people in from out of town to see the show tonight."

"Oh, really?"

"Yes, it..."

Chris pulled Iysha through the door. "C'mon, girl, so we can get seated."

The Closet was packed. The walls were bursting at the seams with people, and there were twice as many lined up outside waiting to get in. Rudy had been told to go all out for the evening's main attraction. There were no seats anywhere...except in the mezzanine. That was the VIP section, where Chris and Iysha would be sitting. Rudy, the operating manager, was at the forefront, but, as of yesterday at 2:34 p.m., The Closet now belonged to Christian Desmereaux. Mr. Tolley, true to his reputation, had come in the club and handled shit. Black granite covered the counters of the glass-bricked bar, complemented with chrome barstools. The floors were painted cement with swirls that gave the floor a marbleized appearance. And because he owed Chris's father some money, he decided to throw in extras at no additional charge. Platinum-colored ceiling fans, a state-of-the-art sound system, a sunken dance floor, polished fixtures, a separate mixed-drink bar, and designer lighting satisfied Mr. Tolley's debt and then some.

"This place is beautiful, Chris."

"Yes, it is," she said, taking her seat. "I want you to meet Rudy. She's good people. Got me out of a few jams while we were in college. I asked her to make tonight special."

"Whatever you saying about me better be the truth," a voice said, coming from the back. "You know I got a reputation to protect." That voice belonged to the most beautiful woman that Iysha had ever seen.

"Iysha, this is Rudy."

Iysha was speechless. Never had she seen skin so smooth and silky. "Nice to meet you," Iysha uttered.

"Honey, your sister told me about this being your birthday so, first, let me wish you a very happy birthday and give you this." Rudy handed Iysha a bottle of Cristal. "I would have brought you two, but, between our star and our new owner, we have a limited supply for tonight." Rudy winked at Chris. "And second, on behalf of The Closet, we got you this cake and goodie bag."

Iysha was blown away. "Thank you, Rudy. I wasn't expecting this!"

"I know, honey. I know. Look, it was nice meeting you and all, but the show is about to start. Take care." And she was off to the DJ booth.

"Chris, she is absolutely gorgeous."

Lighting a Swisher Sweet, Chris chuckled. "You think so?"

"Oh, yes, girl, did you see her skin? It was flawless." Iysha stared flabbergasted at this person who looked like her sister with a cigar in her hand. Dressed in a red

Christian Dior pantsuit and matching red satin underclothes, Chris looked like she was hot off the pages of *Marie Claire* magazine. "Since when did you start doing this?"

"Doing what?"

"Smoking cigars."

"It's nothing. I do it on rare occasions. Like when I go out."

"Is it some kinda dyke thing?"

"It could be, I guess. I don't mind smelling like smoke when I'm in here. You really can't help it, though. Shit, that's all everybody's doing."

"I thought that I told you that I didn't want to come to a dyke club."

"This isn't a dyke club. It's more than just dykes in here. There's probably more straight people in here than anybody. So tell me. What did you think of Rudy? I couldn't hear you too good the first time."

"I think that she's gorgeous."

"Well, *he* takes much pride in making sure that his appearance is always tight."

"What?"

"You heard me. Why don't you pour yourself a glass of that Cristal?"

"Girl, you know how much this shit cost?"

"I'll get you another bottle before we leave. You'll probably need it."

Iysha leaned over the table to Chris. "That was a man?"

"Used to be. He's straight-up bonafide all woman now." The lights were starting to dim. "Shhh, the show is about to start."

❧♥❧

When Phyllis Hyman did "Meet Me on the Moon," she probably never thought about a diva like Lady Champaign putting her own little spin to it. Every drag queen in the city of Memphis tried to imitate Miss Phyllis. But only one had mastered it, and that was Lady Champaign.

"Ladies and gentlemen, The Closet would like to welcome you to 'Lady Champaign's Revue.' She's been gone for a long time, but now she's back. Formerly known as Miss Nay, the Madame has been dancing here on Saturdays for a while now, and the response has been overwhelming. The house has been packed all the way back to the kitchen when she's here. Folks all bum-rushin' the stage and shit! In all my days of doin' the runway, I ain't never seen nothing like it!" The crowd went wild. "So tonight, and only for tonight, she's all yours. Please welcome to the stage Lady Champaign." The building rumbled with applause. Chris and Iysha had the best seats in the house. Chris watched Iysha guzzle half of her champagne. Her sister was hurting, and the events of the next half-hour weren't going to make her feel any better.

"You okay?" Chris asked.

Iysha shook her head and joined in with her own applause. She was mellowing out, loosening up for her evening out with her sister.

A black mesh background slowly lowered from the rafters. Attached to the screen-like material was a gigantic hologram of a rose. When moved in one direction, the rose bloomed; when shifted the other way, it blossomed, and when moved again, it wilted and died. *(That was Chris's idea.)* The mesh fabric sparkled as the midnight-blue mural painted on the back wall of the stage was illuminated. The silence and anticipation in the building could be cut with a straight razor.

The prelude to "Meet Me on the Moon" was longer than usual, but no one seemed to notice. Rudy had a hook-up at the 12-inch record shop in D.C. and kept long versions of all the old and new music. As the lights raised just enough to cast a shadow over the orchestra section, a curvaceous silhouette was revealed. The figure, obviously that of a well-shaped woman, was adorned in a sequined cape whose hood slightly hung over the performer's eyes.

"Payhuhr! Pay-huhr! Get dem dollas out! Lemme see that green! Don't want shit that rattles 'cause, honey, change ain't good for nuthin' but the phone booth! Pay-huhr!" the announcer barked as he pointed to the stage. The performer hadn't uttered a word, but spectators flocked to the stage fanning their dollar bills, five-dollar bills, and twenty-dollar bills. The bouncers, all of them instructed to intercept the incoming money, lined the front of the orchestra section. Video cameras captured their every move and, every once in a while, they would allow a big spender to approach the stage. Tonight, there were quite a few big spenders, all hoping to touch or to get a closer look at Lady Champaign. "Pay-huhr! Visa! MasterCard! American Express! Pay-the bitch huhr money!"

The first few lines of the song were performed dramatically with hand movements and flawless lip-syncing. Her face was beat; Lady Champaign dazzled the crowd with trembling lips, Phyllis's facial expressions—the whole nine yards. Dangling notes slurred over orchestration fit for a queen. Ms. Phyllis had been resurrected—brought back to life by the biggest and best drag queen that the Bluff City had to offer. She swayed, she waved, never missing a step. Rudy had been instructed to hire an audio-visual company for the special performance. Cases of Cristal and Moet had been delivered the day before, and a caterer was brought in to offer a little something different. No other gay club in Memphis served liquor, food and entertainment all under one roof. The Closet was classy and destined to become the hottest nightspot in town, and, with an appearance by Lady Champaign—an old familiar face, Chris knew that the club reflected her in every way: the style, the mood, the ambition, and, in a few minutes, the drama.

There was a trumpet solo in the song, and, as Lady Champaign halted all movement and stood frozen in time, a tuxedo-clad gentleman mimed the piece to perfection with a brass trumpet Rudy had found at the pawnshop. During the reprise, Lady Champaign's cape was flung to the stage, and the crowd exploded. Iysha gasped and threw her hand over her mouth. It was then that she saw her missing Parisian dress, her new scarf, her new shoes, and…her new lipstick. All of it on Lady Champaign! All of it on Nathaniel! In a dress or not, there was no mistaking her husband.

His/her eyes gazed up into the mezzanine, courting the big spenders as he/she always did. Misty-eyed from the special effects, the diva couldn't see anything that wasn't directly in front of him/her. Iysha, with furrows embedded in her brow, leaned forward in her seat and forlornly peered at him while shaking her head in disbelief. Her husband had been too damn cheap to buy his own shit to wear, and now this song—the same song that she'd lost her virginity to in the eighth grade—had a totally new meaning. What a birthday this had turned out to be.

With a heavy heart but little remorse, Chris thought quietly to herself, *Payback is a bitch.*

HALLELUJAH! THANK YA, JESUS! AMEN!

Home

The usual Sunday morning gospel hits blasted from WLOK. After all, it was a Memphis tradition, and Nathaniel swore by it. Every Sunday morning Iysha had breakfast ready by 7:30 so that the kids could eat before getting dressed. This morning, though, at 7:30, Iysha was still in the bathroom. There was no bacon frying, no biscuits baking, and no grits bubbling. Iysha was in the bathroom throwing up.

"Iysha!" Nathaniel yelled, banging on the door. He heard her gagging; he heard her dry heaving; he heard her spitting. "You gonna make us run late! You need to hurry up! You ain't even started cookin' breakfast yet!" Nathaniel didn't ask if his wife was okay, nor did he seem to even care.

Iysha was sitting on the side of the toilet holding her stomach, rocking back and forth. As Chris had driven her home from the club, neither of them had uttered a word. She'd been up since a little after 4 a.m., and the bags under her eyes showed it. Even more disturbing was that Nathaniel still wasn't home when she'd awakened. He'd apparently come in while she was in the bathroom. Weary from disgust and anger, Iysha could've cared less that his ass had been out all night. She had figured he was doing whatever it was *they* did after their shows. "I'll be out in a minute, Nathaniel. I'm almost done washing my face." When she opened the door, she couldn't avoid looking into his eyes. "Good morning to you, too," she snapped as she headed for the hallway.

"Where are the kids?" Nathaniel questioned.

"At Momma's. They spent the night."

Following closely behind her—damn near on her heels, Nathaniel grabbed her arm. "Well, they need to go to church with us. Go pick them up after you get breakfast ready."

"Nathaniel, I'm not driving all the way over there this morning. Momma said it was okay to get them after church."

"Iysha, it's not up for discussion. Go get them. I've got to get in the shower."

It took everything she had in her to fight back. "Well, you know what, I'll go get them, but I'm not cooking breakfast. I'll meet you at church."

Nathaniel couldn't understand why Iysha was being so shitty, and standing for it in his own house meant that he was getting soft. "Take your ass over there, and get my kids!" he said, pushing her in the back. Iysha fell face first into the wall and hit her lip on the door facing. "And breakfast better be ready before you leave."

Iysha got a paper towel and wiped the blood from her lip. "Okay, Nathaniel. Whatever you say." As he turned to walk away, she mumbled, "How was work last night?"

Nathaniel gathered the front of his robe, adjusting the belt. "It was okay."

"Get a lot of tips?"

"A few."

"Good. Make sure that you pay the light bill tomorrow. It's almost three months' past due. Go ahead and take your shower." Iysha felt a little bit of her sister coming out in her. "Breakfast will be on the table when you get out."

"Thank you," he said, going into the bathroom. "Oh, and Iysha?"

She sighed. "Yes."

"We don't need to be late for Sunday School."

"I know." Iysha went to the laundry room for a shirt and some shorts. Before getting her purse, she remembered that Massa wanted breakfast. Today, though, was one of those days when she had to do as she'd been told if she was to keep her sanity. Grabbing from the top of the refrigerator the stale box of Rice Krispies that Max had quit eating months before, Iysha poured her husband a bowl of cereal, added some milk to it, and placed the bowl on the table. With a slight smirk, she remembered that Nathaniel loved for his place setting to be garnished with fresh-cut oranges and cantaloupes. Isyha snorted. "Umph." They didn't have any cantaloupes, and she didn't have time to go to the store.

I've got a trick for that, she thought. With self-righteous indignation, she opened the refrigerator to see if her "loving husband" had taken out the oranges that she'd been saving to make homemade orange spice potpourri. They had been in there since just after Easter and had to be dried out for the recipe to be just perfect. Looking past the fresh grapefruits and strawberries, Iysha found them. "Oh, yeah," she remarked with satisfaction. She took two of them, noticing the peels had begun to wilt, and the insides were all squishy. *I'll fix yo' ass!* Iysha smirked as she leisurely cut the oranges into several round slices, carefully arranged each piece on a saucer next to a tall glass of buttermilk, and resolutely stood back in defiant satisfaction to admire her resourcefulness the way a sous-chef relishes his finest creation. Pissed would be an understatement for Nathaniel, but with all that was on Iysha's mind, he'd just have to be the hell all right.

Sunday School

Why Pastor Edmonds had asked Nathaniel to teach a Sunday School class was a mystery to Iysha, for Nathaniel never bothered to open his teacher's manual until they were in the car on the way to church. "You drive," he'd demand so that he could look over his lesson for the day. But, on this morning, Nathaniel was more interested in why his wife had sabotaged his breakfast. "So you gonna tell me what all that back at the house was about?"

Iysha sighed. She really didn't have much to say to Nathaniel, but to keep the kids from getting anxious before church she had to keep things on the straight and narrow. "You know, Nathaniel, I'm really not in the mood for that right now. I've got a lot of shit on my mind."

Nathaniel looked as if someone had bitch-slapped him. "Don't cuss me, Iysha. You *know* how I feel about that." Disrespecting him with profanity was something he didn't allow in his house, especially from his wife.

"You know what? Fuck how and what you feel, okay? I said I—am—*not*—in—the—mood!!!"

With that, Nathaniel left it alone.

While her husband stood at the front of the church ranting and raving about God doing this and God doing that, Iysha relegated herself to the rear pew doggedly contemplating how she was going to handle the discovery of her husband's part-time job. The children were outside running around on the playground, and for that, Iysha was thankful. She didn't want them anywhere near her because the vibes she was emitting were particularly unpleasant. Each one of the usual parishioners steered clear of her, only pausing to ask her to hold Nathaniel's eyeglasses while he bounced up and down during his Holy Ghost dance. Shaking his hands like they'd been burned in a fire, Nathaniel scampered from one side of the church to the other shouting, "Hallelujah! Amen! Thank ya, Jesus!" Usually, Iysha helped him by chasing her husband and embracing him as he went through his weekly ritual. But not today. *Let him run by himself from his own damn demons. Let them catch him, and burn his ass alive.* She didn't care today, and she'd never care again. As Nathaniel fanned himself and wiped his forehead, Iysha mentally replayed how he swayed in that evening gown—his hands eloquently manipulating the air around him; his eyes, his lips, his nails, everything about him from the previous night haunted her. *Just how far did his performance go? Had he been doing this every weekend? Was he sleeping with men since he was already dancing for them?* Knowing that he didn't come straight home after the show, Iysha's mind was doing cartwheels. She was pissed with herself because she'd been so stupid as to fall for his lies and deceit. She was pissed with Nathaniel primarily because he was bringing another lifestyle into their bedroom and disgusted with him for ruining her clothes and make-up. And last on the list, she was pissed with Chris for leaving her. Her flight left at noon, and, there was no telling when Chris was going to come back.

Lady Champaign's Demons

She had packed the house yet again with another flawless and triumphant performance. There wasn't an empty stool to be had at the bar all night, and a line was still around the block after her final encore. During both of her performances, she'd felt a different pair of eyes on her. They weren't there for entertainment, either. She looked to her left and looked to her right. Nothing. The smoke-filled room had cleared slightly as she'd requested the house lights to be brought up. Gazing into the mezzanine, she saw nothing or no one atypical. Dismissing the feeling, she spent about ten minutes taunting and flirting with the mostly male audience and then headed for the dressing room.

Just like any other Saturday night, Lady Champaign was skinning and grinning all up in some man's face when Dallas caught up with her and whispered, "I need to see you." Once in the dressing room, he jumped right to the point, "We're gonna have to let you go."

"What?" Lady Champaign gasped.

"You're done. It's in writing," Dallas said, handing Lady Champaign an envelope. "Effective immediately."

"I don't understand what the fuck is going on! The house is packed with folks hangin' all out in the streets and shit, and I know you just saw me pull in all that money in tips. There's gotta be almost a thousand people out there!" Lady Champaign raged as she wiped sweat from her brow. "After all that, you're telling me that I'm fired?"

Although he had somewhat of a heart when it came to

Lady Champaign because she was always on her shit, Dallas was in no position to change the decision. "Look, this is coming from management."

"Rudy? That qu..."

"No, not Rudy. This is coming from Rudy's boss. Just take your money and go."

"I suppose this means I can't bartend either, huh."

"Look, I'm sorry, okay. Security, meaning Nelson, has packed your stuff and has it waiting for you at the door." Almost pleadingly, Dallas continued, "Please do us all a favor and get out of here with the class I know you got. I was instructed to have security escort you out, but I ain't gonna do that to you with all these people in here." Dallas handed Lady Champaign another envelope filled with money and walked her to the door. Patting him on the shoulder, he sighed, "Inside this envelope is your last paycheck in cash. Take care of yourself, Nathaniel."

The last time Nathaniel had left the club, he left because he didn't want *it* anymore. Now, that he'd once again sacrificed all he had to offer in order to make up for his abrupt exit, it was the club that no longer wanted him. The only reason Chris had let her brother-in-law keep any of the money was because she knew that her sister and her nieces and nephew needed it.

At church Sunday, when it came time to shout and

give God his glory—that fire and brimstone thing again, Nathaniel was the first out of his seat.

❧♥❧

Hallelujah! Iysha thought to herself as she recalled the last time that she'd let Nathaniel run up in her. No one knew that it had been several months since they'd been intimate. Hell, even then, it was anything but intimate. He'd come into the kitchen and brushed up against her behind. She was repulsed; he was enticed. He pulled up her slip (it was just before church) and had his way with her. Anytime after that, he only desired her to stroke him until he was full…until he was happy. The blowjobs had stopped after Max was born. He didn't taste the same; he didn't feel the same.

Thank ya, Jesus! Chris was not a popular person with Iysha right now, but as she prayed and tightly grasped her Bible, Iysha thanked the Lord for her sister. No, Chris wasn't right for how she'd busted Nathaniel, but she knew that it had been the only way.

Amen! I got a man that does his best to take care of me and his children. Can't complain about that.

CURIOSITY KILLED HER KAT

(That same Sunday morning in another part of the city)

Shit! Shit! Shit! I cheated on Manney! Oh, my God, what I am going to do! (Pacing) *Why did I ever come up here? I know I should've left after Mama's Family went off! I bet she thinks that I do this all the time with people I meet on the Internet! Shit!*" (Pacing faster) "*Can't do this! Can't do this! Stop it, Amil! Just stop it! Breathe, girl!* (Inhaling) *Come on, breathe!* (Exhaling) *I can't believe there's someone's kiss softer than Manney's. I mean, damn! Those moves, those strokes…* (Pacing faster) *Okay, this is what I'm going to say.* (Thinking) *No, I better not say that. It doesn't even sound right. Maybe I should throw in the bit about… Nope, can't do that either. Shit!*"

❧♥❧

Amil awoke that morning to a single red rose lying on the pillow next to her. "Happy Birthday," the note read. "I hope that it was as special for you as it was for me." The aroma of fresh strawberries and cream complimented the lingering scent of Chris's perfume. Opening the bedroom doors, Amil was confronted with a space overflowing with seven dozen roses, each of a different color—a dozen for every year that she and Chris had known each other. A lightly browned Belgian waffle, coated in powdered sugar and caramelized apples—accompanied by scrambled cheese eggs and maple sausage awaited her on a silver platter that rested perfectly on the dining table in the suite. To her delight, Chris had also remembered Amil's favorite—fresh squeezed orange juice with a strawberry on the side. Dr. Lindsay had never been showered with such attention, never in her life, especially not ever on her birthday. Exuding a glow of pure delight, Amil smiled, instantly recalling the rapture of the night before.

Opting for third shift was strategic for Amil. Since hardly any administrative activity occurred at night, Amil enjoyed the freedom to do whatever was needed, working anywhere she was summoned. It also provided the perfect solution to a horrendous sound problem called Manney and an opportunity to escape the confines of home while he slept, peacefully—oblivious to any disturbances—as relaxed as a newborn baby. Manney snored something terrible, and many times either he or Amil ended up pissed off and relegated to the sofa or banished to the guestroom. This year she wanted something different. To avoid another disappointing, boring, yet traditional night out, as a present to herself, on the night she turned 40, Amil volunteered to work.

"I sure hate that you've got to work tonight," Manney said as he hugged Amil from behind, caressing her body with his own. "It would've been nice to get out tonight instead of tomorrow night."

"I know," she partially agreed. "I don't know why I even let them schedule me for tonight." Amil reached for Manney's hand and gently kissed it. "I'll try my best to get away early, though."

"Promise?"

"I promise," she whispered. Instead of reporting straight to work, Amil drove around for hours. She'd lied and assured Manney that if she went in early, then she'd definitely get out of the hospital ahead of her usual time. However, at this point, she had no idea what she wanted to do. Fifteen minutes into her drive, Amil took a detour and headed for Oak Court Mall. The closer she came to the entrance, the more she couldn't help but notice that Rafferty's parking lot was half empty—the perfect time for an evening cocktail or two and whatever else she was going to get to eat for free since it was her birthday. "A Corona, please," Amil had told the waitress.

"With lime?"

Chris didn't know that Amil had never tasted a Corona, but it seemed to fit her well. The right kind of chill with a twist of lime brought back memories of years past. The first time they'd chatted; the first time she'd heard Chris's voice; and now, the first time they'd laid eyes on each other. While alone, Amil could reminisce about the night before. Smiling, she graciously replied, "Yes, I'll have it with lime. Hold the glass. The bottle is fine."

"Okay, then. I'll be right back." Glancing over the menu, Amil noticed that, as the birthday girl, she was entitled to a free entrée and dessert. When the waitress returned, she ordered the prime rib dinner with apple cinnamon crisp for dessert, and another Corona with her meal. *Okay*, Amil silently decided. *Maybe I'll have two more Coronas...with lime, evenly spaced out, of course. After all, a girl's gotta celebrate.*

While waiting on her order, Amil wondered if Chris had noticed her peering at her throughout last evening, unable to believe that Chris was actually in front of her eyes. Whether she was peeking over the menu or cutting short her stares whenever Chris made eye contact, Amil was curious. She had definitely remembered her from a few years before but was too ashamed to admit it. Evidently that was an encounter that neither of them was ready to discuss...thankfully. After three beers, Amil's appetite disappeared. Asking for a doggie bag, she packed her food and decided to eat it later at work during lunch. Goldsmith's was one of those department stores that knew how to have a good sale even at the weirdest times of the year. Their extra-savings coupons yielded hellacious discounts for the serious shopper—something Amil prided herself on being. Once she left Rafferty's with a cup of black coffee in tow, she strapped on her walking shoes, determined to walk herself back into sobriety. Looking at her watch, Amil realized she still had time before work; therefore, she decided to make the best of it.

Two-thousand dollars later, Amil left the mall with bundles of bags and a persistent melancholy feeling. In search of any type of "pick-me-up," she drove two miles down the street and caught a movie. If it were boring enough, at least she would be able to sleep off the rest of those beers. *No luck.* The movie ended at 10:00. *Still an hour before I go to work.* "Good evening, this is Dr. Lindsay," she affirmed to the receptionist on the other end of the cell phone.

"Yes, Ma'am, Dr. Lindsay. How are you this evening?"

"I'm fine. Thanks for asking. Look I won't be coming in tonight. I…"

"Okay, I'll inform anyone who asks about you." Dr. Lindsay was never out. Anyone who did ask would be surprised.

"Is there anything else I need to do? I mean I've never been out to know what protocol is."

The young lady chuckled. "Well, since you *are* the boss around here, I think that this will be fine. You have a good evening."

Stupid, Amil thought. *I didn't think about that.* Three hours later, she was still driving around looking for that unforgettable birthday present. Like some wild, uncontrollable force that lived deep within her, Amil found herself sitting outside the Adams Mark Hotel. *What am I doing?*

Three a.m. It was humid, but there was a slight breeze coming off the pond. Amil walked into the hotel lobby and ordered a couple of Coronas before the bar closed. Taking a seat near the piano, she tried to drown the urge that had brought her to this side of town at such a late hour. But it wasn't working. It only intensified. Guests were coming and going; many of them retiring to their rooms for a few hours' sleep before the sun awoke. Still in her walking shoes, Amil made her way to the front desk. "Excuse me," she interrupted two clerks engaged in heavy gossip.

"Yes, Ma'am. Welcome to the Adams Mark Hotel. How may we help you?"

Hands trembling, voice quivering, she inquired, "Would it be possible for you to call Ms. Desmereaux's room?"

The clerk smiled. All of the staff knew Chris and were especially eager to protect her. "Um, I don't think that she's in yet. And you are?"

Amil's shy side began showing. The five beers she'd consumed by now had complicated it. So as to not come across as a disoriented drunk intent on harassing one of the hotel's favorite guests, every word had to be carefully chosen. "I'm a friend of hers. When I last talked with her, she told me she was here but never gave me her room number."

The second clerk conferred with the first clerk and whispered that Chris had returned to her room about an hour earlier. "Ma'am, due to hotel policy, I'll need to call her first. Is it okay with you?"

"Sure, go ahead." Amil stood there and patiently waited.

"Ms. Desmereaux?"

Despite an emotional evening, Chris was wide-awake. She'd left The Closet in a hurry with her sister and hadn't spoken to anyone since. She wanted to ensure that Dallas had followed her instructions. "Yes," she replied into the phone. Cut four, "Sometimes Dancin'," from Brownstone's *From The Bottom Up* album was blasting in the background. She had it on repeat, and was certain, by now, that she had pissed off the guests in every room within a reasonable distance of hers.

"Um, this is Jamal at the front desk. I'm sorry to disturb you at this hour, but we have a lady here who wants to see you. She said she doesn't know your room number."

Puzzled, Chris asked, "Who is it?"

Jamal covered the receiver and asked for a name.

Amil snickered. "Just tell her it's the birthday girl."

Jamal replied, "She said it's the birthday girl."

Chris didn't need to know anything else. "Okay, that's fine. Send her up." Believing it to be Iysha coming to say what she hadn't been able to express after seeing Nathaniel, Chris, wearing only her bra and panties, unlocked the door and returned to her bed to finish packing. She had to be up early enough to pick up the girls and get them fed before their flight departed. The lock on the door clicked. "I'm surprised that you even have anything to say to me," she said, folding her jeans. "I know you're pissed, but Iysha…" "Iysha" placed her arms around Chris's waist. "Girl!" Chris yanked herself from the grasp of those folded arms, stunned to see a slightly inebriated Amil. "Amil?" she gasped, reaching for her robe. "What are you doing here? I thought you had to work."

Smiling at Chris as she'd done so many times before when she'd seen Chris sign online, Amil, clearing her throat, attempted to justify her presence. Unlike with Manney, she wasn't going to lie. "I did, but I called in at the last minute. Don't ask me why I'm here. I haven't figured that out yet." Chris, tying her robe in what, at this point, seemed to be a triple knot, plopped down on the bed and realized that Amil had been watching her and listening to her more closely than she'd first thought. "I've been driving around for hours. I went shopping thinking that I just needed to get out, but before that I went to Rafferty's and downed about three or four Coronas. Did you know that I don't drink beer?" Amil rambled. Chris's eyes began a smile that rapidly spread to her lips. "I've been to a movie and can't even begin to tell you what it was about. The next thing I knew," Amil said, looking into Chris's eyes for approval, "I was here."

"I see. Well, um…" Chris sighed rising from the bed. "You obviously don't need anything else to drink. You want something to eat?"

"Not really. It feels so funny being able to actually see you and talk to you without having to wait on you with your slow typing self," she commented, gliding toward the sofa to take a seat.

"Heyyy." Chris giggled. "It might be slow, but it gets the job done. And you're right. It does feel good to be face to face instead of miles apart." Chris didn't need to waste time asking Amil again why she was at her hotel at three in the morning; it was written all over her face. Despite the overwhelming desire to throw her on the bed and make love to her, Chris was determined that Amil would have to make the first move. "You sure you don't need anything? Room service is open all night."

"I'm sure. I don't want anything." Nestled in a corner of the sofa, Amil didn't have much else to say. She was in the presence of the person that soothed her soul—the person who had made her life seem like a bright light in the midst of Manney's overbearing shadow. Amil let her hand fall on the middle cushion of the sofa, and it lay there limp waiting for some kind of support, some kind of sign.

Chris, taking her cue, moved to the other end of the sofa and took Amil's lifeless hand in hers. Starting with Amil's pinky finger, adorned with a diamond anniversary band, Chris began a trail of kisses from the top of the nail circling around the two carats and then to the base of her finger and traced it with her tongue, making a path to Amil's ring finger. The pattern continued until Chris had circled every finger with a wetness so gentle that Amil moaned and wiggled against the silky fabric of the sofa. Chris stroked Amil's arm and kissed it from the knuckles to the center of her elbow. Amil shrieked in pleasure. Massaging the area with a combination of lips and tongue, Chris's other hand unbuttoned Amil's blouse. Slipping her hand underneath Amil's bra, Chris took a gentle hold of her nipple, tickling it with her fingertips. The closer her kisses got to Amil's neck the more Chris realized that she had to step back a minute and regain some composure. "Amil," she called.

Amil, lying there in ecstasy, hadn't noticed that Chris had stopped.

"Amil?" she called again, stroking Amil's thigh.

Amil couldn't figure out if she were dreaming or if it had all been real. She sat up on the sofa and saw Chris gazing into her face. "Mmmm, that was feeling so good. Why did you stop?"

"We need to talk before we let this go any further. I don't feel comfortable doing this with you. You're drunk, and I don't think that you really know what you're doing."

Amil adjusted herself on the sofa and leaned into Chris, reaching out to pull her closer. Amil hesitated before saying anything. There was no need to carefully choose her words, for she knew that whatever she had to say would be the truth. "I know what I'm doing, Chris."

"Unh-unh, bullshit. I need you to tell me what the hell is going on here. I've got too much happening in my life right now to get caught up in something like this. And then there is way too much on the line where we're both concerned. I really don't need you playing around with me just to get your rocks off with another woman."

"Chris," Amil started, sitting with her bra undone and her pants slightly un-zipped. "I decided on my way over here that I wanted to do something different for my birthday. I wanted to finally do something that *I* wanted to do, and being here with you, no matter what happens, is what I want to do."

Chris stood, reached for the decanter on the table, poured a glass of water, and pondered her next move.

Right now she needed love—love Amil appeared eager to give. Chris yearned for compassion. Amil readily had it for her. So caught up in the complex affairs of Iysha and Nathaniel, Chris had tossed aside her own life and buried her own desires. But now, the same comfort Amil had found in their relationship, Chris had unearthed solace in it, too, for in Amil, Chris had discovered a caring heart, and Amil had found someone who made her feel special, someone who made her feel loved, even if it were for only one night. Considering all these things, unsure of what the morning may bring, Chris said, "Okay, then," as she gulped her glass of water.

By the time they reached the bed, Amil was completely undressed, and, as Chris caressed her body from the base of her ankles to the back of her knees to the inside of her thighs, she tasted the joy that Amil had bottled up inside. The luggage that Chris had taken such care in packing was violently swept to the floor, and neither of them bothered to turn back the covers... until the third time. It was after then that Chris cradled Amil in her arms and talked to her. If they were to never make love again, that was the one thing that Amil would have remembered the most—conversing—communicating—was something that she and Manney had never done after having sex. She'd run to the computer, and he'd pass out on his side of the bed.

"Chris?"

"Yes," she answered, kissing the nape of Amil's neck.

"Nothing." She sighed. "I just wanted to see if you were asleep."

"Noooo, I'm not asleep although I probably should be. It'd be rather rude of me to ignore you like that."

"Can I ask you a question?" Amil felt that she now knew Chris well enough to pry just a little.

"Of course, you can."

Never turning around, Amil questioned, "Who was that girl to you. The one that died that night."

Immediately, Chris thought to herself, *you can ask me anything but that.* However, she'd never kept secrets from Amil and wasn't going to start now. "She was a woman that I loved dearly, and I believed that she felt the same way."

"Were you ever in a relationship with her?"

"Oh, my God, was I ever! It was one of the most debilitating experiences of my life, but it was also one of the best things that ever happened to me.

"That complete experience helped to mold me into who I am today. I don't dish a lot of bullshit because I don't want to get it back. I don't let my guard down for anybody's love until I've been friends with them for a while. Most importantly, I realized that my soul was empty and was crying for help. I just didn't know how to get that help until it was too late."

"Do you miss her?"

"Not really. I did at first, but I don't now. I used to wonder why God ever let her come into my life, and then I started pinching myself, hugging my babies, and admiring my accomplishments. I realized that I'd needed her to bring out the bad in me so that I could remember the good that was in me, too."

Listening intensely to a voice that could melt the coldest heart, Amil tightened Chris's arms around her and rested comfortably in Chris's embrace. "Do you visit her grave?"

"Nope, I didn't want to know where she was buried. I still talk with her mother every once in a while, though. That's about it."

"Okay, that's all I wanted to know. You can go back to kissing my neck." Amil giggled. She felt the hair on her back rise as Chris caressed it with a string of long warm kisses, kisses that led to more of the same passion that they'd already shared over and over anew.

Eight a.m. Chris scurried about her room gathering all of her belongings and tossed them in her suitcase with less care than just a few hours before. Amil, resting on her stomach and exposing the smoothest back that Chris had ever seen, never moved a muscle. Multiple orgasms on top of one beer shy of a six-pack were going to have her knocked out at least until early afternoon. Just before closing the doors that separated the bedroom suite from the large seating area, Chris tiptoed over to the bed and, as she scanned the perfect posterior of Amil's slender body, she couldn't resist kissing her in the small of her back. Then she placed a single red rose and little note card that she'd purchased from the gift shop on the pillow next to Amil, pulled the covers up over her naked body and closed the double doors behind her. The bellhop stood at the door waiting. "Go ahead, and take these things down," she whispered. "I have to make a couple of phone calls."

"Yes, Ma'am."

The first call was to Ora. Chris explained that she was running terribly late and that the girls needed to be ready. Lacking enough time to take the car to Rudy, Chris asked Ora if she would give her a ride to the airport. Before hanging up, Chris inquired whether or not Ora had heard from Iysha. Ora mentioned that she'd just been by to pick up the kids and was in a hurry because she was running late, too. Iysha had left so quickly that Ora really didn't have a chance to notice if something were wrong. The second call was to a nearby florist. When Chris reached the lobby, the bellhop was waiting for her. "Hold on a minute. I need you to do something."

"Yes, Ma'am."

Chris instructed the front desk to have breakfast prepared for her guest and to leave it in the sitting area of the suite. She arranged for a late checkout for Amil and permitted the hotel the discretion to charge an additional day to her credit card if needed. Afterwards, Chris gave the bellhop his instructions, tipped him $100, and told him that she'd clear his temporary absence with his supervisor.

❧♥❧

"*Over ten years I've been with this man. Over ten years! But it was so good with her. So good that I could do it over and over again just as long as I had a drink or two in me. The way she held me at just the right moments, and the way she knew exactly when and where to touch me.* (Thinking yet again) *You know what?* (Looking in the mirror) *I'm not going to tell him shit!*" Clearing the steam from the bathroom mirror, Amil noticed a new sparkle in her eyes. Her smile had a purpose, and her heart pumped a rhythm infused with joy. The only way that she could preserve the roses that had been lovingly left for her was to remove them from their stems and take the petals with her.

When she arrived at home later in the afternoon, Amil placed the petals in an African bowl that rested beside her bed. Running her fingers through the multicolored pile, she was lost in a tranquil daydream when Manney popped his head in the bedroom.

"There you are!" Manney exclaimed. "Did you have to stay late or something?"

Amil's heart raced. "A little."

"I called for you, and no one on first shift had seen you."

"I was probably in the shower. It got so hot and sticky in that place last night." Her curly locks were still wet on the ends. Fortunately, she always kept an emergency toiletry bag in the car and was able to put on some of her own perfume instead of one of the fragrances left by housekeeping. She gingerly raked her fingers through the rose petals once more, this time picking up a handful and bringing them to her nose. These were her memories—beautiful, different ones at that. Later that evening, Amil went through the same ol'-same ol', humdrum plans that she'd had with Manney.

Later that night, after pounding hard enough and long enough inside Amil to ask her whose pussy it was, Manney wrapped up the evening by passing out on top of her. Twirling her fingers, yet again, through that bowl of multi-colored rose petals and dreams, Amil whispered to her soul, "This pussy belongs to Chris."

A little curiosity had killed her kat.

FLIPPING THE SCRIPT...REWIND

A layer of pink rose petals.
A layer of hand-poured votive candles.
A layer of peach rose petals.
A layer of hand-made Parisian soaps.
A layer of fresh lavender.
A pair of French silk panties and lace stockings.
A layer of perfumes, body lotions and bath oils.
A layer of red rose petals.
Another layer of red rose petals.

Chris then placed sheets of floral tissue paper over the contents that she had so tenderly arranged in a box and overnighted it to Amil…at the hospital. Since their interlude at the hotel in Memphis, Chris had gone into full mack-mode. Every day Amil received some type of floral arrangement, many of which contained exotic flowers indigenous to other states and foreign countries. With this newfound thing, Chris wiped her personal slate clean of all previous emotional baggage and pitfalls and started over with what it meant to be in love with a woman. She knew what to say and when to say it. She also knew how to be Amil's friend first and her lover second. In the passing weeks since Chris had returned from Memphis, she had noticed a change in Amil's behavior but attributed it to being overwhelmed by the newness of the next level of their relationship. Blinded by her visions of love, Chris had forgotten that Amil belonged to Manney.

"Lula," Manney said, buzzing his secretary. "Get Ms. Desmereaux on the phone for me." Realizing he hadn't had an opportunity to talk to Chris after dinner that night, Manney had set aside some time to call her the following week. Only now he hoped that she was available. Just as quickly as the thought crossed his mind, Lula rang Manney's extension to announce that she had Chris holding on line one.

"This is Manney," were the first words out of his mouth as he picked up the phone.

"Bonjour." Chris giggled. "How's it going?"

Grinning like a Cheshire cat, Manney replied, "Everything's good. How are you?"

"I'm well. Just going through some paperwork as usual."

"Good to hear that. Look, I was meaning to talk to you while you were here, but you ducked out on me," Manney continued. "Called you at the hotel but couldn't get through."

Chris beamed as she reminisced about her rendezvous

with Amil. "There's no telling what I was doing. It was a busy weekend for me. What did you need?"

Manney's smile lit up the office as he stated proudly, "I'm getting married."

"What?" Chris gasped. *I know he didn't just say what I thought he said.* Chris's mind was racing. Suddenly it was getting hard to breathe.

As if he'd heard her thoughts, Manney repeated his pronouncement, confirming the name of his fiancée. "I'm going to marry Amil. I'd wanted to talk to you about it while you were here but didn't get a chance to."

Chris was speechless. Mute was more like it. Now she needed some air.

"You still there?" Manney questioned as the sounds of silence echoed over the phone line.

Clearing her throat, determined to regain her composure, Chris responded in as business-like a manner as she could muster. "I'm here. Someone was in my office. Um, c-congratulations, Manney."

Excited, like a seafood lover at an all-you-can-eat crab leg buffet, Manney continued, "And guess where we're having it?"

I can't begin to imagine, Chris deadpanned silently. But aloud she replied, "Why don't you tell me since you sound like you're about to pop?"

"I've planned a surprise wedding for her in Paris and was wondering if you could help me with some of the details."

"Manney, I don't know what to say." Chris knew what she *could* say, but it wouldn't have been appropriate. "Does Amil know? You said it was a surprise."

"Well, yes, she knows, but she told me to handle everything and to let her know when and where. She's always assumed it would happen. I just don't think she expected it to be like this." Manney quietly recalled the evening he had told Amil they were going to get married. He didn't get down on one knee, nor did he try to set the mood. "I'm ready to get married," he'd stated. "We're going to do it in Paris with our families and friends there." Amil unemotionally accepted his plans, as if they were merely discussing the weather or finalizing a business proposition, and moved on to the next subject.

"Is she excited?" Chris asked.

"Uh, kinda indifferent about it. She's not as excited as she was when I first asked her ten years ago. We've been doing the common law marriage thing long enough, and I felt she deserved something special."

"I see," Chris responded. "Well, let me know what you need me to do. You should have a wedding planner, though. It's going to be difficult to pull off if you're always there in Memphis." Rushing him off the phone was imperative. He didn't need to hear Chris bawl her eyes out. Chris's affection for Amil quickly turned to something that was hard to swallow. Despite everything Chris had done for Amil lately, nothing ever seemed to be enough. If she sent Amil roses, Amil would ask, "Why are they orange? I thought you might've sent something peach." If Chris sent her candy, Amil insisted it be from Godiva. If Chris sent a letter, Amil complained, "Don't send me anything in writing. He might find it." Yes, Amil was picky as hell, but Chris loved it. Nothing else mattered one damn bit. Now everything made sense.

❦♥❦

As LaNisha dusted the freshly shaven hair from the neck of her next-to-last customer, she noticed Amil pull up in the parking lot and get out of her car with a bounce in her step that wasn't always there. *Oh, Miss Girl musta got herself some this morning.* LaNisha—or as Amil called her, Nee-Nee, chuckled quietly. *I know she got some juicy gossip for me today!* Amil usually came in and greeted Nee-Nee with a hug before sitting down, whether she was with a client or not. Instead, Amil entered the salon, picked up a magazine, and took a seat in an empty dryer chair. Thumbing through the pages, she restlessly glanced at the pictures and tossed the book aside. She picked up another…and another…and another. After letting her previous customer out of the door and sweeping a pile of hair up from the floor, LaNisha walked towards the wash area and said, "C'mon, Amil."

At the shampoo bowl, LaNisha placed a towel in Amil's lap and began to lather her client's tresses. Amil didn't crack her lips. LaNisha hummed a few lines from a song she knew Amil loved. Still nothing. Ms. Lindsay was doggedly mum. LaNisha rinsed and shampooed Amil a second time. Eyes closed, relaxed with her head in the bowl, Amil was content to let LaNisha do her job, refusing to offer a sound. There had never been a time when the two friends had nothing to say to each other. *Oh, sistahgurl gon' be like that today*, LaNisha thought as she clicked her tongue. *Aiight. I gotcha.* Anxiously watching the last employee exit the door, LaNisha, in one swift motion, cocked and locked her forefinger in a thumping position and popped Amil in the temple hard enough for it to sting. "What the hell is wrong with you?"

"Ow!" Amil yelled as the sound of the thump ricocheted inside her head.

"Ohhhh! It lives!" LaNisha exclaimed sarcastically. "What's up with you? You ain't said nothin' since you got here, and you know that ain't you. My breath stank or somethin'?"

Cracking a smile as she massaged her temple, Amil shook her head and replied, "No, Nee. I wish it were that simple. I got some stuff on my mind."

"Okay, and? You talk to me about everything else. So what's so different about today?"

Well, for starters Amil wasn't feeling a lecture today, but she did need to vent. *Oh what the hell,* she thought. She had to talk to somebody about what was happening in her life. "Manney wants to get married." *There. I've said it.*

Surprised by Amil's somber tone, LaNisha snapped, "'Bout damn time, don'tcha think? But you don't sound like the happy bride-to-be. So c'mon. Give it up."

"There's something else."

"I knew it. What?"

"I finally got my kat licked."

"Get the fuck the outta here!" was LaNisha's initial reaction. Then after regaining her composure, she slowly leaned in to Amil's ear and, with a hint of disbelief in her demeanor, inquired softly, as if they were in a room full of people, "Baby, he ain't never licked your kitty kat before?"

Blushing, Amil responded, "It wasn't by Manney."

"Ohh shit. I knew you'd have some juice for me. Who was it? One of them fine doctors you work wit at the hospital?"

"No. And it wasn't a 'he' that did it. It was this woman I met over the Internet."

"Aw shit now! You tellin' me you let a woman touch your thing? A woman you just met?" LaNisha couldn't believe what she was hearing.

"No, no, no, Nee-Nee. It wasn't like that," Amil countered. "I met her several years ago online. Manney was always busy and all I wanted was a friend, someone to talk with. Well, one day of conversation led to the next day and day after that and the day after that. Before we knew it, a few years had gone by and I realized I was feeling something for her, emotions that should have been exclusively for Manney. Nee Nee, I couldn't understand them or explain them. All I know is that I had this compelling urge to talk to her. I thought about her constantly. It was like I couldn't get her out of my mind. I daydreamed about what she looked like. What kind of hair she had. Was it long enough to dangle over my face if she had me in bed? Did she possess long sensuously slender fingers to glide over the keyboard of her computer and type her way into my psyche? What about her touch? I wondered what it would feel like to have those same hands caress my body with fingernails that tantalized all the right places. Hell, I even became aroused imagining myself reaching out touching voluptuously rounded breasts that were pushed up high enough to peep through the opening of a silk halter top. I don't know, Nee." Amil sighed. "These… these…" Amil threw her hands up in the air and let them fall back down to the armrests of her chair. "I don't know what to call them. When she realized that we'd both gotten caught up, she ended it. It was like POOF! One day we were talking about loving each other, and the next day I didn't hear from her for years."

LaNisha raised Amil's chair from the shampoo bowl and wrapped a towel around her head. Periodically reaching up to catch the droplets of water trickling down her face, Amil was determined to unload and at last let someone into her world of uncertain emotions. LaNisha, sensing Amil's need to confide, pulled up a chair, patted her friend on the shoulder and nodded for her to continue. "She's from here but lives in Paris now. As it turned out, I met her at the hospital one night but I didn't know that it was her. As fate would have it, Manney landed a new project with this woman from, of all places, Paris, France. While the woman was in town visiting family, he and I met her for dinner. I be damned, Nee-Nee, if it wasn't her! Anyway, long story short, we did it. We made love, and I can-not-get-her-out-of-my head." Amil rushed the words out in an emphatic staccato and exhaled in relief that she had finally shared her secrets with someone. "We've hooked up a few times since then. Hell, as a matter of fact, I see her more than I see Manney."

Attempting to absorb the facts before giving her view of the situation, LaNisha let a moment of silence dangle in the air. Then she announced, "You know you have just blown me the fuck away. You, Miss Always Got a Stick Up Her Ass, done got a little freaky. Swingin' from chandeliers and thangs. I knew you had it in ya,"

LaNisha cackled. "And ain't nothing wrong with that! Just don't be looking at me."

Annoyed by LaNisha's clamor, Amil disgustedly continued in an I-can't-believe-this-shit tone. "And now Manney wants to get married."

"Does she know it?"

"Not that I know of. She's going to have a fit."

"I bet."

With eyes glistening, Amil smiled. "Nee-Nee, she's been sending me the most romantic stuff. I don't know what to do."

LaNisha spouted off her words of wisdom, "Honey, you talking to the master at games. I'd play that shit to the hilt. Have your cake, and eat it, too. Get love and attention from her, and then get dicked down by Manney while you're with him."

"I don't even want that from him anymore. I told you it's different."

"Well," LaNisha stood and began, toweling off Amil's hair, "if I were you, I'd marry Manney and cut my losses. The niggah's just like the song. He got money, power, and respect. She ain't gotta know how you really feel about her. From what I've heard, them people all about games anyway."

"Don't misjudge her. I don't think she's like that, Nee-Nee. She's made her point very clear."

Reaching to get the comb and styling lotion, LaNisha

said, "You're entitled to have a little fun every once in a while, but your reality is that finally, after all these years, Manney wants to get married. Knowing the stuff I know about y'all, he's never been a favorite of mine. But as your friend, confidante, and hairdresser, I gotta tell you this. You need to do what you know is right."

"I know," Amil agreed. "I know."

❦♥❦

The following weekend Chris and Amil had plans to hang out in D.C. Chris knew Ms. Yolanda, the owner of the District's only strip bar for women, and had told her everything about her dilemma with Amil. Apprehensive about being seen in an all-girl strip club, Amil nixed the idea, stating she'd never be caught dead in one of those places. "Well, I'll have one of the bouncers carry your corpse out after you've seen all the asses and titties in there." Chris assured Amil that no one would know her, and besides, women didn't go there to see who else was there. They came from all over in droves for "The Show," especially to see Quiet Reign. Every curve on that woman's body claimed its place in her costumes. Minimally dressed, Quiet Reign moved delicately across the stage in five-inch stiletto heels. The first time Chris had ever seen Quiet Reign perform, the crowd tossed so much money at her that it had to be carted off in black garbage bags. She climbed atop the four-foot bar and shook her ass so tough that even Amil was a bit moved. Then, without warning, the "exotic" dancer jumped three feet into the air and landed in one of those cheerleader-type splits...and bounced. Maneuvering her legs, she stretched them forward. Pulling her knees up to her chest as she grabbed her ankles, Quiet Reign was able to scoot across the floor on her back with her pussy pulsating to the bass beat of the music. It was a sight that puzzled many but pleased plenty.

Amil squeezed herself between two women and secured a couple of seats at a small table near the railing while Chris shouldered her way through the mass of bodies in an effort to get drinks for them. When Chris reached the bar, she bumped into Ms. Yolanda. "Hey, darling," Ms. Yolanda said as she greeted Chris with a quick peck on the lips. The scent of her cologne, recognizably the male side of Davidoff's Cool Water, mixed wonderfully with fresh soap. "How's my girl?" she asked. Chris returned the hug and kiss and pulled out a twenty to pay for the drinks. "You know your money isn't any good in here. Put that away."

Obviously not in the mood for disputes, Chris replied, "I'm not going to argue with you about it today," as she picked up some extra napkins and sampled her Pineapple Malibu. She sipped it slow a second time, and motioned for the bartender to replenish her glass.

"That's Amil you came in here with, isn't it?"

"Yep," Chris answered.

"She's a cutie." Ms. Yolanda signaled the bartender to bring her a glass of wine. "Has she said anything about it yet?"

Chris watched the ice in Amil's Coke float around the rim. "Nope." She was in the mood to give only one-syllable answers.

"You need to let her know that you're aware of the big day."

Chris took another gulp of her drink, swallowed and leaned in close enough to Yolanda to lick her face. "It's not my place to say anything. I'm on this kick now where I mind my business and let folks do what they want to do."

"Even if it means you getting hurt in the process? C'mon, now. Get real!"

"I'm already hurt, Yo'."

"Well, apparently, the wedding isn't that important since she hasn't said anything about it."

"No, it's important to her all right. She told him yes. That's enough for me." Amil's drink had gone flat. "I'm going to get her another drink." Chris ordered another Coke for Amil and left Yolanda standing there.

Placing the glasses on the table, Chris nudged a distracted Amil in the back to let her know she had returned.

"You sure were gone a long time."

"There was a line." Chris finished off her drink and started on the hot wings Yolanda had sent over. Dipping a wing in ranch dressing, Chris asked, looking at the meat to make sure it was completely done, "When were you planning to tell me about the wedding?"

Amil's expression instantaneously morphed into the deer-trapped-in-headlights stare. Lifting her glass to her lips, she said, "I figured you already knew since you talk to Manney all the time."

Chris chewed twice before swallowing. An insinuation was being made. "Excuse me?"

"He talks to and about you more than he talks to and about me."

Wiping her fingers on a napkin, Chris said, "You're mistaken. I don't talk to Manney that often. It may appear that I do, but I don't."

"Yeah, right."

Turning the stool until she was square in the face with Amil, Chris snapped, "Look," grabbing Amil by the arm. "Your husband-to-be called me in Paris to ask me to help him plan a wedding…a marriage to the woman I've been in love with for the past five years, and *she* hasn't said a word to me about it."

Pausing for a moment, Amil asked, "You've loved me that long?"

Chris had overreacted. "Maybe not that long. I was fine with having a friend like you. I thought you didn't want anything from me other than friendship. Then you started letting me flirt with you, and the next thing I knew you're flirting back. That's when I knew it was time to stop this silly game before one of us ended up devastated."

"I'm sorry," Amil allowed. "I was under the impression you already knew about the wedding and was just making the best of whatever time we had left to spend with each other." Taking advantage of a perfect opportunity to talk about LaNisha, she continued, "I told my friend LaNisha about us."

"So, what are you telling me for? And come to think of it, ain't that your damn hairdresser?"

Fidgeting with her glass, Amil said, "Yeah, but she's my friend, too. I mean so you won't think I'm keeping us this big secret."

"Okay, whatever you say." Chris, at this point, was edging toward hauling off and punching Amil in the face but thought better of it.

"What's wrong with you?" Amil asked, as if she didn't have a clue.

"I..." Chris began, but, in fear of completely losing what she had with Amil, gave up the argument. The grief of a lifetime of lost loves slowly began to make its presence felt. And this love was the closest she'd ever been to real happiness. "You know what? Never mind. I think I'll have another Pineapple Malibu." And with that, Chris rose from the table and fought her way back to the bar.

❧♥❧

Nathaniel rolled over in the bed and noticed that Iysha wasn't there. The television wasn't on, and no noise came from the other parts of the house. *She's gone.* Leaving the bathroom, Nathaniel noticed shopping bags from Dillard's being used for trash…relatively new shopping bags. He scurried over to Iysha's closet and, after digging through all of her clothes, discovered a new Kasper suit. *Nice. I know she bought some shoes. She never buys a new suit without buying matching shoes.* Beneath the hems of Iysha's clothes was a stack of shoeboxes. Nathaniel picked up the box that was purposely thrown in the very back of the closet. He smiled with his find because they were a perfect match. He was going to be sharp.

While he bathed in his lavish bubbles, Nathaniel thought about the ass he'd gotten since he'd come back on the scene. Iysha wasn't setting it out anymore, so he had to do something. He'd even managed to get Patty to forget about God one night by seducing him in the back of the club. Often lurking in the alley behind the club, Patty might've never gone in, but he made it a point to be in the area on nights when the club was popping. Nathaniel, no matter how disgraceful his actions, was comfortable with the place he was in now. His undercover life gave him the zest he needed to get through whatever he had left with Iysha. But which side represented what was real? Did he want to be a gay man living in a straight man's life, or did he want to be a straight man with gay tendencies? Which one was easiest to deal with?

STRAWBERRIES AND CHAMPAGNE

Although she knew the wedding was inevitable, Chris had actually begun to believe that perhaps, with a little persuading, Amil would change her mind about marrying Manney. For three months, they'd courted each other, going far beyond just emails. Phone calls, flowers, stuffed toys, and anything else symbolizing new love was exchanged with neither of them ever really expecting anything in return. Forsaking Manney's trust, if only for a moment, Amil took several trips to D.C. for "medical conferences" and "meetings." Once there, she and Chris, who'd flown in from Paris, shopped and made love in the city that was the home of their alma mater. Chris was finally able to comfortably frequent the clubs she'd ducked and dodged while in college. Quickly discovering she'd outgrown the club scene that now boasted more of a teenybopper crowd, Chris and Amil chose to attend the National Symphony and even managed to catch a rare Kennedy Center performance by the Dance Theatre of Harlem.

During their last rendezvous in the District, Amil's seven-day "conference" was succeeded by another week devoted to an American Medical Association "meeting." Next on her agenda was a non-stop flight out of Reagan National. Destination: Paris, France. That's where Manney had been for the last fourteen days, busily putting the finishing touches on arrangements for their wedding.

Chris, however, had other plans. Ringing Amil's cell phone moments after her flight arrived from Memphis, Chris instructed Dr. Lindsay to meet her at Legal Sea Foods in the airport. When Amil spotted Chris running toward her, her heart fluttered. "You just getting here?" Amil inquired.

"No," Chris said hurriedly. "C'mon, we're going to miss our flight."

"What?" Amil gasped. "What flight?"

Taking her by the hand, Chris replied, "We're going to France for two weeks."

"Chris, what's going on? I thought we..."

Chris stopped to catch her breath. "Whewww! I need to start back working out! I did just get here, but I flew in to get you. I bought you a seat on the plane...next to me, of course, so that we could have a change of scenery."

Blushing, Amil quietly replied, "I should've known that you were up to something." She stood beside Chris hoping that she'd be able to come up with a reason why she shouldn't get on that plane, but for the life of her, she couldn't think of anything. "Does Manney have you in on this wedding thing?"

Offensively, Chris said, "No, he doesn't. You know I'm not a big fan of that event, so why would I even offer to participate? Besides, he believes that I'm in L.A. on business."

"So," Amil said happily. "I suppose I'm going to finally get to see your place."

Chris laughed. "Uh, no, actually you're not. We're not going to Paris." She started walking toward customs, pulling Amil's luggage behind her.

"We're not?" As Chris flashed her passport that she kept with her at all times, the security guard frisked her and directed her to the other side of the customs counter to wait for Amil. They checked her luggage and passport. Then it dawned on Amil that she'd once told Chris that she always kept her passport in her purse. Amil realized that Chris had been planning this little getaway for weeks. The flight Chris had arrived on was refueling to return to France. When they got to their first-class seats, Amil noticed Chris's attaché case underneath the seats in front of them. "Sooo, if we're not going to Paris, then where are we going?"

"We're going to Champagne. I've always wanted to go there to taste the finest champagne that the world has to offer. I also thought it might be a neat little wedding present for you."

"And how am I supposed to explain why I'm coming in from Champagne instead of D.C.?"

"I'm quite sure you'll come up with something before

then. Is he supposed to be picking you up from the airport or something?"

"Yes," was Amil's wistful reply as she gently caressed the leather seats and inhaled the aromas of fresh fruit and gourmet coffee being prepared by the stewardesses. This was luxury, and it was nothing that Manney would have ever thought to do. "But like you said, I'll have plenty of time to figure this one out."

Their flight arrived in Paris at 9 o'clock at night with two well-traveled women who were thoroughly exhausted. After retrieving their luggage, Chris strolled out front to a waiting limousine. "Je suis Mademoiselle Desmereaux," she declared rapidly, as she greeted the driver. "Parlez-vous anglais, Monsieur?"

The driver smiled and replied, "Yes, I do."

"Good!" Chris chuckled. "I'm too tired to try to figure out whether or not I'm saying the right thing." Chris's French was so-so when conducting business, but more casual atmospheres found her doing more cussing and fussing in English than most natives cared to hear. "We're going to the Ville de Reims in Champagne." Reaching in her purse, she added, "Here are the directions to the chateau."

❦♥❦

Their last day together began differently from the

rest. “What should I wear today?” Amil asked Chris as she thumbed through the closet.

“I don’t know,” Chris replied. “Wear what makes you feel comfortable.”

“What’s up with the attitude? For the past ten days you’ve picked out all my clothes, ironed them, and did all but dress me. Now, I can’t get you to say more than a few words to me. You didn’t even run my bath water this morning.” Amil had become spoiled. Chris had waited on her hand and foot the entire time they’d been together. The odd thing was that Amil couldn’t get Chris to touch her. Several evenings Amil had come to bed nude, but Chris never reacted. They’d spent every moment talking like old girlfriends who’d stolen some time away from their families. They slept comfortably next to each other, sometimes in each other’s arms but most times not. Chris, protecting her heart more than she ever had, was laying the groundwork for whatever was to come. Amil danced around the reality that she’d be married in less than seventy-two hours and wanted Chris to be happy for her. In order to keep things pleasant, Amil ignored Chris’s attitude, picked out her own clothes, ironed them, and looked forward to a long awaited day of sightseeing and shopping.

That night they had a quiet dinner at Le Chardonnay. At the table next to them was an elderly American couple celebrating their fiftieth-wedding anniversary. Chris's eyes watered as she heard them toast their commitment and love for each other while Amil, just as she'd done other times during their trip, whined, "Awww, that is just soooo sweet. I hope that Manney and I are like that one day."

"What did you say?" Chris asked in disbelief.

Amil, giggling like an out-of-control, underaged hoochie-mama at a house party, replied, "I said that I hope that Manney and I have a life like that." Then she took another sip of champagne.

"I can't even see that happening because you're fucking every piece of booty you meet over the Internet."

Appalled, Amil contested, "That's not true. Why would you say something like that to me?"

Chris lived in France, and Amil didn't, so Chris knew it was time to call it a night. She didn't need the embarrassment of being in the company of an intoxicated American woman who was having an affair with another woman three days before she was to marry a well-respected real estate developer. "Monsieur." Chris signaled the waiter and asked for the check. "We need to leave, Amil. You've had a lot to drink, and it seems to be fucking with your head."

For Chris, conversation had been minimal most of the day, but Amil was making small talk at every available opportunity. Chris stopped outside the entrance to their chateau and took Amil by the hand. Amil, amused and aroused by Chris's candor, this once allowed Chris to hold her hand outside the confines of their accommodations. "What is it?" Amil asked softly, gazing into Chris's eyes. "We've been walking for quite some time now, and you haven't said a word. Shoot, we've been walking so long that I need another drink."

Chris always shot from the hip. "Why is it that you have to be drunk to be with me? Do you realize the few times we've had sex that you've been drunk?"

Amil knew she was busted because she had been drunk every time she'd been with Chris…while in Memphis, in D.C., and now in Champagne. "Really? I didn't realize that. I guess it means that I'm always having such a good time with you." She smiled.

Chris raised Amil's hand to her lips and kissed it. "I don't think so, Amil. You're ashamed of me, and you're ashamed of what you've been doing with me."

"No, I'm not. I just want to feel good. That's all."

"No, you want to be numb, so that your mind can be all right with this. We've been walking this long because I wanted you to sober up." Then Chris leaned forward and kissed Amil on the lips. Amil was trembling. "I want to make love to the person I fell in love with. No Coronas, no wine, no champagne. Just you."

Amil, on the defensive, was caught with her guard down. "I don't know if I can do that, Chris."

"Have you tried?"

Standing there as the once midnight-blue sky began to welcome a thundershower, Amil confessed, "I have tried, but it's different when I'm right in front of you. It's..." But she didn't finish the sentence because the rain poured from the clouds, forcing them both to run for shelter inside the chateau.

Just after they crossed the threshold of the dwelling, Chris, heart palpitating and clit hard as a rock, grabbed Amil from the back, pulled her hair over her left shoulder and kissed the nape of her neck. Chris felt Amil, still trembling but surrendering to a passion of which she refused to let go, collapse in her clutches. The hair on Amil's back tickled Chris's nose as her hands massaged Amil's breasts and torso. Amil, engrossed in Chris's intimacy, masturbated just enough to make it beautiful...over and over again. She then whisked Chris around and covered her in kisses from her face to her neck to her bosom. Neither of them paused when Amil tore the dress that Chris had picked out just hours before at a nearby boutique. Neither of them flinched when a strand of pearls snapped, sending beads scampering across the floor. Nobody uttered a word when Amil's tongue entered the walls of Chris's drenched pussy. Saturating Chris's thighs with kisses as she caressed her breasts finding her way back to Chris's lips, Amil whispered, "I'm not drunk now, Chris. I'm sober, baby, as sober as I can be. I love you and want to be with no one but you." She then embraced Chris, holding her tightly, repeatedly vowing to never let her go.

Much later, Chris lit the fireplace and spread a blanket over the ceramic-tiled floor. "Let's have a little picnic." She sliced some cheese, cleaned some strawberries from the refrigerator, and pulled crackers from a gift basket that came with the accommodations. "In order to keep shit real, I'm serving sparkling white grape juice."

Amil chuckled and responded, "Okay. I feel you. Sparkling grape juice is fine with me." As she sipped her juice, Amil reclined on a stack of oversized pillows and listened to the fire snap, pop and crackle. "You know, that's always been a fantasy of mine."

"What has?" Chris inquired as she sat her nude bottom on the hearth.

She sighed in delight. "To taste another woman like that."

"Well, I have to admit. You seemed to know what you were doing, especially for someone who has only fantasized about it. I've never been a fan of oral sex, but you sure made it worthwhile."

"You mean as a gay woman you don't like oral sex?"

Chris took a minute before responding. "Well, maybe that's not what I was trying to say. I don't mind doing it, but it just kinda blows it all to hell for me when I come across someone who doesn't know what they're doing. A lick the wrong way or in the wrong place doesn't feel too nice. That's why I made that comment."

Amil relaxed a little more and said, "I just did it the way you've always done it to me." It was after midnight, and although Amil still had much more passion to give, she knew she needed to get to bed. Polishing off her juice, she stood and strolled towards the kitchen. Amil had recalled seeing Chris wash her face with lemon juice after oral sex, particularly around her mouth, and then cleanse it with alcohol and maybe a little vinegar.

"What are you about to do?" Chris questioned. "We still have the rest of the night ahead of us."

"Girl, I need to get cleaned up and pack my bags, so I can get some sleep before we head out in the morning."

Chris knew it. This little game was coming to an end. "Wait a minute. Amil, you've got to tell me what's going on here. Not even two hours ago, you told me that you wanted this and that you wanted us."

"Yes, I did, but then I came right behind that and said I'd always *fantasized* about this type of thing."

"So, this was a fantasy of yours? A damn game?"

Amil stood in the kitchen, squeezing fresh lemon juice into a cup. "I wouldn't call it a game, Chris. I really do like you." She saw that Chris was furious. Was she missing something? "I know that you didn't believe that I was going to walk out on my marriage to Manney… something that I've been waiting on all my life."

"What!" Chris screamed. "After everything he's put you through...making you perm the hair on your pussy, so it would look like some damn white woman's ass in a strip club? Wanting you to get a fake, big toe nail so that you could look like some scantch he saw in the mall?"

Something wasn't right. Taken aback, Amil tearfully questioned, "How do you know that stuff? Those are things that only Manney should know."

With her arms folded, Chris offered nothing. She'd promised Manney that she'd never repeat the things he told her. So what if she'd lied. "I thought you understood that this is my life you're playing around with. It hasn't been a fly-by-night thing for me."

Remorseful but prepared to move on, Amil stated, "I thought you knew. I really believed that you would be able to walk away if you had to."

Chris retaliated with, "If you were some piece of stray pussy off the street, then I would've run away from you a long time ago just to avoid the drama."

Amil unwaveringly insisted, "I can't believe that you were expecting more. I mean, a relationship? If that's what you're looking for, then I'm here to tell you... it's not going to happen. You've been a wonderful friend to me, and if you'd let me, I can be a damn good friend to you."

"A friend? You went through all of this—years of

emails, phone calls, gifts, and eCards—just so that you could have a damn friend?"

Amil saw that Chris was bleeding on the inside. "The last thing I've ever wanted to do was hurt you. I…"

"You can't even begin to comprehend what you've done. If friendship was what you wanted, then you were looking in the wrong place."

"If I'd told you that, then we wouldn't be here," Amil whimpered.

"Damn right, we wouldn't be here," Chris snapped as she lit a Swisher Sweet.

Taking Chris's cue that the discussion was over, Amil traipsed wearily to the closet and removed her suitcase. As she battled with her conscience for closure, she placed her garments on the bed. The obvious devastation she'd caused Chris was eating away at her soul. Amil, wiping her tears, peeped into the living area and saw Chris still sitting on the hearth. She trudged over and eased down beside her. "I thought we were friends."

"Know this about me," Chris declared, taking a drag from her cigar, "I don't fuck my friends, nor do I fuck them over. Too bad I can't say the same for you."

Tearfully extending the ring finger of her left hand for Chris to see, Amil exclaimed, "Chris, you knew this about me! You knew I was engaged!"

"And that's supposed to excuse you? Amil, I love you because we had a friendship, a good one, before we ever got physical. I was okay with never touching or feeling you, and I respected the fact that you were with a man. You don't know how hard it is for me to sit and listen to Manney rant and rave about marrying you and having babies with you. I don't want to hear that shit, Amil. I have sacrificed so much for you...for us, and you haven't done shit but sit and make fucking friendship bracelets. I knew you weren't going to leave him."

Clearing her throat, Amil confessed to Chris, "Maybe I did perm my hair down *there* to get his approval, and yeah, it all fell out. But it grew back a little straighter than it was. And maybe I did do the fake big toe thing, but the good thing is that the fungus is almost gone. Despite all of that, society is gonna accept me being married to Manney much quicker than it would if I were committed to you. Chris, I could never spend the rest of my life waking up in the arms of a woman."

A freight train had run over Chris. It had stopped, put itself in reverse, and had run over her again. She couldn't take the pain anymore. "Amil..." Chris's voice, now barely audible, was eerily calm, but had it not been for love, would have been laced with a deadly venom. "Don't ever speak to me again until you're ready to tell me that you want to be with me," she snapped. "The airport shuttles run all night. I'll call them while you finish packing your things. Remember this, though. If I am to ever have anything to do with you loving me, then I have to let you go. If you don't come back, then I'll know this was never meant to be." She could've told Amil that she never would have ignored her, the way Manney did; or take her for granted, the way Manney did; or even ask her to relax her pubic hair, the way Manney did. But all that would've just wasted more time. Chris flicked her cigar into the blazing fire, rose from the hearth, and called the limousine company.

As Amil made her way to the door with her bags, she hesitated, gazing at Chris wrapped up in the same blanket that they'd made love in some hours before. "Ummm, I hate to ask you this, but are you still coming to the wedding? You know how much Manney wants you to be there," she said softly.

The limo's headlights reflected in a mirror that hung over the mantle. Chris heard the driver's door open, but she didn't budge. She'd heard Amil, too—having the fucking nerve to ask such a question—and felt that there was nothing else left to say.

PARIS IN THE SPRINGTIME

Vera Wang wedding gowns weren't commonplace for ordinary people. Celebrities like Tamia, Vanessa L. Williams, and Mariah Carey had one, and despite her affluent, cosmopolitan lifestyle, Amil wondered what the hell she was doing in one. Her concerns had nothing to do with stature, but they had everything to do with principle.

The last fifteen months had been a whirlwind romance for Amil, but the honors should have gone to Chris, not Manney. As she sat peering out the open window that overlooked the church's courtyard, Amil inhaled several breaths of fresh air and prayed for a miracle. Limos lined both sides of the blocked-off street like chainlink fences, but as she watched each guest, dressed in his or her finest after-five attire, approach the steps of the church, she realized she still hadn't seen Chris. Manney mentioned that he had had an invitation hand-delivered to her the day before, and he was certain that she was going to attend. He'd come to admire and respect Chris more than he did his own partners in the company.

The surprise guest for the festivities was LaNisha, the only person Amil trusted to do her hair. Plus she was the only other person besides Amil who knew about Chris's real connection to the bride.

"Knock-knock." LaNisha smiled as she entered the bridal room. "You all dressed yet?"

Amil had to tear herself away from the window, giving up on ever seeing Chris again. "Yeah, I'm dressed enough for you to do my hair."

"Don't get nothing on that dress, girl! You know Manney paid a pretty penny for that gown." The dress was made of silk, satin, and ivory organza and was an off-the-shoulder, form-fitting creation made for a princess. It was beaded by hand with thousands of iridescent sequins.

Manney had selected it from a little boutique a couple of blocks from the church. Also featuring a twenty-foot detachable train, the dress incorporated a veil made of sheer tulle netting imported from London. "This thang is so damn sharrrppp!"

"It is nice, Nee-Nee. My man sure did this up right," Amil commented solemnly. "A spring wedding in Paris."

"Well, then, why you trippin'? Your face is draggin' the flo' like a wet mop."

Amil burst into tears. "Nee-Nee, please tell me that I'm wrong. Please tell me that I don't need to marry this man."

"I been tellin' you that shit for years. But who listens to their hairdresser?"

"I *have* been listening to you. I just was ignoring you."

LaNisha took a seat on the chair next to Amil. "Lemme me holla at you 'bout sumthin'." Her demeanor shifted from jocular to serious. "I saw Chris this morning."

Amil's face lit up. "Where?"

"At the hotel. She came by to drop sumthin' off. Since Manney had asked her to help with the hotel accommodations, she knew where I was staying. Seems like you had told her we were best buddies and shit, so she gave me this to give to you." LaNisha pulled out a white box that had a gold-ribbon tied around it. "Amil, if you ask me, I wouldn't open it."

"Why not?"

"Cus it might make you change yo' mind. I think that's what she wants."

Amil was puzzled. "You talked to her?"

"Dayum, y'all got me caught up in this shit!" LaNisha exclaimed. "You know I ain't just one hundred percent okay with this girl-doing-girl thang, but I don't like Manney's ass either. He treats you good when he wants to, and you and I both know that's not all the time. He didn't ask you if you wanted to marry him. He *told* you he was flying you to Paris so that *he* could give you a wedding. He's had eons to do this, and, when you finally start doing something that gives you more pleasure than he does, he decides that it's time to do the right thing. That way you're obligated and expected to be loyal to him and not to, well, you know. He might not *know*, but he knows enough to feel threatened. Instead of discussing this wedding with you, he went about it his way. So what, he flew five-hundred guests out here for this lavish wedding and paid for all the accommodations. Whoop-the-fucking-do! Shit, I needed the vacation and woulda needed to do a whole lotta hair just to pay for my flight here. Needless to say, she's not coming, and I think that somewhere in the back of your mind, you knew that. That's why yo' ass been watching that window. Lemme ask you sumthin'."

"What?"

"What does he do for you that you can't do for yourself? You coulda afforded to do this wedding on your own. You got mad loot! Manney wants you to feel like you owe him something when you really don't owe him shit! In the last three years, how good and how often has sex been for you? C'mon, tell me! Was your kat wet? Were your nipples hard? Prolly not!"

"Umm, well..."

"See!"

"But Nee-Nee, I owe this to him. We've been together so long that it's like a routine."

"Uh-huh, and what did you tell me about routines?"

Amil laughed. "I don't like them."

"Riiight." LaNisha took Amil's freshly manicured hand. "Look, me and my freaky ass ain't got no business tryna tell you what to do in your bedroom, but—and I never thought I'd be saying this to one woman about another one—but that girl loves the shit out of you."

"I know, but this...this whole marriage thing...the frills and stuff, I could never have with her. Five hundred people wouldn't come to see two women get married. Society condemns that, Nee-Nee, and I don't know if I could go through the rest of my life wondering who knew that I was in love with a woman."

"So you do love her."

"Nee, I've loved her the whole time, and," she sobbed, "I still do."

"And you gonna walk down that aisle knowing this? I wish I woulda had the kinda love that you two have for each other. You wouldn't be able to tell me shit."

"I have to marry him. I didn't get my period last month," Amil confessed as she adjusted the bow atop the white box.

"DAMN! I see you been lettin' him hit it."

"Shhh! We're in a church, remember?"

"Oops! My bad!" she whispered. "After all this time?"

"Same thing I said." Amil put the little white box inside of her garment bag.

"Al-righty then." LaNisha sighed. "Lemme get started on your hair," she said as she got up from the chair. "You don't want to keep the man waiting."

WHEN IT RAINS, IT POURS

Rachel sat down at her desk breathing a sigh of relief. The staff meeting for which she'd been preparing for over a month was finally over. They had to do an entire PowerPoint presentation, in French, on the progress of the new dormitories. Granted, Chris, who was fluent in the language, preferred to use her skills only when absolutely necessary. Rachel offered to help out this time in the event that Chris got hung up on the dialect of some of the native Frenchmen who were now major stakeholders in the new development. Fortunately, the questions were minimal, and Chris managed to get through the presentation by herself. As Rachel prepared to put away the remaining handouts from the meeting, Chris's private line rang. "Mademoiselle Desmereaux's office."

There was an American man on the other end. "Yes, is Ms. Desmereaux available?"

Rachel stopped for a minute and thought before responding. "No, she's not in at the moment." It was no one's business that Chris had stepped out to the ladies' room. "Is there a message?"

"Yes, this is Trey Withers, her daughter's father. Can you give her this phone number?" Trey gave Rachel a local number. "Tell her I'll be awaiting her call."

"I sure will." Just as she laid the pen down, Chris walked in. "Your private line rang." Rachel's English was impeccable. "It was a Mr. Withers. Here's his number."

Chris took a look at the number. "Wait a minute. This is a local number. He's here?"

"I guess so. He really didn't say, though."

Chris, after having one of the most difficult presentations of her career, knew that the last thing she needed was a call from the shit-starter. She took the note and placed it in her pocket. "Thank you, Rachel. You can go home if you want. I know I am after I return this call."

Apprehensive about leaving her boss alone, Rachel replied, "I need to clear away the board room and put some other things away. I'll wait on you. Hope you've got your umbrella. It looks like it's going to pour down any minute now."

"I think I do have one in the car. I'll be ready in a little bit, okay?"

"Okay."

Chris, sorting through the papers on her desk and passing over several copies of her resume, quickly found a clean sheet of paper, so she could take notes from the shit-starter. "Bonjour, parlez-vous anglais?"

"Yes, Ma'am."

"May I have Trey Withers's room, please?"

"One moment."

❧♥❧

Trey sat on his bed, reading through the *The Black Man's Guide to Being a Better Father* that he now considered to be his bible. For three months, Trey had read each page from front to back hoping to improve his relationship with his daughter. He knew that he hadn't been a good father up to this point and wanted to try to make up for it. It was going to be hard to play catch-up, so Trey felt it might be a good idea to share custody for a while. Maybe Chris would entertain the thought since it might actually give her a break every once in a while.

"Trey?"

"Yes, this is me."

"What do you need?" Chris had nothing to say to him. He'd stayed away for over half of Chelsea's life, and Chris preferred that it stay that way.

Trey, taken aback by Chris's abruptness, replied, "I want to see Chelsea."

"Okay, but why did you come here? I would've met you in D.C."

"I just wanted to see how everything was going."

He was lying, and Chris knew it. "I don't believe that, and you know it. Cut straight to the chase."

"Why do you always have such an attitude?"

"Trey, I don't really have an attitude with you. I'm just a little peeved at the thought of you coming here out of nowhere demanding to see Chelsea like I've kept you away from her." Pausing for a moment, Chris heard a woman's voice in the background but made nothing of it.

"Can you hold on for a moment?"

"Sure." *No he didn't bring a woman over here*, she thought.

Trey kept Chris on hold for over a minute. "I'm back."

"Uh-huh."

"Look, I don't want to argue. Can we get together and talk?"

"Where are you?"

Trey hesitated. "Um, well, I was thinking maybe I could come to you."

Tapping her nails against the desk, Chris replied, "Okay, Trey." She gave him the address and told him to ask the hotel's concierge for directions. When Chris picked the girls up from school, she immediately told them that once they got home, they needed to make sure their rooms were clean. She also wanted them to keep on their school clothes and to make sure that their hair was neat. "Chelsea, your daddy is in town to see you," she said as she unlocked the front door.

Chelsea looked like she didn't understand what her mother had just said. "What, Mommy?"

"I said your daddy is in town to see you. He'll be here shortly."

"Okay but..."

"But what?"

"Do I have to go anywhere with him? I mean I want you to go with us."

"Sweetie, I don't know what he's going to want to do. Just be your usual wonderful self and that will be fine."

"Okay, Mommy."

Chris looked out her bedroom window and saw a taxi pull up to her door. *There's the shit-starter now.* The doorbell rang.

"Hey," Trey said reluctantly as Chris opened the door.

"Hey," Chris responded. "Wipe your feet, please." Chris knew she had to change her attitude before one of the girls detected it. "Let me take your coat." She took his coat and hung it in the front closet. "Would you like something to drink? We just got in, so I haven't started cooking yet."

As he checked the house out, Trey answered, "I'm good."

Good, I didn't want to get shit for your tired ass anyway. Turning her chair to face Trey, Chris took a seat at the desk and crossed her legs. She was glad that Trey had to see her super sharp—just in from work—so he could observe what he'd missed out on. "Before I call her down here, I need to know what your intentions are."

Adjusting himself on the sofa, Trey asked, "What do you mean?" He'd aged a little with a few gray strands in his beard.

"Just what I said. What do you want?"

He pulled out his "bible." "I want to strengthen my relationship with my daughter."

"Okayyyy."

"I want to be a part of her life."

Slightly agitated, Chris sat swinging her leg back and forth. "You're acting as if you've never had that option. You're the one who's chosen to stay away. I've written letters to you, made phone calls, and you've done nothing in return. She's asked me several times about you, but I truly believe that she felt that she was obligated to do so."

"I wasn't ready."

"You weren't ready?"

"No, I wasn't."

Chris was aware of the many Christmas presents that Chelsea had been given by Trey's family, but because he was pissed off with Chris, Trey never sent them. "One problem I see in this whole thing is that you take your anger with me out on Chelsea."

"I don't."

"You do, and you have. Did you bring all of those

old Christmas presents with you?" Chris was never going to tell him that his sister called Chelsea on a regular basis.

"They're at home. I'll send them when I..."

"Don't bother. She hasn't missed them, and I'm sure that she's outgrown most of them anyway."

Trey wanted to go ahead and get this over with. "I'm engaged."

"So."

"So? That's all you've got to say?"

"Oh, my bad. Congratulations. Is she here with you?" Chris already knew the answer to that.

"As a matter of fact, she is."

Chris was livid. "How the hell can you come here to spend time with your daughter when you've brought some woman with you?"

"She's never been to Paris, and I thought this would be a good time for her to meet Chelsea."

"You don't even know Chelsea."

"Chris, would you please just hear me out!" Trey demanded angrily.

"Trey, you have nothing else to say worth my time. Let me get your daughter for you."

"Wait a minute. I want to run one more thing past you. I want joint custody."

"Go to hell, Trey. If you ever make any attempt to make me look like a bad mother, I'll make you pay for it."

"I'm just asking for equal time with her."

"So you can create this façade that you're the perfect father just to impress whoever she is?"

Trey tried not to raise his voice. "You moved across the globe and never asked me how I felt about it."

"I didn't give a shit how you felt about it, and I still don't."

"Will you just think about it?"

Chris had a counteroffer. "I tell you what. Up her child support $150, and I'll do it." Even if she agreed to the custody arrangement, Chris knew that Trey wasn't going to stick to it.

"It's always about money with you."

"This isn't about money. It's about the fact that you've gotten away with paying $200 in child support from day one, and you know that you can afford more than that."

Looking around the living room, Trey commented, "Hell, you make enough money. I ain't giving you any more than the $200 unless you give me a receipt. If we need to go to court, then…"

"Fine." Chris had made up her mind. "Do whatever makes you happy. I'm done with it."

The day was going nowhere near what Trey had planned. He was eager to show Chris that he was trying to change. "Chris, I've been reading this book."

Pouring herself a glass of wine, Chris interrupted, "I

know you aren't going to sit there and tell me you've been reading a book on how to fix this mess you've created?"

"Well, it..."

"Please don't. I don't want to hear it. Let me get Chelsea for you."

Chris called Chelsea downstairs, and she looked just as her mother had hoped... like she wasn't needing for shit! Trey walked to her and gave her a hug and a kiss. Taking her by the hand, he guided Chelsea over to a seat next to him. For a brief moment, she was glad to see him. She smiled and played. But as soon as Chelsea saw her mother preparing to leave the room to give them their privacy, Chelsea quickly pulled away. "Mommy, where are you going?"

"Honey, I'm just going to change my clothes and to check on your sister, and I'll be right upstairs, okay?"

Chelsea didn't like that at all. "Okay."

❧♥❧

Trey returned from Chris's house just in time for dinner. Deana had already ordered room service for them. "I thought it'd be a good idea to have dinner in the room tonight, so we could have a chance to talk." She took his coat off his shoulders and put it in the closet. Deana was a petite woman with more attitude than Chris had, but unlike Chris, she never gave any of it to Trey. He loved her for that. Having no children of her own, Deana was especially anxious to meet Chelsea but knew that it wasn't going to be easy getting past Chris. "How'd it go?"

One thing Trey realized was that he still had feelings for Chris. He didn't know if they were good or bad feelings, but he was absolutely certain that they were there. "I don't really want to talk about it. Chelsea was, of course, a joy to see, but her mother was a different story."

"What did you expect?" Deana asked. "You probably walked in there expecting her to forgive you for being absent all this time. I know I'd definitely be pissed with you."

"Deana, I don't expect her to forget how I've been over the years. All I'm asking for is a chance. I told her about the engagement."

"Why? That's not the reason you came over here. You shouldn't have even been discussing me and you."

Trey was frustrated. "I don't know why I told her. I guess I wanted to see what her reaction was going to be."

Deana smirked. "If she's like you say she is, she didn't care."

"All she said was congratulations."

"You were wrong for that. This trip was supposed to be about your daughter."

"Well, we talked about that, too, and she's not going for joint custody."

"I wouldn't either, Trey. I told you that you were asking for too much too soon. That little girl hardly knows you."

"It didn't stop her for asking for more child support. Can you believe that she wants more money? You should see her house!"

Deana knew that Trey was immature, but this was ridiculous. "Let it go. You should've agreed to give her more money, so that she can continue to provide for your child. Hell, it's not going to kill you."

"Nope, I'm not doing it."

Deana got up and prepared a place setting for Trey at the tiny table by their bed. "I hope while you're reading that book you don't skip over the chapter about respecting your child's mother. She's done a hellified job with those girls and has done pretty well for herself given the circumstances she could face with her lifestyle and all. I hate the fact that you brought me to her on a garbage-can lid because I really would have liked to have met her."

Trey didn't know what he wanted. Deana Bettis had become the love of his life because she loved him dearly and had no great expectations of him. She was fine with Trey being a flight attendant but not satisfied with his distant relationship with his daughter. Deana was raised in a single-parent home and knew about the trauma and the drama a child in that situation could possibly face. Deana and her father were very close which was mostly due to her mother and father being really good friends with a mutual respect for one another. Chris and Trey were far from that. He hated Chris, but he loved her. "Let's have dinner. I really don't want to talk about Chris right now."

Deana didn't press the issue. "Okay, baby, we don't have to talk about it."

❧♥❧

As the sun glared through the blinds, Chris lay there and wondered what else could happen in her life. Amil was gone. Chris had changed her email address and made it a point to stay away from the computer whenever she was at home. Iysha wasn't speaking to her; Darcy, at some point, had to have been tired of hearing Chris and Trey stories; and Rudy's shoulder was too far away to cry on. Chris was going to have to carry this one alone. After dropping the girls off at school, Chris called in sick.

Rachel knew her boss wasn't sick and wondered if there was anything she could do. "I don't know much about what's going on, but I am a good listener."

"Merci beaucoup, Rachel, but I'm fine. I just need a little down time."

"Okay, I understand. A woman was by here to see you this morning. She didn't leave her name."

"Well, she must not have wanted anything. Oh well, I'll talk with you tomorrow."

"Au revoir."

❧♥❧

Chris couldn't make sense out of anything. *Why is this man here? What does he want from my life? Why did he have to come all the way here to tell me he's getting married? Why do I care?* Ding-dong.

Just as she snuggled comfortably in the right spot and buried herself far beneath the covers, she heard the faint sound of her doorbell but had no intention of answering it. No one but Rachel knew she was home. Ding-dong. Chris took her pillow and covered her head and ears with hopes that whoever the agitator was would go away. Ding-dong. Ding-dong. Ding-dong. Ding-dong. Dinga-ding-dong!

"Damn! Who is it?!!" Chris screamed out of her window.

"It's Deana."

"Deana?" *Who the hell is Deana?* "And you are?"

"Trey's fiancee."

Shit. Why is this happening to me, Lawd? What did I do? Why is she here? How does she know where I live? Trey's ass is forever trying to start some shit.

Before Chris could open her mouth, Deana blurted, "I know I'm wrong for being here, and trust me, he'd kill me if he ever found out. But I had to do this before you got the wrong impression of me."

Chris was in an oversized pair of men's boxer shorts, decorated with a rainbow elastic band, and had on a rainbow-laden tank top to match when she opened the door. She had on a pair of white socks with her favorite black Fila shower shoes. Her hair was pulled back in a ponytail with a rainbow clasp holding it together. She looked like a dyke straight from the Pride of Paris. "You're right. You're really wrong for being here." Chris opened the door and asked Deana in.

"He's still in bed. I got your address from his pocket."

Oh, she's a creeper, Chris thought. *My kinda girl.* Chris went into the kitchen to put on a pot of coffee, since she obviously wasn't going to be able to go back to bed. "Do you drink coffee?"

"Yes, all the time. Trey hates it, though."

"He'll be all right." Chris pulled a small blanket from a decorative trunk she used as a coffee table and took a seat on the sofa. "What's up, Deana? Why have you taken this huge chance in coming over here unannounced? I'm quite sure Trey has told you all about me and my infamous attitude."

Deana took off her jacket and reclined in the chair. "He *has* told me a lot about you. Seems like almost too much sometimes. It hasn't been all bad, though."

"That's a surprise."

"Now, don't get me wrong. He's said some rough stuff, but as a product of a single-parent home, I draw the line when it comes to certain language about the other parent."

"I guess he told you I was gay. That is, if you hadn't already guessed it by my colorful attire."

"He did, but that's your business. I've never wanted to discuss that with him. I came over here to let you know that I didn't come to Paris with him to make you feel bad but to help him make amends with you and Chelsea."

The coffee had finished brewing, and Chris got up to pull mugs from the dishwasher. "Cream and sugar?"

Deana was taken aback by Chris's house. Trey was right. It was gorgeous. "Yes, please. Chris, you have a beautiful home."

"Thank you." Chris handed Deana her coffee and sat the cream and sugar on the table next to her. "If you call waltzing in here demanding joint custody after over six years of being gone a way of making amends, then…"

"He told me what happened, and I didn't agree with him one bit." Deana daintily sipped from her mug and placed it on its saucer. "What do you want from Trey?"

"Not shit. I just threw the child support in his face as a matter of principle."

"I want to see him and Chelsea have a better relationship."

Well, do you now? Chris had to catch herself before she clicked. "Has Trey not told you about his track record with me and this playing daddy thing?"

"No."

"The girls and I lived in Philly for a little over two years. We were all of maybe two hours from him. He'd call and say that he was on his way, but he'd never show. One weekend Darcy and I drove the girls to D.C. to visit the zoo. He met us there but only stayed for about an hour. Then another time he met us down on the Mall for the kite-flying thing they have every year. He was pretty cool there—I guess because we were doing kids' stuff. A month later he was supposed to come to Philly for her birthday party; yet again, he didn't show. As long as it's convenient for him, he might participate, and that's not fair to my child. Trey's got to be consistent. If not, she's better off without him."

Deana obviously didn't know the whole story. "I'm shocked. I wouldn't expect that from him."

"Me either."

"So what do you need me to do to help make this situation better for everybody?"

Chris couldn't believe what she was hearing. This woman was acting like all she needed to do was put a big Band-Aid on the situation and everything would miraculously improve. "Deana, please don't take offense to this, but I'm trying to figure out why you're here and not Trey."

"I just want to help."

"You know what you can tell Trey?" Chris inquired. "You can tell him to leave us the hell alone."

Surprisingly, Deana wasn't offended. "I can understand why you feel that way, but I don't think that's going to happen. He's really serious about this."

"Deana, dear. Please do us, especially me, a favor and stay out of it."

Respecting Chris's wishes, Deana backed off and got her jacket. "I wish you could see him when he's trying to do the right thing," she said, approaching the door. "I really think he means it this time."

Chris, finishing off the last of her coffee, assured Deana that her visit hadn't been in vain. Given all the gloom that loomed over her personal life, the last thing Chris wanted to do was to start more drama. "I tell you what. I'll consider some visitation, but I'm keeping sole custody. I still want the child support, though. It's only $150. If we go to court about it, they're going to hit his ass up harder than that for it." Chris wasn't worried about Trey and his antics because, whether the visitation be on paper or not, he wasn't going to stick to it.

"I will. Can Chelsea and your other daughter have lunch or dinner with us before we leave? I'm a firm believer in doing for both…not just one."

"Sure, they can." Chris felt that someone had to be the bigger person, and she wasn't going to be outdone by her ex's new woman. "Deana, thank you for coming by. Trey's a lucky man. It was nice talking with you."

Smiling, Deana replied, "Thanks for the coffee."

❧♥❧

Saturday afternoon was the perfect time for the girls to be away. It gave Chris an opportunity to do some shopping and to get her house clean. She took in a movie and returned some phone calls to her family. Ora was especially surprised when she heard about Trey's visit. "'Bout damn time he came around. Hell, that baby would've graduated from high school and still not known who he was. Now, Chris, you didn't act a fool with him, did you?"

"Not really. Just made some things clear." Chris was holding something back. Trey had asked her how she felt about him. He wanted to know that if things had been different, would they still be together. "Momma?"

"What?"

"Trey wanted to know how I felt about him."

Ora exclaimed, "Does he not know when to quit? Didn't you say that he was over there with another woman?"

"Yeah, he is here with someone else, and she seems to be really good for him."

"What did you tell him?"

Before Gayle died, she'd asked Chris how she felt about her. Chris had been brutally honest, and she'd treated Trey no differently. "I told him I couldn't stand him, but with my lifestyle and all, I don't understand why. I surely don't want him. I also told him that I was pissed with him for not being a better father than what he has been, and that it was going to take a while for me to get over it. My feelings for him should be moot at this point because his focus should be Chelsea. I further explained to him that I'm gay. Although I'm far from a man-hater, I have no interest in any intimate feelings toward any man."

"I bet that didn't go over well."

"It might as well have. We can work on a friendship for Chelsea's sake but nothing else. I mean, I think this girl really likes him."

"She must if she came over to your house like that."

"I suppose. Look, Momma, I want to get off this phone, so I can enjoy what little time I have left. Can you do me a favor, though?"

"Yes."

"Tell Iysha hey and that I love her."

"Will do. Kiss those babies for me. Bye-bye."

THIS IS WHO I AM

"Mommy?"

"What, baby?" Chris answered, sipping on a cup of espresso while reading through her mail. She'd just gotten in from a long day at work.

"Are you a dyke?" Chelsea asked harmlessly. Gaylon stopped playing with her Barbie dolls, anticipating a serious tongue-lashing or slap across the mouth for Chelsea from her mother.

Now choking on her beverage, Chris managed to ask, "Where did you get that word from?" Never raising her voice as Gaylon had expected, Chris put her mail aside and continued, "That's a pretty harsh word for someone your age to be using." Chris was calm as she took a seat in her favorite chair.

Embarrassed but desperately curious, Chelsea responded, "I got it from my daddy. He said you were...well, um...you know."

"A dyke." Chris realized that this was what had been bothering her daughter. Since Trey's visit, Chelsea had been withdrawn and moody, retreating to her bedroom as soon as she got home from school. A peacefulness had fallen upon Chelsea's eyes, and the sadness that had been in her smile had lifted.

Relieved, Chelsea confidently replied, "Yes, a dyke."

Determined to stick to what she'd always said about telling her children about her sexuality, Chris didn't hesitate to answer Chelsea's question. Before starting, Chris gestured for Gaylon to come and sit on her lap. "Come on, Li'l Mama, you're old enough to hear this, too." Chelsea climbed on to her mother's chaise lounge and stretched out across Chris's legs. "First, I don't like the word dyke. Some people do, but I don't. I'm a lesbian."

"A what?" Gaylon giggled.

"A lesbian."

"What does that do?" Gaylon asked. Chris wondered if Gaylon was ready for this. Quickly, she thought of a way to break it down into kiddie terms for the girls. There was no need to complicate the issue.

"You remember the talk we had about the birds and the bees?"

"Ewwww, I remember," said Chelsea.

"This is kinda the same, but there is no man. It's actually two women making love and going through almost the same things as men and women do."

"So you're gay?" Chelsea questioned.

Chris was floored. "And how do you know that word? Let me guess. Your daddy told you."

Blushing, Chelsea said, "Actually, I saw it on TV. They were talking about it on this kids' show."

Shit. "And what else did you learn?"

"Oh, well, I learned that gay people can be men or women and that they have sex with members of the same sex."

Double shit. "I see. Did you tell your father about this show?"

"No, but besides calling you a dyke, he said some other pretty mean things."

"And how do you feel about those things?"

As she peered toward the ceiling, Chelsea responded, "Pretty bad, I guess. He's never really been around for me, but you have. He never calls, but you're always here for me. I know that you two don't get along, but in my own way, I can understand why. I've been unhappy these last few weeks because he called you out of your name. Despite how angry he's made you, I've never heard you say anything mean about him."

Chris knew better. Trey had been all kinds of sons-a-bitches and MFs for as long as she could remember. She'd just been careful not to let Chelsea hear it. She fessed up. "Baby, I've said some nasty things about your father, but I just didn't discuss them with you. I'm angry, though, that you had to hear something like this from someone other than me."

"Mommy, I've known for a quite a while. I just figured that you'd tell us when you thought we were ready to know."

Chris's heart warmed as she looked upon Chelsea

and Gaylon attached to almost every part of her body. "I was waiting until one of you asked me. There was no need to burden you with a lot of big-people stuff. You need to be focusing on being a child and enjoying it."

Chelsea looked puzzled. " I have another question," she interjected.

"Sounds serious."

"What about Auntie Rudy?"

Triple shit. She knew it was coming. It was just a matter of when. "Um, Auntie Rudy is a different subject altogether. I don't want to touch that today."

As she gripped her mother's thighs with all her might, Chelsea said, "I love you no matter who you love. Just as long as you're happy."

Gaylon turned around and grabbed her mother's head and planted a big, sloppy kiss on her cheek. "I love you, too, Mommy, but I have a question."

"Oh, you do?" Chris asked playfully.

"Yes." She giggled. "Can we still go to Disney World?"

Chris pulled Gaylon to her and began tickling her underarms. "Sure, baby, we can still go to Disney World."

When Chris arrived at work the next morning, she was so damn mad she could spit fire. *How dare he tell my baby that?* It wasn't his place to say a word about it. Since her brief meeting with Deana, Chris had decided that it was time to push aside the bullshit and be an adult; therefore, she refrained from calling Trey and cussing his ass out.

Two months had passed since Chris had first considered applying for the position of University President. Her boss had encouraged her to do it, and so had every other administrator on staff. The job required a lot of extra time that she wasn't prepared to give because of her commitment to the girls. It also would keep her tied to the office, and she wouldn't be able to hop on a plane anytime she felt like it and show up in Memphis. But as she thought about the emptiness in her life, Chris reconsidered. She could make time for Chelsea and Gaylon—that's a perk in being the HBIC, Head Bitch In Charge. Hell, she was able to drop everything in a split second to attend to the girls' needs now. Chris had never missed a classroom party, a play or a recital. She was there when Gaylon first jumped off the diving board, and she was there when Chelsea gave a speech on the history of United States government. All of this with two classes shy of having her Ph.D. Chris had herself together professionally, but emotionally, she was quietly a wreck. More work would leave less time for anyone else but her daughters, so she typed up a cover letter and had Rachel to forward it, with her resume, to the university's Board of Trustees.

"Chris?"

"Yes, ma'am," Chris responded, never looking up from her computer.

"There's a call for you on line one. It's Amil."

"I'm not in."

"Are you sure?"

Although she meant well, Rachel's line of questioning sometimes got out of hand. "What part of that is confusing to you?" Chris snapped and turned her attention to the bookshelf behind her desk.

"Okay." Rachel couldn't resist. "Are you going to always be out when she calls? You haven't talked to her any of the times she's phoned."

"Rachel, if you want me to tell you that I don't want to talk to her, then fine, I will, but I've always thought you were astute enough to read between the lines. No, I don't want to talk to her when she calls."

"Okay." Rachel remembered a time when she was reprimanded for not putting Dr. Lindsay's calls through quick enough, and now she was getting a severe tongue-lashing for trying to do so. "Dr. Lindsay?"

Chris never skipped a beat after chewing Rachel out. As a matter of fact, Chris worked well into the evening, managing to return a week's worth of phone calls and emails. She was hurting but refused to ever let the rest of the world know it.

CUNNILINGUS 101 (I TOLD YOU SO!)

Rudy stood in the doorway shaking her head in disbelief. Removing her sunglasses with the left tip of the arm stuck between her crimson red lips, she touted, “What am I going to do with you? So beautiful but always so unlucky with love.”

Chris let her pass and then jetted to the curbside to pay the taxi driver. “Please don’t start with me, Rudy.” She sighed as she headed back into the foyer. She’d flown Rudy to Paris to go over the books from The Closet and was hoping to explore the possibility of making Rudy a partner instead of merely an employee. But Chris had to make sure that Rudy had her head on straight; it wouldn’t take too long to find that out. “Sorry I couldn’t pick you up from the airport. I’ve been busy.”

Rudy saw all of the papers strewn about the room as well as tons of dry cleaning that needed to go out. Apparently, Chris had never made it to her bedroom because all of her suits and lingerie were piled up on the end of the sofa.

“Got pussy on the brain, I see,” Rudy sassed.

Sighing again, Chris asked, "What are you talking about, Rudy?" She plopped down on the sofa and rested against her pile of laundry.

Rudy strutted around the room running her white-gloved fingertips through the dust on the mantle, shaking her head at the stacks of dirty dishes on the coffee table.

"Didn't I ever tell you?"

"Tell me what?"

"The cardinal rule of being a lesbian." She laughed. "Don't be lickin' on no straight woman. She'll fuck your head up every time." Rudy put her purse down and untied the scarf from around her chin that covered her fresh French roll. "More appropriately, it's Cunnilingus 101."

"Girl, you're a trip. It wasn't even like that. Amil *really* does like me."

"Okay, and that's why she *really* married Manney."

Chris lugged Rudy's Louis Vuitton bags to the guest-room and shoved them across the floor, wishing to escape Rudy's interrogation. She continued what she thought were elusive movements, but Rudy was switching right behind her. She'd arrived in town like Josephine Baker reincarnated. Tight key-lime dress hugging the curves of her sculpted body like a 1969 Harley-Davidson Easy Rider grabbing the esses of a narrow mountainside road; scarf tied around her face reminiscent of Jackie Kennedy during her days in Camelot, and drenched in the finest perfume that money could buy. In her six-inch heels, she towered above Chris and was able to look downward without obstruction into her friend's sullen eyes. "I'm sorry. I shouldn't have said that."

Chris buried her head into Rudy's bosom, and although the pain was great, she refused to shed another tear. A hug was all that she needed. "Don't worry about it. I should've known it was coming."

"They all just devils. Wanting their needs taken care of at the expense of someone else's. She was prowling; you know that, right?"

"She's called me several times since the wedding. I don't have anything to say to her."

"Good."

"I guess the best thing about being in this funky-I-don't-wanna-be-around-the-rest-of-the-world mood is that I've been able to get some stuff done around the house. I mean, it obviously could stand a little tidying up, but..." Abruptly changing the subject as she looked at the piles of dishes and clothes, she asked, "Did I tell you that I came out to the girls?"

Stopping dead in her tracks, Rudy commented, "Knowing them smart ass babies, they probably told you all about yourself, and, yes, my dear, your house is junky," Rudy observed. "Ain't your ass like borderline mega-rich? I mean, you can't get some half-French, half-Mexican muthafucka to come clean this house? *Ah-choo!* This dust is makin' my asthma act up!" She sniffled.

"Rudy, asthma doesn't make you sneeze." Chris chuckled.

"Whateva the hell...it's making me sneeze in this bitch. *Ah-choo!* Oh, my Jesus, I need some tissue." Sitting on the sofa, wiping her nose with a silk handkerchief she pulled from her purse, Rudy asked, "Now, what were you saying about coming out to the girls?"

"Actually, it was Trey's black ass that referred to me as a dyke. The conversation went on from there from what I understand." Chris rose from her seat and wiped off the mantle with a damp paper towel that had been sitting underneath a sweating glass of ice water, feeling a tad bit paranoid after Rudy's comments.

"How'd they take it? And by the way, what you just did with that paper towel was triflin'!"

"Everybody's cool with it. My babies and I talked, and although they seem to know what gay means, there are some things I know they're not ready for."

"Such as?" Rudy asked, batting her eyelashes.

"Their minds are not mature enough to understand the likes of you. I mean, I told them to respect you for being true to yourself."

"Seems like you had a chore and a half on your hands. Some folks would tell their kids about me as if I were some God-awful person."

"Unh-unh. No, I didn't. I ain't tellin' them shit like that right now. Damn kids would be on a couch in a minute trying to tell some shrink about how their Auntie Rudy fucked up their lives. You ain't trying to get with nobody's husband or anything like that. You're just being you, and I respect you for that. When the time is right, I'm not going to mind telling them one single thing about you."

Rudy took Chris by the arm and pulled her out onto the veranda. "From what I could tell through the filth, you done hooked this dirty bitch up! You should bring your depressing ass back to Memphis and work some miracles on your condo."

"Well, that was what I was trying to do before a friend of mine moved into it!"

"Oh, hell, here we go. Well, then, moving right along. Where da clubs at?"

Chris was amazed at how refined Rudy could be, and in a split second without warning, when she wanted to, she could just as easily remind you that she put both *t's* in the word *ghetto* and the *O* on the end for good measure.

"There are quite a few along the Champs-Élysées, but let's go get some food first. Unpack your shit, and I'll go get dressed."

"Not so fast. Where the girls?"

"With my assistant. She has two little girls about the same age as my two. They'll be with her until Monday. So that gives us plenty of time to hang out and to get some business taken care of." Chris had an opening where she could now spring the partnership thing on Rudy. "Before we do that, though, I want to ask you something."

Caught completely by surprise, Rudy kept her seat. "Ask me what?"

"How are you doing? I mean, with the club and everything, you rarely have time for yourself."

Rudy, brushing the lint from her lap, gave a sly grin. "It's under control, and so am I. I thought I might lose it for a minute, especially after Nathaniel was let go. But I regrouped. As you'll see, we didn't lose any money or anything like that, but a lot of people missed him...her...whatever. I auditioned some new talent and hired a couple of new bartenders. I added some new rules. One which I think you'll like."

"And what's that?"

"No gospel performances."

Chris cut her eyes at Rudy. "You've been allowing the queens to do gospel songs?"

"There was only one or two. The crowd started responding to it pretty decently. I mean, they did some Kirk Franklin stuff and some Patti stuff, but then after Devine did Tramaine's "A Wonderful Change Has Come Over Me," it was all downhill. It was like complete silence after she got through. I thought maybe it was because folks were speechless because she sounded so good. But it wasn't that. The words really fucked people up. Don't get me wrong. Devine's shit was tight now, but the timing just wasn't right."

"Seems like you made a good decision without having to consult me."

Rudy joked, "I didn't want to hear your damn mouth, and besides, I wasn't that all right with it in the first place. Anyway, that's that."

"No, it's not. I want to talk to you about something else relating to the club."

Puzzled by Chris's tone, Rudy inquired, "What's wrong?"

"Nothing's wrong. I want to know if you'd be interested in being my partner in The Closet. I mean, you've gotten things in order, and you've become quite a businesslady. You've helped the club get the respect it deserves."

Blown away, Rudy replied, "I don't know what to say. Partner?"

"Partner. Basically, half of my interest in the club is now yours if you want it."

No one had ever taken a chance like this on Rudy. "Are you sure?"

"I'm positive. I don't trust anyone but you to do this. I'm swamped over here, and I know you won't let me down. Besides, I only signed on to help you out, and this is my way of saying, 'Job well done.' You don't need to do anything but say yes."

"I'll do it."

"Good." Chris smiled as she pulled out a stack of papers. "Sign here. Fifty-percent of the profits will be transferred to you in the morning." Little did Rudy know, but a tremendous burden had been lifted from Chris.

Rudy took a breath for her next question because there was a likelihood that she was going to get cussed out. "You been thinkin' about her, ain't you?"

"Not as much as I used to. Mainly because I've kept myself so busy. The girls have been wonderful. We took a trip to London last month for some shopping, and we're going to Italy later this month."

"Must be fuckin' nice! Hell, the only way folks back home know how to unwind is to go across the state line to drop a coupla hundred at the casino."

"True," Chris agreed.

Rudy, always the wise one, gave Chris a few consoling words. "You've been through a lot of shit and have pulled through like a champ. I just want you to finally be happy. You've been so caught up in trying to make everybody else's dreams come true that you've tossed your own shit aside. I hate to see you in all this pain, but now that I see that you're doing better and have put this woman behind you, I can now honestly and truthfully say this."

"Say what?"

Rudy winked. "I told you so."

EVERYBODY PLAYS A FOOL...SOMETIMES

Dearest Chris,

When we were growing up, people always referred to us as being as different as night and day. I was ever the quiet one who would occasionally mutter a word or two. I had that sly but shy grin that was so often overshadowed by your wit and amiable personality. You could do anything you put your mind to and was always good at it. And sma-r-r-rt! You were so smart that even your best friends hated you. They knew they couldn't compete with you so they dissed you. Now that you Ms. Money and shit—a woman 'bout bidness, all those playa-haters are saying, "Oh, I know her. We went to school together." They don't mention that they used to put red food coloring in your seat whenever you wore those too-little ass white pants you had or that they booed you when your name was called for the 20th time at the Honors Day Program. I hate people like that. I am most upset with myself, however, for not defending you when people talked about you even when those people called themselves family. Since I'm telling shit, I might as well admit that it was me who tore up the letter you got from that famous news reporter. Jealous? I was. I got tired of people telling me that they'd heard my sister's name on the evening news. I guess now that you know the truth you're going to be ready to give me that ass whipping you promised me if you'd ever found out that I'd had anything to do with the letter's mysterious disappearance. You should have picked better role models, Chris. That lady ended up having a really bad drinking problem. Her husband left her with all the bills and this monstrous house in Germantown that she couldn't pay for. I think she's still in and out of rehab. You sure knew how to pick'em. Even though you have the strangest ways of doing it, I know that you've always done whatever was necessary to protect me—like the time you told Momma that you were the one who was burning matches in our bedroom closet and throwing the burnt matches in my tennis shoes. She lit your ass up for that one. Then there was the time that I brought home those condoms from school and left them in your room. When Momma found them in her precious honor student's dresser drawer, I thought it'd be near your high school graduation before you got off punishment. I have to laugh, though, because had we known then what we know now, those three months of your life would have been a little more pleasant, don't you think?

You probably don't know this, but I know why you told Momma and Daddy about that man molesting you when we were little. One day after school I was in the kitchen getting a drink of water from the refrigerator. I was trying to sneak and drink straight from the bottle to keep from having to dirty up a cup that I had no desire to wash. And you know how only Big Mama supposedly drank out of that juice jar in the freezer? I drank out of it, too, whenever I could. It was like she kept the temperature just low enough to keep the glass from freezing up and bustin' open. I always opened both sides of that "side-by-side" refrigerator and stood right smack in the middle and guzzled away. But that day when I closed those doors, "he" was standing right there with this look on his face: the kind of look that a ravenous hyena gives a lion cub who has wandered away from its mother's watchful eye. I moved around the table and made my way to the sink. It was closest to the back door, and, at that moment, it was my only way out. But then, "he" started trying to corner me by pushing the kitchen table toward the doorway leading in to the hall. Realizing that exit was the only other way for me to escape, I hastily darted for the back door. I thought that "he" might be just playing around until "he" lunged at me from the other side of that island that Big Mama had sitting in the middle of the floor. "He" was too old to climb over it, and I was too scared and frail to try and push it on him.

As I backed into the hot stove desperately trying to get away from him, I bore the heat and eventual burns from the cast iron pot full of greens. Had you not walked in, I would have picked up that pot and tossed it—fatback, water, and all—at his ass. The look on your face was one that I'd never forget because I knew that you had then reached your limit with him. I knew about him touching on you because you stayed away from him no matter what the cost. In the dead of winter, you'd sit on the porch so as to not be in the same house with him, and I watched you damn near fall out from heat exhaustion in the summertime while trying to play outside all day until Momma picked us up. I used to see him try to take your hand and place it between his legs, and I'd watch him slide you five-dollar bills for kissing him on his dingy ass cheek. Chris, when you walked into the kitchen that day, you saved my life. I know that it must be pure torture to have to live with the memory of that nasty old bastard putting his hands on you. I guess you finally told Momma and Daddy because you wanted to protect me from him, and what you don't know is that I cried for you in my room the day they made you go to his funeral.

When I met Nathaniel, I noticed that he had a lot of sway in his seemingly manly way. His high-pitched voice, the way he batted his eyes. His wrist was so broken that he probably should have kept a cast on it. His wardrobe and taste in clothes were impeccable. I don't think that I ever saw him in the same thing twice. I listened as the football players teased him in the cafeteria and watched them turn over his tray every single day. I started packing two lunches every morning and shared one of them with him during our study hall period after lunch. Despite the other just down-right, low-down things that used to get done to him, I was most hurt when I saw him bawl like a baby. His name was on the nomination list for Homecoming Queen, and, since it was the football team that had orchestrated it, Nathaniel won unanimously. The principal, Mr. Olsson and his geriatric ass, threatened to expel him if he didn't fulfill his duties as queen. The night of the game wasn't as bad as you'd think, though. Nathaniel gave his adversaries and hecklers what they'd asked for. Tashiba, Nathaniel's cousin from Little Rock, was in town with the cast of La Cage Aux Folles*—the ethnic version.*

Girlfriend was the cream of the crop when it came to make-up and costumes, and, when the producer approached her to do the make-up and wardrobe for the show, Tashiba commanded a pretty penny and also the title of Creative Director. She had heard what had happened at the school and called Nathaniel up with the quickness. "Baby, if they want a damn queen for that game, then we'll give'em one! And when I'm done with you, they'll all be on their knees givin' all praises to you. I promise you that!" And she ain't never lied. The football team expected Nathaniel to be booed and disgraced that night, but when he stepped foot on that field in Crump Stadium, you couldn't hear a thing…not a word. A satin train, carried by two male members of the production's cast, adorned his full-length white, sequined gown. Traditionally escorted to the sideline by the principal, Nathaniel gracefully extended his hand to Mr. Olsson and proceeded to claim his spot in the Queen's Court. The fans screamed and cheered as Nathaniel walked to mid-field, and they wholeheartedly gave my boy his props. His pompous ass commanded respect, and I be damned if he didn't get it. I guess that's how all this got started.

Respecting his privacy, I never asked him about his personal life. All I knew was that whenever I needed someone to listen, he did. Whenever I needed a shoulder to cry on, he gave me his. I knew that whenever I needed an opinion on what to wear to school, he was there. He knew what was best to wear in any season. After spending so much time with him, I realized that he was a lovable man if I just stayed away from his private life; and I guess, out of respect for me and my femininity, he never volunteered any information. Knowing all of this, I married him anyway.

A marriage of convenience was what it was at first. He needed money to pay for his escalating credit card bills, and I wanted out of Momma's house. He had his own place, so we combined the few personal assets we had and gave it a shot. The sex was good, but probably because I made myself believe it was. I can't remember a time when there was ever any passion in our lovemaking. Between you and me, I don't mind doing it doggy-style but not all the time like Nathaniel wanted. I even let him talk me into letting him stick it in my rectum, and I'd never seen or felt him cum like that before. After a while, it got to the point where he wanted his dick sucked at the drop of a hat. Like I said, I got a little freak in me every now and then, but something was wrong. He never cared about my needs or about my feelings. He spent hours in the bathroom jacking off, and, if I walked in on him, naturally I'd scared the shit out of him. To play it off, though, he asked me to help.

Then there were the days that he didn't want me anywhere near him. At first it was every once in a while, but then it became all the time. His second job was providing us with extra money to pay off bills and to do some things for the children. But once we paid off the bills and the children were more than provided for, he refused to quit that job. If he wasn't at either of his jobs, we all were in church—not really with a purpose, either. We were just there. It seemed that every other time we were there he had a testimony. Nathaniel confessed that he had sinned, but those sins never left his lips. I thought that maybe he was repenting because he'd been such a jackass to me just hours before or maybe even because he'd said a cuss word or two. But then later on, I realized what the problem was. Everything started making sense to me when I watched this documentary one night on HBO. It was about male prostitutes, hustlers, and all this stuff that had been going on in my house...in my life. It was then that his spontaneous trip to Santa Monica made sense to me.

A lot of people have teased me, including you, and some have even snickered when I've walked into a room with him. It was like they all were saying, "Damn, she's so stupid. How you ain't gonna know that niggah's a punk? Look at him!" But you see, I do know, and I've always known. Sometimes, however, it's just easier to play the fool. That's one reason why I've always quietly admired how you'd never let yourself be anybody's fool. And if you did, it was because you were blindsided and never saw it coming. Unlike me, you bounced back with a vengeance. I fight with my own demons about why Nathaniel still hasn't told me about his secret, but I am glad that you did. By the way, I want to thank you for my birthday present. I guess that you probably thought I was mad at you about it by the way you just left town afterwards. Well, I was pissed but not for what you think. I was mad because you left me here to deal with everything by myself. How could you do that to me, Chris? I needed your sense of humor and strength to get through this madness, and I still do. There is something else going on right now. Something even more pressing.

Max is sick. He has AIDS, and you're smart enough to figure out the rest. For years I thought it was asthma and maybe, even from to time, a cold, but Vicks, Robitussin, Triaminic, humidifiers—none of that stuff—ever worked. He's in the hospital now with pneumonia, and all I can do is just pray. Afraid that I'd miss his last breath, I haven't slept in weeks. Nathaniel hasn't been seen in about twice as long. Since he's been gone, bill collectors been calling me about all this money we owe. They've already taken his truck. Nathaniel knows about everything, but he still hasn't said a word to me. I didn't do anything to him, Chris. The doctors have been asking me a lot of questions about Max being sick with this, and the most baffling thing is that I don't have the virus. But I know who probably does.

Max has been asking for you whenever he's able to gather enough strength to speak. Here lately, though, that hasn't been too often.

Hug and kiss the girls for me, and we hope to see you soon.

All my love,

Iysha

WAKE-UP CALL

A midnight phone call to Chris was inevitable. Several days had passed since Iysha's letter had been mailed, and there still had been no response. She knew that Chris would be quite peeved with her for not calling her sooner. For over three months, Iysha had asked questions and begged for immediate answers concerning Max's illness. But no one had any.

The last time that she and Chris had spoken, an argument ensued and many hurtful things were said. Iysha knew that Chris had meant every word she'd said and had only been waiting for the right time to let it all go. Chris called Nathaniel a sissy, a punk, a queen, and anything else that came to mind. Hoping that her sister and her husband could be, at the very least, civil toward one another, Iysha concluded that they'd never be one big happy family. So, in order to respect her husband's house, she didn't call Chris nor did she ever mention her sister's name in front of her husband.

None of that drama mattered now to Iysha. She needed her sister more than she ever had before. Iysha, having confessed the real deal to Chris, was ready for anything and had to start facing the reality that her son was sick. With all the love that Chris had for Max, Iysha knew that her sister's heart was going to be broken… yet again.

"Hello," a scratchy voice answered. Awake since 4 a.m., Chris was up helping the girls get ready for their swimming lessons. Her throat was raw from sinus drainage, and once she'd gotten the girls off, she was praying for a short nap.

Holding back tears, Iysha took a deep breath. "Hey, Chris."

Chris was surprised to hear her sister's voice. Their last argument had been so tumultuous that Iysha had gone so far as to block Chris's phone number from the phone. Although she was aware that Nathaniel had been fucking men before and apparently during their marriage, Iysha had made a vow to him and to God. Despite the deception, she couldn't let him go. Chris, nonetheless, played off her anger and disappointment and played the martyr. "Iysha?"

"Yeah, it's me. Did you get my letter?" she said, sniffling. It wouldn't be long before the sniffles turned to sobs.

"I might have. As a matter of fact, I just picked up my mail from the post office. I'd had a hold on it for a few weeks while I was out of town. Ain't shit but bills anyway." Taken aback by her sister's tone, Chris stopped packing the children's gym bags. "What's wrong, Iysha? Is Momma okay?"

"Yes, she's fine. How are the girls?"

"Fine. Getting ready for swimming lessons."

"I see." Iysha thought it best that Chris read the letter because there was no way that she'd be able to articulate what was happening.

"Iysha, what's going on? You're upset about something. You're crying, and I know you. You've never called me crying." *Oooooh, if that mutherfucka has…*

Iysha regained her composure for a minute. "I'm at the hospital right now. Momma let me use her calling card to call you." A lot of noise was coming from the background where the nurses were changing shifts. By this time, Chris was restless.

"Iysha, what's going on? Who's in the hospital?"

There was no need to hold back. "Max."

"Max?" Chris heard the name reverberate through her head. "Is he hurt?"

"No. Did you get my letter?"

"I probably did, Iysha, but you've got me on the phone now, so tell me what's wrong?"

"He was positive and I didn't know."

"What?"

"He was HIV-positive; now it's progressed to AIDS."

Chris didn't need to ask from where, but she did. "From where?"

"They don't know."

"Where's Nathaniel?"

"I don't know. I haven't seen him in a while. He hasn't been sleeping at home for the past few months. He's called to check on the girls but never asks anything about Max."

In disbelief and anger, Chris responded, "Is that what this letter is about?"

"Yeah, but there's some other stuff in there, too. I wrote it after they gave me his test results. I wanted to scream but couldn't. I wanted to fight, but no one was around to punch. I wanted to cry, but I couldn't find the tears. So I sat down and wrote you that book." She laughed. It was the first time she'd been able to crack a smile in months.

"How is he?"

"Not good, Chris. Not good at all. His asthma was acting up a while back, but he recovered and seemed to be doing just fine. Then a week or so later this flu bug started going around. The girls had it, I had it, and Nathaniel had it. Max got it, too. Two weeks after that, Max still wasn't any better, but everybody else was fine. Nathaniel took him to the doctor and said that they'd given him a shot. A week later he was still having trouble breathing. They took X-rays and found some fluid on his lungs. The fluid was drained, and I took him home a few days later. Another week passed, and I saw that he had grown exceedingly frail. I could barely get him to eat a bowl of soup let alone anything else. Last week, I brought him in here because I found him in his closet having trouble breathing again."

"What kind of tests have they run?"

"All kinds, Chris. I can't stand to see all the shit they do to him."

"You're at LeBonheur?"

"Yes."

"Have they run any blood work?"

"Every day they're doing something."

"What kind of doctors have they got working with you?"

"Well, a pediatric HIV specialist is on his way over here. Hopefully, he'll be able to tell me how Max got this because I don't have it, and neither do the girls."

Chris hesitated. "What about your husband?"

Quickly changing the subject, Iysha said, "I don't know him like I used to. I need you to read that letter, though."

"I will as soon as I get off the phone. Look, I'm going to go ahead and try to get a flight out. The girls won't be able to come with me because school is in session now. I'll call my babysitter, and try to get on the next thing out of here. Where's Momma?"

"At home with the girls. She wanted to call you when he first got sick, but I told her that I wanted to do it. I knew that you should've gotten the letter some time ago, but I just assumed you didn't want to call me."

"Now, you know that's not the case. I wasn't here,

Sweetie. Let me get off this phone, so I can get some things done."

"Okay, I'll see you when you get here. Oh, and Chris?"

"Yes?"

"I love you."

That did it. The strength Chris was trying to have had left the room and the tears started flowing. "I love you, too."

The seven-hour time difference between Memphis and Paris gave Chris the opportunity to read her sister's letter over and over again. Chris had known for years about Nathaniel's trip to Santa Monica for its Black Pride Celebration, and she was ill with guilt about having harbored that secret. She'd been under the impression that he'd gone to perform on behalf of the club. Rudy had tried to tell Chris that, nine times out of ten, if a queen is dancing and making crazy money at the club, then she is tricking and getting her dick sucked, too. But Chris didn't want to hear it. "Rudy," Chris said. "That's my sister's husband, and being all up in their business is something that I don't want to do anymore. So whatever he does, I don't want to know about it. Let her deal with it." Chris, now that Max—the apple of her eye—was fighting a war he surely wasn't going to win, was faced with the reality that this was one time she shouldn't have minded her business.

❧♥❧

"Mrs. Alexander," Dr. Endicott started as he placed his arm around Iysha's shoulders. "We need to talk." A short, balding man, Dr. Odell Endicott had over ten years' experience in dealing with HIV patients, but he'd spent the last five years handling HIV-positive children. With what he needed to discuss with Iysha, Dr. Endicott knew that she shouldn't be alone. "Do you want some coffee? You look like you need a cup."

"No, I'm fine." *Get on with it.*

"Is your husband available?"

"Um, no, he isn't. Why?"

"I thought you might want him or another family member to be here with you while I go over some things about Max's condition."

Chris is on her way, and Momma can be too dramatic sometimes. "I'll be fine. Just tell me what's wrong with my baby."

Dr. Endicott wasted no time. "Max has full-blown AIDS, and we need to determine who, when, where, and how he got it. Have you ever been tested?"

It was time to come clean. "I'm tested every three months." Iysha sighed.

Bewildered, Dr. Endicott continued with his interrogation. "When was the last test?"

"Last month."

"Okay. Assuming you're negative, I need to know what's happened to make you feel that you need to be tested."

Iysha swallowed. Dropping her head in shame, she responded, "Nathaniel has a double life."

"You mean he's bisexual."

"I don't know what to call it, but I believe it's deeper than being bisexual. I know for a fact he's a drag queen. I don't know if he's gay or just sleeps with men from time to time. I really don't think that he's ever wanted to be with a woman." *There, I said it.* That release made her feel like an alcoholic taking her first step toward sobriety.

Dr. Endicott was confused. "Why are you still with him?"

"For my children and for me. God says it's wrong to divorce your husband."

Assessing the situation further, Dr. Endicott continued, "The first thing we need to do is get you into counseling, but I have to ask you something."

"Yes?"

"When was the last time you were intimate with your husband?"

Iysha shocked even herself when she responded, "Over two years ago." She recalled that last time when she'd pushed him away just as he was about to cum. "I got tired of him wanting to stick his dick in my ass." Although she tried her best to answer the doctor's questions, she was still in need of some answers of her own. "I don't understand, though. How can Max be sick and not me?"

Crossing his legs and disgusted by what Iysha had disclosed to him, Dr. Endicott proceeded. "There has to be one of two explanations. One, your husband—who is apparently unknowingly positive—is or had been sexually abusing your son; or two, Max received infected blood during the transfusion he was given as a preemie. I want to believe that it happened during the transfusion. I know that rushing to judgment about your husband seems a little unfair, but I'm simply going on the facts you've given me and by the information I have in your son's file."

"Wait, I've known Nathaniel most of my life, and yes, he's done some questionable things, but I don't see him being a child molester. In my mind, he's a-many-a-sons-a-bitches right now, but I don't see him being that kind of monster."

"Mrs. Alexander, ethically, I'm going to have to document something, and, without proof that your husband hasn't abused your son, I'm assuming that he did."

"And what about the transfusion theory?" Dr. Endicott was fully aware of who the donor had been, but although a stickler for the rules, he believed that Iysha should know the truth as well. "Did you know that your husband donated his blood for Max's transfusion?"

Iysha jogged her memory, recalling the critical hours

just after Max was born. She knew she hadn't been a match. O-positive ran in Nathaniel's family. "Um, I never asked about that. I was just glad they found a donor on my husband's side of the family and not from some stranger."

"Well, according to his chart, your husband gave blood."

"Oh, my God." Realizing that Iysha understood that Nathaniel had given blood for Max, Dr. Endicott asked again if there were someone Iysha wanted him to call.

"My sister is on her way in from Paris, but pushing that aside, aren't y'all supposed to test any blood that's donated?"

"Looking at the records, the blood was screened and tested negative. Meaning, your husband was negative—at that moment. You see, with HIV there is an incubation period of two weeks to six months where the antibodies may or may not show up in an infected person. In some cases, it may even be years."

Reflecting deeply on Nathaniel's medical history, Iysha thought back to the blood tests that they had taken when they got their marriage license. It was negative for HIV, so she knew that this had to have happened just before or after Max was born.

Dr. Endicott continued, "Your husband could've contracted the virus any time between the time your son was conceived and now. But if you don't have it, then it's likely that he contracted it during the transfusion, or well, you know. Max's symptoms are like those of someone who's had the disease for years."

Iysha thought about the trip to Santa Monica—the trip Nathaniel was on when she had gone into labor. It had been after that that things really began to change.

Dr. Endicott explained, "Although your husband may not have had it then, he could have it now. Do you know whether or not he's been tested?"

"I haven't seen him to ask him."

Flipping through Max's chart, Dr. Endicott noticed that Max supposedly had asthma. "What doctor diagnosed Max's asthma?"

Iysha pretended to ponder. No one had ever told her Max had asthma. "Nobody did. I just assumed that was what was wrong with him since he was coughing and wheezing all the time."

"Mrs. Alexander, after looking at his chest X-rays, he had pneumonia...not asthma."

She didn't know how much more she could take. "Just tell me what I need to know to get my baby better."

"Come out to the courtyard with me, so we can have a little more privacy and get some air." This was going to be harder than he thought.

"Okay." Twenty-seven floors towered above them and the buildings' shadows allowed a slight breeze and provided shade from the afternoon sun. "It feels good out here," Iysha whispered. "I didn't realize how long I'd been inside." Squinting her eyes at first, she was finally able to focus on a bench sitting just south of Max's window. "Let's sit over there. I want to be close to him."

"I understand," Dr. Endicott replied. "Have you noticed that Max isn't getting any better?"

Iysha's heart pounded, and her stomach fluttered. "Yes, I have." Her sullen, bloodshot eyes—finally resting from tear-filled days and nights—were watering again.

"Before I go any further, do you need me to try and call your husband? I really think that he needs to be here."

"No, I don't. I need Jesus right now. Not Nathaniel."

"Okayyy. Max isn't going to get any better. The HIV incubation period for children is typically two to six years, maybe more…maybe less. He's had no treatment since he was infected, so his chances of surviving this are nil. Had we known about it sooner, we could have had him on cocktails and some other things to make him feel better. That rash you told us about is not a rash; those are lesions. Max has AIDS now. How long had he been sick before you brought him in?"

"A couple of months, I guess. At first he was just sniffling all the time. We all had colds, so I didn't worry about it. But then everyone but Max got better."

"What about your husband?"

"What about him?"

"How has he been?"

"Since Max has been in the hospital, I haven't seen him. I know that he hasn't been up here because Max keeps asking for him. We were barely speaking anyway. And please, please, out of respect for my son, don't ask me anymore about where my husband is because right now I don't give a damn where he is." Tears streamed like running water down Iysha's face.

"I'm sorry. I won't ask you again. Are there any questions that you have for me?"

"What is the treatment going to be from this point on? Is he going to come home?"

Pausing for a moment, Dr. Endicott thought about where he'd want his child to be if the situation were reversed, but with Max's condition so progressed, the doctor responded with an honesty that he'd previously given to no one else. "I will speak with admissions about moving Max to a more comfortable room, meaning we'll get a cot put in there for you and some chairs for visitors. Bring anything he wants in there, okay?" It was the most comforting way he could tell Iysha that Max couldn't go home and that his time on this earth was limited.

A SURRENDERED SOUL

Standing barefooted on the cold, hospital room floor, Iysha looked out the window, watching traffic pass on the streets below. She'd just come back from MLG&W with a final disconnection notice. Nathaniel had drained all the bank accounts, leaving them each at zero balances eventually causing them to be closed. Sitting in the chairs this time hadn't worked, and the utilities would be turned off by the close of business. The girls were with their cousins at Ora's and were welcomed there until the whole thing with Max was over.

In and out of consciousness, Max asked for his daddy, but all Iysha could do was promise to get Nathaniel there. She called his family, and no one had seen him. She even rode by the club to see if his car was there. Iysha paged him but never got a return phone call. Desperate to satisfy the dying wishes of her son, Iysha asked Chris if she could put in some calls to see if anyone had seen Nathaniel. Contrary to what she felt, Chris made an effort to find him and wasn't surprised to find out that Patty knew where he was.

"Chris, don't go over there."

Angered by Nathaniel's secrecy, Chris snapped, "How can you expect me not to?"

"I promised him I wouldn't tell anyone where he was. Besides, it ain't exactly where I'd want folks to visit me."

Chris was livid. "For heaven's sake, Patty, his dying son wants to see him."

Patty, trying to sympathize with Chris's request, asked, "Do you actually think that he wants to be a father to that little boy? He's a queen, Chris. I don't care how many women he marries or how many babies he makes, he's a queen whose first line of business is to be fabulous. Nathaniel can't be a diva and at the same time try to make a man out of your nephew."

"Do you know how cruel that is to that baby? Have you seen how mean he is to Max?"

"I've heard, and sometimes he even feels bad about it. But most times he doesn't."

"All I want him to do is to say good-bye to his son. Max asks for his father almost constantly."

"I doubt if that's going to happen," Patty replied. "Here's the address. There isn't a phone over there, so I can't call him to tell him you all have been looking for him."

Exasperated, Chris snapped, "Max is better off without his ass anyway."

Wiping his forehead with a handkerchief, Patty suggested, "He probably is."

Pacing the floor, Chris asked, "Can I ask you a question

since you seem to know more about Nathaniel than his own wife?"

"Yes, go ahead."

"Did he stick his nasty-ass, perverted dick into Max? I know it sounds horrific, but my sister has a son with full-blown AIDS lying up there in that hospital bed. He got it from somewhere."

Patty pleaded with Chris, "Let it go. You're the smart one here. Has it occurred to you that Nathaniel might be sick, too?"

"And who gives a shit? Hmphf. You, maybe, but no one else."

"His wife just might."

Chris threw up her hands in disbelief. "He left her in that house with no food, no phone, and, if it hadn't been for me, she would've been without utilities! He drained all the bank accounts!"

"He needed it for medicine. He lost both his jobs, and now he doesn't have any health insurance."

Cupping her ear as if she were listening for something, Chris joked, "Shhh, Patty. I think I hear violins."

"You can be such a bitch sometimes. You're reminding me of what you were like when you were with Gayle."

That was low, and Chris knew it. She'd done everything in her power to change. "You know, I could've told Iysha about him years ago, but I didn't because I was trying to respect her wishes and stay out of her business. Doing that was obviously a big mistake."

Patty, wiping his forehead again, commented, "Having said that, don't you believe he deserves to be free?"

Chris stood there and listened to Nathaniel's former lover take up for him. But all she could think about was how, in his lucid moments, Max called out for his daddy but never got any response. "Fuck him, Patty. If he's as sick as you say he is, then he's getting what he deserves."

Leaving the whole matter alone was unheard of at this point. She had to finally confront Nathaniel.

The house was a wreck just like Patty had implied. The gutters were falling off because of the leaves and pine needles trapped in the water's path. Shutters were hanging by a nail or two and hadn't been painted in what appeared to be years. The mesh in the screen door was torn from the wood frame and hung by a thread. Trash was thrown about the yard, looking as if no one had bothered to take it to the curb. The mail slot on the front porch was full of old mail and newspapers. Chris turned the doorknob and cautiously entered the dilapidated house. The door was hard to move because of the stack of mail piled on the floor. With all her weight she pushed the door back, revealing something she'd never expected from someone like Nathaniel. The house looked and smelled like shit.

Chris was on a warpath. She knew that when she was face-to-face with Nathaniel she was going to do her best to kill him. Being who he was, Chris knew Nathaniel wasn't going to put up a fight, so she was determined to bitch-slap his ass South Memphis style until he bled to death.

As she walked through the house perusing each room and closet, Chris came upon the only bedroom in the house. Strewn about the room were ladies' clothes and shoes, elaborate headdresses, sequined gowns, and expensive lingerie. Stepping over the many trunks and suitcases propped open on the floor, Chris stumbled into the bathroom where the reality of Max's illness smacked her right in the face. There were so many medicine bottles that it looked like a pharmacy, and all of them had Nathaniel's name on them. Now realizing that Nathaniel wasn't there, she reveled at the stacks of make-up and nail polish. Chris couldn't take anymore. Paper was all over the place. Pieces of mail strewn from room to room. Beneath her left foot, she felt something on her shoe. *Please, please, don't let this be a condom. Oh God!* Holding on to a nearby door facing, Chris lifted her foot and saw that an envelope was stuck to the bottom of her shoe. The return address read, "Tennessee State Department of Health: Open Immediately." The letter was addressed to Nathaniel. Dropping the envelope, Chris picked up another envelope and another. "California Department of Health: Open Immediately," "Arkansas Health Department: Open at

Once," "Atlanta Commissioner of Health: Immediate Attention Required." In her mind, Chris knew what these letters wanted. *This bastard hasn't opened a single one*. The mail slot was filled with letters from nearly every health department in the country. Most of them dated back to just after Max was born. When Chris returned to her car, she cleaned her hands with hand sanitizer and wiped them until they were red.

❧♥❧

Iysha was sitting on the side of the bed when Chris returned to Max's room. Her voice shook with pain as she told her sister that Max was now breathing on a ventilator. While holding Max's limp hand, Iysha questioned her sister, "Where have you been?"

"Uh, I was running an errand. What's wrong?" Chris asked as she noticed that some of the machines had been turned off.

"They said he's brain-dead," she whimpered. "I was waiting for you to get back before I pulled the plug. I don't want him to suffer any longer." Iysha knew her son was headed to a better place. She'd grown tired of seeing him struggle for a miniscule breath of air. This weary mother was at peace with letting her only son go.

Sobbing, Chris walked over to Max's bed and kissed his forehead. She rested her head on his tiny chest as

Iysha reached for the plug. The sorrow that she'd had bottled up inside since Gayle died surfaced. All of the pain of seeing Trey with another woman made itself known. The loss she'd felt after Amil left had finally cut into her soul.

As the ventilator pumped its final stream of air, Chris whispered, "It's okay to go now, Max. Tee-tee loves you."

IN MY DARKEST HOUR

The family cars left from Ora's with Iysha, Jessica, Erica, Chris, Chelsea, Gaylon, Ora, Carlos, and Ora's mother, Marie, in the first limo. It seated ten, and hoping that by some chance he'd show up, Iysha left a space for Nathaniel. Admiring the luxurious interior of the car, the children's laughter was missing Max's sweet, familiar giggle that had once resonated with such joy and youth. While she wanted so desperately to tell them to be quiet, Iysha couldn't. Someone had to laugh and live for Max.

Chris hadn't said much since the night they had left the hospital. She'd escorted Max's body to the hearse, and during that long walk, she'd pinched herself repeatedly making sure that she wasn't in some sick nightmare. Fortunately, Iysha, with assistance from Ora, was able to make the funeral arrangements without having to bother Chris. Covering the funeral expenses was the last thing that Chris could do to let her nephew know that somebody else loved him even when his father wouldn't.

The service was held at the Tennessee Funeral

Home with the interment across the street at the funeral home's cemetery. The family entered, walked down the center aisle, and stood in front of the casket. Carlos, who'd made his stint as a grandfather relatively meager, had bought a white tuxedo for Max. The mortician had done an excellent job on Max's face, covering the lesions without darkening his complexion. Each of his sisters placed one of his favorite stuffed animals in the casket, and standing there clutching a picture of Max, Prince, and her, Chris pressed her fingers against her lips, touched Max's hand, and slid the picture underneath it. As she turned to walk toward her seat, Chris noticed a woman clad in a black dress, black gloves, and black veil sitting in the back of the chapel. Chris took a seat but kept a watchful eye on the woman. At every opportunity, she turned to cast a glimpse at her. Chris wanted to see her every move. The last time she looked back, the woman wiped her eyes with a black handkerchief, stood up from her seat, and left the room.

Max's tiny coffin was carried across the street by his grandfather, his two great uncles, and a cousin. Prince was brought to the burial where he sat with Erica and Jessica. Just as the minister said his closing words, Prince got up and scratched the side of Max's coffin whining and crying like everyone else.

Gazing across the cemetery, Chris noticed that woman

again, and this time Chris was determined to have a few words with her. While everyone filed past the casket, Chris excused herself from the family and walked over to the woman dressed in black. "How dare you come here," she snarled. Chris saw Iysha's bewilderment at the presence of the mysterious guest.

"I had to," the woman replied.

"No, you didn't. You came trying to make some statement. I've held my tongue with you out of respect for my sister. You've put her through all of these changes because you were too shallow to be true to who you really are. Max loved you because you're his father, and you didn't have enough man in you to even notice it. I can't stand your ass." Chris never changed her facial expression. "You could've at least put on a suit and tie today out of respect for your son." Then she turned and walked towards the car. Chris knew she was obligated to tell her sister that her husband was there. "He's over there," she said, gesturing to Max's coffin.

Her heart thumped fiercely. Iysha hadn't seen her husband in months and wasn't sure what to do first. The last time she really had seen him was the night of his "performance." Since that time, he had only been a dark shadow to her. There was no desire to look at him in his eyes and no urge to kiss his lips. For allowing her to be where she was…alone…she hated him. Iysha tried her best to look beyond his sculptured nails, Stuart

Weitzman heels, and Versace black dress. Clenching her fists and closing her eyes, Iysha privately wished him away, but for the sake of her son, she said, "You could've called, Nathaniel. He asked for you up until his last breath."

Quietly weeping, Nathaniel took Iysha by the hand. "I did what was best for him."

Iysha, looking over Nathaniel's presence as if she couldn't believe he'd said that, commented, "That's not true. All he ever wanted from you was for you to be his daddy. Nothing else. For some reason, you wouldn't give him the love you gave the girls."

"It's complicated, Iysha. I only came here to say good-bye to him hoping that no one would see me." A slight breeze had begun to blow Nathaniel's veil, revealing three lesions on the side of his face. "I didn't want anyone to see me, Iysha, especially you."

She didn't know what to say. Her love for him wanted to pull him to her and cradle him as they grieved the loss of their only son. But then, as she looked at him in his pumps and nail polish, there was the hate. "In my darkest hour, I've clung so tightly to the one thing you gave to me that no one can take away, and that's my faith in God. All I have to say is that you let my son leave here wanting something you were never willing to give."

"And what's that?" Nathaniel asked.

"You," she answered solemnly. "And that's something I'll never forgive. Good-bye, Nathaniel." Iysha turned away from the being that had once consumed her life, making her way to Max's casket for a final good-bye.

GOOD THINGS COME TO THOSE WHO WAIT

At the age of 35, Christian Desmereaux—graduate of Howard University, Temple University, and most recently the University of Paris—was poised to become the first African-American president of the University of Paris, but she didn't know it. During her leave of absence, the Board of Trustees had unanimously elected her to the post. Her credentials left all of the other candidates in the dust, particularly after she'd just earned her Ph.D. in International Business. From *Ebony* to *Jet* to *Essence*, Chris's picture was set to grace magazine covers and the society pages of newspapers all over the United States. But she didn't know it.

Chris had not been selected because of her outstanding academic track record (she barely got out of Howard with a 2.5), nor was she selected because she had all those extra letters behind her name. She stood out because, in the essay part of her application, Chris dismissed the fact that she was highly educated and adequately trained for the position. Instead, she humbled herself by admitting that she'd made many mistakes… MANY of them, but, like the rest of the world, she was only human. She also acknowledged that she'd been in a mental institution (the question was asked in the application), and, while hospitalized, she concluded that she wasn't mentally incapacitated, nor was she, for the lack of a better description, "crazy." She had merely examined and analyzed herself just as she felt the rest of the world perhaps should do. Fortunately for her, there had been a doctor who supported her opinion and sent her home to resolve her own issues. In an effort to win the affection and attention of her family who'd never sought to be anything more than what was socially expected of them, Chris had, at one point, stooped to a level that had given her the ability to get along with her family. Sure, life with them had become easier, but she had compromised who she was and who she was destined to become. Her essay boasted of the downfalls in her life, but she'd reflected on them as stepping-stones. And, at this point in her life, she welcomed all challenges and faced them with unshaken faith and determination.

"Have you tried reaching her in Memphis?" Jean-François asked.

"I did, but I can't get an answer," responded Michelle.

"Well, did you try her cell phone?"

"I tried that, too. She doesn't seem to have it on. I can try her mother's house if you want me to."

Jean-François and his staff had been trying to reach

Chris for over a week. The University had released Chris's curriculum vitae and picture to the media since the items in her application packet had become the school's property. "I would like to let her know about our decision before she reads it or sees it anywhere." Jean-Fràncois was one of the few white men that Chris had ever trusted. Always a straight shooter, this man had grown to admire Chris for the shrewd but respectful businesswoman that she'd become. During a late night at the office, Chris had confided in him about everything in her life, and that everything included *everything*. Jean-François, a Canadian-born gentleman who'd never seen a black person until he was 15 years old, kept exchanges equal that evening, and he coyly revealed his personal history to a woman whom he knew was destined for greatness. She listened to him intensely, never questioning his past or those involved in it. They had become inseparable colleagues, for he'd stood behind her every decision. Their mutual respect for one another had paved the way for a friendship that had, in no way, influenced selecting Chris for the position. After all, it was Jean-François who'd encouraged her to apply for the job in the first place. Now, at a crucial hour, he was terribly concerned about his friend. Chris had a lot on her plate lately, and, Jean-François wondered if she were handling it okay. With Chris's faith and spirit always unshakable, he knew that whatever was going on with his comrade was only a temporary setback. "Did she ever say when, or if, she was coming back to Paris? It'd be nice to talk to her before these stories run."

Michelle sighed. "I think it's too late for that. *Jet*'s story runs next week, and the AP's coverage begins Sunday."

"Merde! Shit!"

"What's the big deal? The University owns the pictures and the vitae. I don't think that Chris will mind. It'd be different if it were trash being printed about her."

Shaking his head as he reached for his coat, he responded, "I mind, though. With all that she's been through these last couple of months, she deserves some good news, and I know that this would do the trick." He remembered that when Chris had handed in the application, she smiled at Jean-François and calmly said, "It's in God's hands now. He's gonna put me where He wants me to be."

"I am sure that she's just out of reach somewhere. You know, her nephew's death hit her pretty hard."

"I know it did, and that's what I'm afraid of." Jean-François retrieved his briefcase and laptop from the conference room. "Michelle, I'm going to go on home. If she calls, tell her to please call me immediately. Okay?"

"I will."

❧♥❧

Two weeks after Max's funeral, things were pretty much back to normal for Iysha. During Max's last days, she conditioned herself to accept God's plan and to be prepared to move on when He told her to. Iysha had lost much: first a husband and then her only son.

Chris had hooked her sister up with a job at Lindsay, Locke, and McKay. Chris and Manney played that game of scratch my back and I'll scratch yours. Professionally, Chris had the utmost respect for him, but, on a personal level, she knew firsthand that the brother had some issues. Nonetheless, they had come through for each other. His company had redeveloped three apartment buildings within three blocks of the University that were quickly filled with American exchange students. Although their business relationship had proven lucrative for Manney, there were only two things that Chris actually wanted from him: one had been a good job for her sister; and the other was his wife.

Chris often thought about the last time she'd spoken to Amil, which was at Ora's house the night before the funeral. Early on when Chris first saw her that evening, conversation with Amil was avoided. She'd made it clear to Amil that she had nothing to say until Amil had come to her senses about their relationship. If Amil walked into a room, Chris walked out. If Amil joined in on a conversation, Chris instantly became mute and left the room. Chris didn't want to see her, smell her, touch her, or hear her. There was no need for uncertainty anymore because they'd slept together too many times to say that it was a mistake or that it'd happened because they were both drunk. Alcohol didn't always play a part in their interludes: Chris had made sure of that. If Amil wanted to be on the D-L, then so be it. But Chris wasn't having it.

Most of the guests had left by the time Chris finally found a moment to sit down. She took off her heels and escaped into a quiet moment on the patio. While trying to be there for everyone else, she hadn't taken the time to realize that there was no one there for her. She'd smiled through some of the most uncomfortable moments—the hospital, the funeral home; but it was expected of her. As she buried her head in her hands, she felt an arm gently embrace her shoulder. The intoxicatingly familiar fragrance announced that it was Amil. "Why are you here?" Chris sighed without even looking up.

"I wanted to be here for your family," Amil responded. "But I mostly wanted to be here for you."

"On behalf of my family, thank you for coming," Chris said as she wiped away tears. "As for me, you shouldn't have bothered."

"Why not?"

"You know why, Amil. I gave you my terms, and you ignored them. You can't have us both. Life doesn't work that way."

"It could if you'd let me explain." Amil grinned.

"Let me clarify it for you then. *My* life won't work that way." With that said, Chris left for home. She'd given up on trying to cash in on the second thing she had wanted from Manney.

❧♥❧

Rudy's last issue of *Jet* was due any day. It was the first time that she'd ever pre-paid for a magazine subscription, and she dared it to be late. When the mailman slid the mail into the slot, the magazine hit the floor face-up. "Well, I be damned. Ain't this some shit?" Rudy put the magazine under arm and scurried for Chris's room.

Tacky but nonetheless doing the job, Chris had put newspaper up to her windows to keep out the sun. Was it day or was it night? She didn't know and frankly, didn't care. Alternating between guilt and wretched despair, Chris desperately needed this alone time away from the kids, who were with Ora getting spoiled like nobody's business. Max was the son that she'd never had, and no one seemed to understand that. His innocence was tainted through no fault of his own. *If only I hadn't minded my business,* Chris thought, *Max would still be alive.*

Rudy walked over to the window and yanked the newspaper down from the window facing. "Do you know how damn ghetto this looks from the street?"

Chris rolled over and grabbed a pillow. "Damn, Rudy!" she yelled into the pillow. "What do you want?"

"You need to get the hell up. You've been cooped up in here way too long."

"Am I bothering you in MY house?" Chris snapped.

"No, BITCH, you ain't, but you need to get up. We're worried about you," Rudy said as she made her way around the room to the other two windows. "All you do is take baths and sleep. When was the last time you ate something?"

"I don't know," she said, sitting up in the bed.

"Well, judging by the way your breath is smelling, it's been a few days. C'mon, get up." Rudy threw the covers back and grabbed Chris by the arm. Meeting some resistance from Chris, Rudy threw the mail to the floor and grabbed Chris's other arm. "Get your big ass up outta this bed!" Rudy pulled so hard that she lost her grip and balance and flopped to the floor. She grabbed the magazine and put it back under her arm.

Chris, sitting on the edge of the bed by now, had to squint from the sun's radiance. She hadn't seen in it in days. "You all right?" she asked as she reached for Rudy's hand.

"Don't touch me," Rudy joked, struggling to her feet. "When are you going to snap out of this?"

"Who knows." Chris yawned. "No phone, no TV, no kids, and, up until today, no you. I was doing just fine."

Rudy went into the bathroom and started a bath for Chris. She got some candles from the bedroom, lit them, and placed them along the side of the tub. Then she took Chris's cell phone from the dresser and placed it in the bathroom next to the toilet. Finally, she got tape from the nightstand drawer and tore off four long pieces. After setting out fresh towels from the linen closet, she sat down on the bed next to Chris with a serious frown that Chris had never seen. "I think you need to take a long hot bath to wash this self-pity off you. You've been wallowing in it for too long. I got you some fresh towels and lit you some scented candles. Chris, contrary to what you've been making yourself out to be while lying in here in this bed, you're really a good person, and you know what they always say?"

"No, I don't," she said reluctantly. "And I'm not in the mood for a guessing game."

"Fine, then," Rudy said, smiling like the cat that swallowed the canary. "Be that way. Incidentally, your Highness, I put something in there for you to read."

Peeping over at the dresser, Chris asked, "Why did you put my cell phone in there?"

Rudy got up and placed the towels in the bathroom. "Well, that's in case you need to call somebody. I'm going to leave you alone." And then she was out the door.

Chris pulled off her nightshirt and walked to the bathroom. The dirty clothes hamper was full, so she hung the shirt on the door. The room was filled with candlelight and smelled of fresh peaches; the water resembled ground after a fresh snowfall. Rudy didn't believe in using bubble bath because you couldn't get good bubbles from it. She used good ol'-fashioned dishwashing liquid and lots of it.

Jean-François and the University's staff had been so nice to her despite the fact that she had often accused them of being racist and sexist. After the first two years, she concluded that she was just being bitchy and needed to lay off the bullshit before she ended up losing her job. Jean-François had been there for her when it seemed that no one else was, and Chris was quite sure that he was climbing the walls by now. She often thought about how ridiculous it was for her to apply for the President's position. There was no way that a woman, especially a Black woman, would ever land that job no matter how qualified she was. On the flip side, there was nothing but hardcore facts in her favor. Chris had brought in over $20 million in funding for the school, which included the renovations, for which Manney had been responsible. The new apartment-style dormitories guaranteed the University at least an annual half million-dollar return on the investment. Filled to capacity, the complex could fetch over $2 million a year. There was no doubt that Chris had finally made it professionally, but, with heartache and heartbreak seeming to always find her, she knew that she had to get a grip. God's way of reminding her that He wasn't finished with her yet was to punish Chris with a nuisance named Rudy. If Rudy hadn't burst into the bedroom, Chris probably would've just continued to sleep and bathe all of her pain away. For nearly a month, Chris had considered herself unreachable. The University didn't need her for anything, and she wasn't due back for another two weeks.

The steam from the bathwater was unbearable but welcomed. Rudy had talked Chris into putting a whirlpool bathtub in the master bedroom because it was fitting for Chris's sometimes stressful environment. As Chris settled into the cocoon of water and pushed the buttons for the jets, she reveled in the beauty of the candles and the flowers. It reminded her of the night that she and Amil had made love, and that thought reminded her of the night that they danced at The Closet and how Tracks 3 and 4, "If You Love Me" and "Sometimes Dancin'," from Brownstone's first album would never mean the same. Without regard for the wall décor so gently hung by Rudy, Chris closed her eyes again and sunk further into the massaging waters. She dreamed of Amil—the love that she'd never have; she dreamed of the fun times that she and Max had shared; and she dreamed of her job. She needed to call them. Just as she opened her eyes to reach for the phone, something fell in the tub. "What the hell...?" Chris was breathless when she saw her picture on the cover of the magazine. Rudy had used just enough tape to slightly secure the magazine to the tiled wall above the tub. With merely a hint of moisture, Rudy knew that it would fall. Chris's heart raced, and tears flowed into the perspiration running from her chin. She opened the book and saw that inside was a note from Rudy that read, "They always say good things come to those who wait."

❧♥❧

Manney arrived in Paris two days before the grand opening of the new dormitories. Since he and Chris had not seen each other since they'd finalized the details of his contract, Manney was anxious to spend time reminiscing and catching up. On the contrary, Chris was anticipating seeing a business associate and had no interest in knowing about Manney's personal life. Surprisingly, there were no calls from Amil nor any online communication. Chris was finally glad that she'd been able to move on, forgetting about what almost was. "Hey, Baby Girl!" Manney shouted as he entered Chris's office.

Chris got up from her desk, walking swiftly toward the man whose innovative ideas had played a big role in the progress of her career—despite the fact that he was the husband of the woman that Chris most desperately wanted. "How you been, Manney?" She smiled as she graciously embraced him. "It's good to see you. Come on in, and have a seat. You want a glass of wine or something?"

Placing his briefcase on the back of the plush office chair next to the window that opened to a breathtaking view of the Eiffel Tower, Manney took a seat and accepted a glass of Moet. "Moet during business hours?" He laughed. "That's all right."

Chris sat next to him, crossing her legs and pouring herself a glass of Moet as well. "It's strictly for the occasion."

"I'm surprised that you don't have someone in here waiting on you hand and foot with all the pomp and circumstance going on about you."

"Actually, I do have an assistant, Rachel Dubois, but I don't want her waiting on me hand and foot. She's out taking care of some last-minute details for the gala tonight. I don't need her to do all of my typing and lazy shit that I can do myself. She appreciates the fact that I treat her as if she has sense and not like some high-paid servant. I haven't forgotten where I came from, so I insist that she involve herself in all aspects of the University, and let me be self-sufficient." Chris was putting up that smokescreen—the one that would keep her from asking those "How's the family" questions, and, so far, it was working. "So, I know you're coming to the gala tonight, right?"

"Of course, I am. I wouldn't miss them honoring you. You deserve it."

"Thanks, Manney, but I didn't know that I was being honored for anything." She smiled.

"You didn't? Oh, dayum, my bad!"

"Don't worry about it. I figured they were up to something anyway. So, enough about business." Chris couldn't take it anymore. "How's the family?"

A huge grin exploded from Manney's face, and Chris did a superb job of disguising her disappointment. "Fine, fine. You know, I have a son now. He's a little over a year old."

"Oh, really! Well, congratulations! I know he looks just like you."

"Actually, he looks just like his mother. I believe her flight arrives in the morning around 9:00. She was looking forward to seeing the new complex."

"I see," Chris said softly. Time to change the subject. Chris had taken about as much as her heart would allow in one day. "Glad to hear everything's going well.

I wanted to try one more time for perhaps a son, but sometimes things don't always go the way we want them. I've been so busy this past year that I forgot about having babies. The only pressing thing on my mind now is how to keep this gray hair from coming in so fast."

"Speaking of gray hair, how are the girls? Did you and their fathers work things out as I suggested?" Manney believed that a child needed both parents no matter how the adults felt about one another.

"Well, let's see Gaylon's father almost went postal on me. His marriage was on the rocks after I took him to court for child support. He demanded a paternity test even though Gaylon looks just like him. The judge laughed at him but granted him the right to have the test done. It came back 99.9% positive that he was her father. His wife tripped out because they'd been trying to have kids. Anyway, he tried to hide his pastor's salary, and, when the Court found out, they arrested him on a contempt charge. It didn't have to go that far, but it did. She gets over $1,500 a month in child support. Probably, the most hurtful thing is that he doesn't want to have anything to do with my baby. Her attitude has pretty much been like mine—she's better off without him. As for Mr. Trey, he caught wind of the child support that I was getting for Gaylon, so I guess that somebody advised him that he might want to make amends with me to decrease the chances of the same thing happening to him. We talked, and he even offered to come back to the relationship and put all of that drama behind us. I explained to him that I couldn't be with him, and I didn't want him to be offended by that. I honestly and truthfully just didn't want to be with him. So we've become good friends, which has been good for both girls. Although Gaylon isn't his, he understands the situation and loves both of them."

"So what did you decide about child support from him?"

"Oh, now, I still handled business. He pays a little more than Gaylon's father. I stuck with it in case he stopped wanting to be daddy. There's a fine line between playing daddy and being daddy. Trey has a bad habit of going back and forth."

"Did he ever get married?"

"Almost once or twice. He said he got cold feet." Things were getting too personal, and Chris was a little uncomfortable. "Look, Manney, I have a lot to do before the dinner starts, and I'm quite sure that you want to take some extra time to go by the complex to see the final product."

Manney never took hints well. He continued asking questions about Chris's personal life. "So are you dating? A beautiful woman like you should be. I know you weren't the last time we spoke."

"No, I'm not actually. I don't have time for it with

my schedule and all. I spend the majority of my spare time with the girls." Chris got up from her chair and headed to her desk. "That reminds me, I need to get ready to get out of here because they're coming with me tonight." Chris hoped that would mean good-bye for now.

"Okay, well, don't let me keep you. I'm going to head on back to the hotel before going to the dormitory. I'll see you tonight, then."

"Good, we can talk some more later. " Chris smiled as she, once again, hugged Manney. "By the way, thanks a million times over for making this happen. I couldn't have done it without you."

"No, Chris, we did it together," and he turned and walked toward the elevator.

❧♥❧

Approximately an hour after Manney left, Chris heard the elevators door open. Everyone else had been gone for nearly half an hour. As far as she knew, none of them had planned on returning. Chris was focusing on the evening's activities while wrestling with the possibility that she may see Amil. Whoever it was that had come up on the elevator was of no consequence to her.

"Good evening, Chris," a sultry, female voice intoned softly as its owner closed Chris's office door.

Recognizing the presence of the only woman that had ever truly possessed her heart, soul, and mind, Chris resisted the urge to spin around. She'd been gazing out the window for nearly an hour, and her thoughts of Amil had become abundant. She couldn't help but think about what people meant when they said be careful what you wish for. "I thought that you wouldn't be in until tomorrow," Chris said as she slowly swiveled around in her office chair. After all that had been said and done as far as the two of them had been concerned, Chris never once believed that she'd see Amil again—especially alone.

"I caught an earlier flight because I wanted to talk with you since you still aren't taking my phone calls."

"Look, I don't think you should be here."

"Well, I do. You've closed the door on me for two years now, and I won't let you do it again. You're going to let me talk this time. Okay?"

"For some reason, I feel as though I have no choice but to let you do that. Say what you have to say."

"You're not going to interrupt me?"

"I promise." Being quiet gave Chris the opportunity to reflect on the beauty of a love that had transcended everything she ever knew. "If you love someone, let her go" was the last thing she had said to Amil, and, as Chris turned and walked away from LaNisha that mild spring evening in Paris, she thought to herself, *if she never comes back, then it was never meant to be.*

"Chris, we've known each other for a very long time. Longer than I'd ever imagined we'd be in one another's lives. I've tried day in and day out to forget about you and to hopefully forget about those nights we spent together. I wasn't afraid of what you were feeling. I was afraid of what I was feeling. I mean you have been the only person to make love to me without touching me, without penetrating me. Sometimes my panties got so wet that I'd have to take them off in the car, so that they could dry out before I got home. There was no telling if Manney was going to want to get him some before he went to bed. That's why I stopped making myself available to you. I had unexpectedly become physically attached to you, and, because I had no one to tell at that time, I just cut it off in my mind, but my heart had other plans. I'd wanted so badly to chat with you, but I no longer knew what to say. I had reached the point where the only person I wanted to touch me was you. Having been with Manney for so long, I felt that I had betrayed him, and, then, without any forewarning, he wanted to get married and wanted to do it right away. I got pregnant with Parris the night after my birthday. I named my son Parris to remind me of what I really felt that night. Parris Christian is his birth name. I may have been caught up with Manney, but my mind was thinking of you."

Shocked but respectful of Amil's wishes, a tearful Chris didn't say a word.

"Manney surprised me with this whimsical fairy-tale wedding in Paris...of all places. When I spent those nights with you before the wedding, I never expected to feel as I did. My heart was pounding out of control, and my soul was uplifted. If anyone had ever told me that I'd feel like that about another woman, I would've called them a bold-faced liar. And, then, when you turned from me and let me walk away from you, I felt my soul enter a darkness that did not see any light until the day my son was born. I walked away from what would have been a lie to me."

Chris had to interrupt. "Wait a minute. You're trying to tell me that you didn't marry Manney?"

"Yes, I am." Amil spared the details of how she summoned Manney to the bride's room just before the ceremony was supposed to start to tell him she was pregnant. Amil let him know immediately that although she could deal with being a mother, she knew she couldn't deal with being his wife. Manney, embarrassed but tearfully grateful, walked away and offered to tell the guests that there would be no wedding. After the baby was born, they'd agreed to remain friends for the baby's sake. "When LaNisha came to do my hair, she told me she'd seen and talked to you. She told me I'd be a fool to give up the kind of love you were willing to give me, but she understood what society had dictated for me to do. Despite her love for all fine,

Black men, she couldn't stand Manney because of the way he'd been treating me. Rondell, with his big mouth, had started dating her—my hairdresser, of all the women in town, and told all of Manney's business. He was afraid he was losing me. LaNisha also knew that if she'd ever had anyone to love her the way that you told her that you loved me, then she would be a lot better off in this world. 'So, what it's a woman? Doing it with another woman has always baffled me, but I understand now that Chris's love for you has nothing to do with sex,' she said."

Chris chuckled. "Leave it to the hairdresser to not be able to keep her mouth shut. She's never been able to hold water."

"Chris. You promised."

Chris buttoned her lips like she used to when she was in the first grade.

"She brought me this." Amil smiled, tossing the little white box on the desk. "I've kept it all this time. I wanted to open it when I was with you."

Chris, sitting on the edge of her seat nervously shaking her right leg, recognized the little white box but opted not to remove it from the desk.

Realizing Chris was not going to touch it, Amil picked the box up, and after two years of waiting, she opened it, finding a platinum diamond anniversary band with a half-carat stone for each year of their friendship. The clarity of the diamonds spoke volumes about the love Chris had for Amil. "Damn! I've been carrying this around with me all this time?" Amil cried, removing the ring from the box and placing it on her finger.

No response from a beaming Chris.

Amil continued, "Where was I? Oh, now, I remember. The night we exchanged words at your mother's house did something to me. I wanted to run away and be alone. After leaving the house, I drove around Memphis for hours and ended up at The Closet. Fortunately, there was no one in there…so I thought," she said, glancing at her finger.

Chris remembered she'd gone by the club to help Rudy finish up the books that night.

"I didn't want to be around anybody," Amil affirmed. "When I got ready to leave, I spotted you on one of the dance floors just doing your thing to that reggae-flavored jam by Brownstone. Until then, I'd never noticed the beauty in a woman's body when it grooved to reggae music. Your waist, your hips, and the graceful movement of your arms have been comforting thoughts in my time of need over these last several months. In my mind, I've embraced you so many times on that dance floor and taken breath from the woman who had unselfishly given me life. Then, I think about how 'If You Love Me,' the song that followed, echoed every communication that we'd ever had. I'd wanted to leave that night without you ever knowing I was there, but, instead, you came to me and danced with me, never saying a word. And when the music stopped, so did life for me." By this time, they were both crying. "You've never given me the chance to tell you that I didn't get married. I came here today not only as an invited guest but as a woman who knows who and what she wants. I came to make things right with you and to do what you told me to do when and if I was ever ready to talk to you again." Wiping away her tears, Amil asked, "Do you remember what you said to me?"

Shaking her head in disbelief tinged with joy and anticipation, Chris responded, "That night at the chateau I told you not to talk to me until you were ready to be with me."

"Yes, you did. I didn't realize you meant it until you refused to let me say more than five words to you at your mother's house, and then you didn't speak while we danced. Most importantly, though, I remember you uttering that you loved me enough to let me go, and, if I never returned..." She sniffled.

"Then it was never meant to be." Chris whispered the end of the sentence for her.

Amil had unloaded what had been a heavy burden for way too long. Relieved that she had finally rid herself of the emotions that had kept her awake at night, Amil could breathe again. "I love you, Chris, and I always will. I'm here now, and I will always be here. I know how much you've always wanted a son, and Parris and I are ready to come home to you if you'll say you'll have us." With that she walked over to Chris and pulled her from her chair. Taking a clean piece of tissue from her pocket, Amil placed the palm of her left hand around the bottom of Chris's face while her other hand wiped Chris's eyes. "Now, you can say whatever you want. I've said my piece." Then she gently kissed Chris on the nose.

So many thoughts crossed Chris's mind as she stood there with the woman that she'd longed to be with for what seemed to have been an eternity. Staring into Amil's eyes, Chris asked, "Are you sure you're ready to wake up in the arms of a woman?"

Amil, resting her head on Chris's shoulder, replied, "I wouldn't have it any other way."

TO THINE SELF BE TRUE

With the Parisian moon glaring through the atrium of the Marriott Renaissance Hotel, Amil walked into Manney's hotel room as if he were a stranger. Her ball gown shimmered and sparkled in the dimness of the room as she searched for the words she should've spoken years before. She gingerly eased onto the sloping edge of the bed, and when Manney offered her a drink, Amil calmly said no. It had been a beautiful evening with him and Chris receiving accolades for the completed project. Amil beamed with pride as both Manney's and Chris's names were called. "I need to talk to you, Manney."

Their relationship had evolved more into a friendship than that of ex-lovers. Manney felt that Amil could tell him anything. She had given him a handsome son, and they'd agreed to raise him together. "What's up?" he asked, taking a seat in the chair.

"The best way to get this over with is to simply tell you what's what."

"Okay," Manney replied as he took a seat in the chair next to the bedroom door.

"During the last few years of our relationship, I was having an affair."

Manney wasn't shocked. He figured she was doing something. "Surprisingly, I'm all right with that. I wasn't giving you the attention you deserved. You did what you needed to do."

Her eyes repeatedly sketching an imaginary line from the floor to the ceiling, Amil sighed and interjected, "Stop it. It's more complicated than that. I was having an affair with a woman. I mean..."

"A woman?"

"Yes, a woman, Manney."

There wasn't much to say about it. They were now history. The damage was done. "All right then. I mean, what do you want me to say? That was a long time ago. We've sorted through our differences and moved on."

Amil wasn't expecting Manney to be so amenable. "I was having an affair with Chris, Manney."

Bolting upright, Manney gasped, "What?"

"I knew her before you ever introduced us. But we'd never met face to face. I fell in love with her through innocent conversation over..."

"Wait a minute. You met her over the Internet, didn't you?"

"Yes, I did, but don't be mad at her for this. I was the one who was searching." Amil knew it would come to this, but now that the moment was here feelings of anxiety washed over her. She could hear the sound of her heart pounding inside of her head, the rhythm accelerating with each word spoken. She had to be calm. *Get a grip*, she thought. Amil closed her eyes for a second to think, then stood and slowly began walking back and forth across the room. Somehow, she had to convey to Manney that this wasn't just some light-hearted Internet affair. None of this was meant to hurt him. It wasn't planned; it was fate. She and Chris were real. Amil knew that now. She accepted it finally. And her acceptance fueled the remainder of her explanation. "Of all the people on God's green earth, Chris ended up being a business associate of yours. She didn't even know that you and I had a connection."

"You never told her you were involved with someone?"

"I did."

"You never told her my name?"

"No, I didn't. She never asked. For years she didn't even know my real name until you introduced us. Manney, please understand that I fought the way I felt about her for so long. But after a while, I couldn't... fight it, I mean. I had to stop and think about all the things that attracted me to her. She never tried to change me into something or someone I wasn't. She made me laugh. She made me feel special. She was never predictable. But most importantly, she gave me something that I wasn't getting from you."

"And what was that?"

"Attention."

That one word brought a deafening hush over the room, a hush accompanied by a stillness that neither Manney nor Amil could seem to break. Finally Manney emitted a long sigh and was the first to sever the silence when he said, "I can't believe this shit. Chris is a lesbian?"

"That's not for me to affirm or deny, Manney. I'm telling you about me."

"I guess I'm to assume this whole thing is the reason for us not getting married."

"You're a smart man."

"You've been seeing her since that time?"

"No, actually, this is the first time Chris has spoken to me in a couple of years. She didn't want to talk to me because she thought I was married to you. She respected you too much and wanted nothing to do with me while I was with you. I had to be sure of what I wanted, and, after all this time, I know I want to be with her."

Manney realized that he had never told Chris about his wedding fiasco. He was too embarrassed, and plus, there'd never been any time to discuss it. Chris had gotten to the point where she'd only talk about business and nothing else. Now he understood why. "So what happens next?"

Amil inhaled deeply and continued haltingly. "Well, she and I discussed it, and we're going to see where it all goes, but we determined it best I talk to you about her and me first."

Feeling slightly betrayed, Manney asked, "Why couldn't she tell me? I thought we were friends. Was she afraid of what I'd say?"

"Chris's and your relationship is professional, and you know how she is about handling her business. She didn't want to hurt you. Besides, this is about you and me."

Manney respected Chris and Amil's decision to tell him. His business with Chris was finally done. There was no need to dwell on something that should have never been. Amil was obviously head over heels in love with Chris, a woman who had managed to keep her personal life undercover, totally separate from her professional one. *What an ass* was the one phrase that kept reverberating through Manney's head as he pictured himself constantly skinning and grinning in Chris's face, never once thinking that she wasn't the least bit interested. And furthermore, he felt like a fool for having made love to Amil when she really wanted to be with a woman. Glancing across the room, preparing for what he was about to hear, Manney had to ask the question. For some reason, he had to know. "Can I ask you something?"

"Sure."

"The last time we were together in bed where was your head?"

Amil's eyes teared. "Don't make me answer that."

"I want you to."

"My head was into trying to keep you happy, but my heart was with Chris."

All he could do was calmly get up and take Amil by the hand, pressing his lips against her soft skin. "I hope you two will be happy together. As always I'm here for you." Manney wasn't about drama. He was far too educated for that as was everyone else involved. Amil was the mother of his child, and he'd always have a bond with her—no one would ever change that.

Walking to the door and exiting the room, Amil paused to caress Manney's arm and said, "Thank you for understanding. Parris is going to be just like you."

Nodding his head in acceptance and simultaneously giving her a small wink of the eye, Manney gently shut the door on any unresolved issues that had been lingering in the air and walked away with his dignity, setting the mold for the man his son would one day become.

Later that night, Manney awoke from hours upon hours of endless tossing and turning. His sheets were wet with sweat, and his heart was racing. Although his parting words to Amil seemed to make everything kosher between the two of them, Manney needed more closure. He had questions he'd never pose to Amil, and there was only one person who could give him what he was looking for. He reached for the phone.

A groggy, agitated female voice answered the phone. "Hello?"

Sitting up in the bed, adjusting his covers, Manney hesitiantly asked, "What's up, Chris?"

"Manney?" Chris was alarmed but had quietly expected the call. She rolled over and adjusted her head on the pillow for a good cussing out. "What can I do for you at 4 in the morning?"

Sarcastically, he replied, "You have to ask?"

Silence.

"I talked to Amil earlier this evening, and she..."

Chris stopped him before he could get started good, and the funny thing was she never moved from her position in the bed. "Manney, I need to let you know that I'm not about to get in the middle of your business with Amil. I've never wanted to discuss it with her, and I have no intention of discussing it with you."

"Chris, after everything we've been through, you're going to do me like this? This is my life I'm trying to talk about. I thought I was your boy."

"In our line of business, you had my back, and I had yours. That's just how I am. Chris couldn't hurt the man's feelings any more than what had already been done. Manney, now think about it. Other than when it concerned Trey, have I ever discussed my personal life with you?"

Manney reflected for a moment and realized that Chris had actually never discussed her personal life. "I can't say that you have, but..."

"And I'm not going to start. I will admit this, though. I've never meant you any harm That's one of the reasons I've kept her at a distance all of this time. I have loved Amil for quite some time, but that was something I needed to deal with. I've been hurt a lot in my life, and

I don't get into returning the favors. I can understand your frustration with this, and I can understand you hating me right now."

Manney knew his feelings were far from that. "I feel like I failed her, Chris."

"And to be perfectly honest, you did. She should have never needed to look outside of home for love and approval, but Amil's issues were of a different nature, and I can't get into that with you."

The question was burning in his mind, and before he knew it, he blurted it out. "Is she there?"

"Manney, if it were anyone else, I'd cuss you out for being nosy, but it's you. No, she's not here."

Breathing a sigh of relief, he answered, "Oh, okay."

Chris couldn't resist the temptation. "So you want to fight me now? Meet me out in the parking lot?" She chuckled.

Manney started laughing, too. "Naw, it's all good, Chris. Besides you'd probably kick my ass anyway. Still buddies?"

"That's your call."

"Still buddies, then. Good night." Manney hung up the phone and got up to take a piss before going back to bed.

And Chris rolled over, kissed Amil's shoulder and got up to brew a fresh pot of coffee.

FREE

Nathaniel arrived at the pool party wearing a tight spandex T-shirt with matching biker shorts. A pair of Cole Haan leather slip-ons, one of Nathaniel's many finds on his West Coast shopping spree, covered his supple feet that had just received one of the best pedicures that money could buy. He was fragranced from head to toe in Issey Miyake, and the tiny Coach leather travel bag he carried matched his ensemble to a tee. There was no use trying to get into the men's' room to pee because every stall was occupied by two or more. Nathaniel was determined to make the best of his last few nights in Santa Monica. He stood in the doorway of the patio, making his statement, "You want some of this? Come and get it."

A business trip he'd called it. Well, while Nathaniel conducted his "business," he got a piece of ass from every Theron, Dickson, and Juan that came to pass. True enough, he had been hitting the bathhouses and the pool parties, but he'd been safe. Tyrell, a fine, young tight-assed pancake known for his beautiful smile and charm, had caught Nathaniel off-guard. Earlier that day during brunch, Tyrell had slithered over to Nathaniel's table and claimed a seat without saying a word. Nathaniel had seen him at all the parties earlier in the week; never once had he arrived with the same guy twice. More importantly, Tyrell had never left with the person he had come with. Knowing all of this, Nathaniel couldn't risk taking any "souvenirs" back home with him, so he'd managed thus far to steer clear of Tyrell and his fine, luscious ass. "And what do I owe this pleasure?"

Flashing his gorgeous, mesmerizing smile, Tyrell responded modestly, "You don't owe me anything. I just didn't want a good opportunity to go to waste. I've been watching you."

"I know," Nathaniel said coyly. "I thought that you were far too busy for little ol' me."

"Well, actually, I've been saving the best for last. Wanna do the Strip and then watch the sun set?" Yes, Tyrell was very swift. He skipped all the bullshit and went straight for the gusto.

"I was actually going back home today. My wife…"

"Oh, let's not get into all of that. Are you down or not?"

Nathaniel had gotten Iysha's message about not feeling well, but he hadn't received an answer when he had tried to call her back. He figured that she was just in a deep sleep and decided to not bother her again. It never crossed his mind that she had gone into labor and was on her way to the hospital. With all of this fine, hunka man in front of him, it didn't even matter. "Let me take care of my bill, and I'll meet you in the lobby."

"Okay, Sweetness, I'll see you in a few." Tyrell strolled along the poolside and watched the ladies drool over him. It gave him great pleasure knowing that they could never satisfy his tastes. He loved being a tease but loved being a hustler even more.

Nathaniel was completely smitten with Tyrell. His honey-coated chest was buff with a six-pack across the middle. His eyes were light brown, and the natural arch in his eyebrows made this conquest all the more intense. The two of them walked along the beach hand in and hand for hours like newlyweds on their honeymoon. They had tasted each other in every vacant bathroom they could find. Reckless yet addictively intoxicating, their lovemaking was spontaneous and inexcusable. Caught up in a fire that had him burning from beginning to end, Nathaniel had lost all consideration for the lives he'd left in Memphis. When the condoms ran out, there wasn't a time-out or a run to the drugstore. The passion simply became more intense; so intense that Nathaniel quietly crossed into the realms of harsh reality.

Returning to Memphis only a couple of hours after Iysha had given birth, Nathaniel zapped back into his doting husband and loving-father routine and swiftly stepped up to the plate to donate blood for his newborn son. Shortly after the blood was taken, it was given to the new community service volunteer, Jessie Townsend. His only job in the hospital was to run blood work to the lab and to run errands as assigned. But Jessie, being the con artist that he was, had figured out ways to get out of doing practically everything so he could go to the roof and smoke a joint.

Jessie was placed in the neonatal ICU that day stoned out of his mind, but he was two days shy of completing his community service and refused to miss a day of work. When he took Nathaniel's blood from the nurse, he was instructed to rush it to the lab for testing and to wait for the results to be hand-delivered back to the floor. The computers had been down and waiting for them to come back up wasn't an option. Instead of doing as instructed, Jessie went to the roof and rolled a blunt. He sat there for an hour smoking weed and snacking on Funyuns. After he was done, he reached in his pocket and pulled out a roll of stickers that read, "TESTED–O.K." He took one from the roll and stuck it on the packet. The blood was returned to the neonatal ICU and delivered to the nursing team to be administered to Max.

❧♥❧

The stomach cramps started a year after Max was born, and then the daily vomiting began. With every episode, Nathaniel looked into his past to see if he should be concerned about an interlude or two, but he couldn't think of one right off.

Although he was proving to be a less-than-perfect husband, Nathaniel took out a no-strings-attached life insurance policy on himself for the sake of his family. And then, on his way home, he stopped by the health department for his quarterly, routine blood test. This time the usual staff nurse did not give the results over the phone. Nathaniel was asked to come in. Instead of the usual nurses that greeted him at the triage counter, there were two doctors and one community liaison when he got there. "Mr. Alexander, we need to talk." From that moment on, Nathaniel felt his life was obsolete. He was now pretty sure that he was responsible for Max's illness and realized his punishment was to live, for as long as God allowed, with that on his heart and mind.

❧♥❧

The house had been willed to Patty from his aunt, and during the last year of his relationship with Nathaniel, the two of them had begun to redecorate it. Nathaniel had started hanging new window treatments and mini-blinds on all the windows, and Patty had purchased cartons and cartons of hardwood flooring. They had major plans for their new home together, but then Patty's mother died, and he yearned for something different. The day after their break-up, Nathaniel got himself an apartment and put anything that would remind him of his past in storage.

Patty left the house, too, and went to live in the house where his mother had resided. One afternoon, Patty decided to stop by the house and check on things, to make sure no vagrants or crack-heads had broken in. The front of the house looked fine, so he drove around to the side door and noticed that it had been kicked in. Taking his flashlight from the glove compartment, Patty, without an ounce of fear, left his car and climbed through the doorway. He heard someone coughing. "Who's in here?" Patty demanded as he continued walking through the house. He followed the hacking cough until he came upon the bedroom and found the love of his life sprawled out on an old, mildewed mattress. "Nathaniel?" When Patty touched Nathaniel's cold, clammy skin, he recognized his lover's illness and tenderly covered him with his coat. "How long you been like this?"

Nathaniel, whose skin had broken out in lesions so horrific that even Patty winced as he glanced over his body, answered, "A while."

"What are you doing here? It's damp and musty in here."

Pulling the coat tightly around him, Nathaniel said, "I had nowhere else to go."

"Don't you have a home?"

Attempting to swallow but settling for a spittoon sitting on the floor next to the mattress, he responded, "Not really. I fucked that up."

Patty wanted to be spared the details. "I'm not even going to ask what you meant by that. I've got to get you out of here. This is no place for you to be in this condition. I'm taking you to the hospital." They left the house, but Patty didn't take Nathaniel to a hospital in Memphis. He bundled him in blankets, put him in the back seat of his car, filled up his gas tank and drove Nathaniel fourteen hours to the Whitman-Walker Clinic in Washington, D.C. While they were on the road, the two talked, in between Nathaniel's catnaps, about what was going on with Max. "Why are you taking me to D.C., Patty? It's too late for a honeymoon." Nathaniel grinned.

"You need more than just medical help. There's some serious stuff going on here, and the people at this clinic can help you. They're known to be the best at what they do. And they're confidential. They believe in keeping your business just that, your business. I'm going to get us a hotel room, and then we're going to spend some time at Whitman-Walker...together."

"I see," Nathaniel whispered. "All I can say is thank you."

They spent two weeks in D.C. Nathaniel was put on cocktails to make his suffering bearable. Once back in town, Patty got in touch with Chris at the hospital, and to soothe what yearning she had to destroy Nathaniel, Patty told her where her brother-in-law was, knowing full well Nathaniel wouldn't be there. He was at a support group with other terminally ill AIDS patients where he'd been spending most of his days since their return from Chocolate City.

Finding comfort in the home that held so many fond memories of their life together, Nathaniel had made the bedroom his own, furnishing it with all his gowns and make-up to make him feel complete. Everything was now out of storage. Patty had bought a new mattress for him and attempted to give the room some life, so that Nathaniel would feel at home. Fresh bouquets of roses were put in there daily to drown out the odor and cover the dismal appearance of a dilapidated pharmacy.

Patty arrived back at the house to find it spotless. Nathaniel had somehow found the energy to scrub the linoleum floors in the living room and to finally hang the mini-blinds. "I'm too tired to hang the window treatments. It got hot all of sudden."

Cupping his hand over Nathaniel's forehead, Patty said, "You've got a fever. Get back in bed." He walked through the living room and was amazed at how he could see himself in the floor. "Why did you do this? You didn't need to do this."

As Nathaniel shuffled to the bedroom in his navy-blue furry slippers, he replied, "I got tired of not being able to walk around the house barefooted. It was too damn nasty in here for me."

"I would've cleaned it for you, but I've been running back and forth and..."

Climbing into bed, Nathaniel responded, coughing, "Let it go. I did it because I wanted to."

After leaving the drugstore earlier, Patty stopped by Baskin-Robbins to pick up a pint of mint chocolate chip ice cream for Nathaniel. But before spending that money, it occurred to Patty that Nathaniel hadn't eaten the last two pints. Normally, he'd inhale it in one sitting. Nathaniel's appetite was withering away, but his spirit was suffering even more. Patty's call to the Lord, despite his indiscretions, was unusual since it had been someone in the church that had turned him out. Scripture insisted, however, that he heed his calling and do as he was told. And that he did. But no matter how many sermons he preached or how many times he read the Bible from front to back, Patty still loved himself some Nathaniel.

Looking around the bedroom as he tucked Nathaniel's sheets under the mattress, Patty noticed a black dress and veil lying on the floor. He walked over to the pile and smelled Estee Lauder's Beautiful, one of Nathaniel's favorites, all over the clothes. Then he pulled the covers up from the mattress and saw that Nathaniel was wearing nail polish. "Please tell me you didn't."

Nathaniel just lay there, rocking back and forth in the bed.

"Tell me you didn't go to the funeral."

Nathaniel stopped for a minute as the tears mixed in with his mascara. "He was my son, Patty. I had to go."

"Dressed like this? Did anybody see you?"

"Chris saw me first."

"Oh, hell, I know she went off on you."

Nathaniel wiped his eyes with a piece of wadded tissue from under his pillow. "You know she did, but I was kinda expecting it. Then I saw and talked to Iysha."

"I can't believe you. Do you know how she must feel with you showing up in drag at your son's funeral?"

Nathaniel's weeping eyes turned to gut-wrenching sobs. His soul wanted to be free, but God was working him over good-fashion. "I want to die, Patty. I quit taking my cocktails some time ago, but I took one yesterday and today, so that I'd feel well enough to make it to the funeral. I want to be put out of my misery. Take me out back and shoot me like the dog I am! You hear me! Please!" he wept. "I have ruined my life. I ruined Iysha's life, and I've ruined my children's lives. I've been undercover all my life, Patty. I want it to end. I came back here to kill myself by taking every damn pill I had in there, but instead I decided to clean. I wanted to scrub the floors until my fingers bled."

Patty didn't know what to say. Nathaniel was hysterical, but Patty knew his heart, and that was what was killing him. "Is there anything you want me to do?"

Nathaniel wiped the caked make-up from his face with a cold towel and then looked at himself in the mirror. "Yeah, there is one thing you can do for me."

❧♥❧

Two days after Max's funeral, Iysha received an anonymous call and was summoned to the house at 567 Baker Street. She was told that the door would be unlocked when she got there. Walking in, Iysha saw that the house was spotless…not one thing out of place. She recognized the layout of things and immediately knew her husband was there.

The bedroom door was slightly ajar, and peeping through the opening, Iysha saw Nathaniel lying in the bed wrapped in several blankets. He turned his head from the stack of down pillows it rested on and smiled. "I didn't think you would come."

Iysha, in amazement at the severe condition of her husband, allowed tear after tear to fall. Her husband, her best friend, was, for all intents and purposes, dead.

As he lifted his trembling hand to reach out for her, she walked over to him and took his hand into hers. "I needed to."

Nathaniel cleared his throat. "I'm going to try to talk to you as best I can. I'm a little weak today since I stopped taking my medicine over a month ago."

Iysha strugged to not be upset with Nathaniel. She wasn't there, by his side, as his wife. She'd come to ease this nagging feeling she'd had inside of her since she had seen Nathaniel on the stage that night. "Why did you do it, Nathaniel?"

"I don't know. I can't say any more than that."

"Do you know how much you've hurt me?"

"I do know, and I made up for it, trust me." Nathaniel pulled an envelope from underneath the covers. "This is for you and the girls." Inside the envelope was a life insurance policy for $500,000. "Don't spend it all in one place," he kidded.

It was more money than she'd ever seen, but the gesture didn't faze her. "Guilt money, is it?"

"Yes and no," Nathaniel wept. "I knew Max would be sick at some point, but it was too late for me to do or say anything. I didn't find out I was positive until a year or so after he was born."

Angrily, Iysha inquired, "Did you not even think about me, your wife?"

"Oh, I did, Iysha, I did. But what was I supposed to say?"

"All you had to do was tell me the truth so I wouldn't have to find out about it in ALL the different ways I did. I know now why you wanted Chris to stay away from us."

As he shifted in the bed, Nathaniel responded, "I'm sorry about everything, and I'll understand if you don't want to be here."

Iysha's memories of her relationship with Nathaniel spanned from the good to the bad, and now the ugly. She reached within her soul and did what Max would have wanted her to do. "Nathaniel, I'm not going to leave you here because before we were lovers, husband and wife, or parents, we were friends. Right now, you need a friend, and I'm not leaving you alone to die."

As the morning sun's brightness peeped into the eastern window of the bedroom, Nathaniel took his last breath cuddled in the arms of love and friendship. He was finally…free.

The End

ABOUT THE AUTHOR

Laurinda D. Brown is the author of *Fire & Brimstone*, *UnderCover*, and the forthcoming *The Highest Price for Passion.* A graduate of Howard University, she lives in Hampton, Virginia with her two daughters. You may visit the author at www.ldbrownbooks.com or email ldbrown1@aol.com.

The Memphis native writes about life…not lifestyles.